AFTER THE END

Ω

BRUCE GOLDEN

Portions of this book previously appeared in: *Enter the Apocalypse* as "Adrift" (Mar. 2017); *Enter the Rebirth* as "Holiday" (June 2018); *On The Premises* as "The Harvest Christ" (Oct. 2017); *Young Explorer's Adventure Guide* as "After the End" (Dec. 2017);

Cover Art   Jonny Linder

ISBN-13: 9798625262859

Shaman Press

Also by Bruce Golden

**MORTALS ALL
BETTER THAN CHOCOLATE
EVERGREEN
DANCING WITH THE VELVET LIZARD
RED SKY, BLUE MOON
TALES OF MY ANCESTORS
MONSTER TOWN**

http://goldentales.tripod.com/

*For all my grandchildren and their progeny.
May they always love the written word . . . but never
have to face a world as bleak as the one herein.*

AFTER THE END

Words dissemble, words be quick
Words resemble walking sticks
Plant them, they'll grow
Watch them waver so
I'll always be a word man
Better than a birdman

James Douglas Morrison

Bruce Golden

It came from beyond Pluto, from deep within the great Oort Cloud--the badlands of the solar system. No one knows why or how it was jostled from its eons old nest, and no one ever will. But whatever the unknown force that propelled it to leave its brother comets behind and begin its long journey, the rogue came with a vengeance. Some say it was divine retribution, others believed in random mischance. In the end it didn't matter. Rationale and reason were lost in the maelstrom of survival.

ASYLUM

THE HARDEST PART WAS THE WAITING. At least that's what it seemed like to Brett. Even though he'd served seven years on a sub, the empty hours, the tedious passage of time, reinforced the claustrophobic aspect of a submariner's life. Not enough to overcome his love for submarine service. Just enough to occasionally make him think about his days of growing up in the wide open spaces of Montana, his work on his father's horse ranch. He'd long ago admitted to himself it was a strange dichotomy. But now, submerged in the Atlantic, waiting for a comet to come crashing into Earth, he felt more confined than usual.

Command had not been very forthcoming about the comet and what would happen when it hit. Though the theories and opinions he'd seen from the scientific community varied by extremes, he'd read enough to know that, unless a miracle occurred and Smith-Kim somehow changed course, it would have such a devastating effect that things would never be the same.

He thought about what would happen to Wendy, his on-again off-again girlfriend in Norfolk. Things had been strained between them for some time, and they'd drifted apart, but he still cared about her. His parents were dead, and though he'd always wanted a family, kids, he was glad, now, he didn't have anyone else to worry about.

The captain didn't have a wife or kids either, but most of the crew did. The tension aboard the *Savannah*, since it had deployed two weeks ago, had been palpable. Two men had gone AWOL even before they left Norfolk, and he didn't doubt if they weren't at sea, more would have left by now. Despite the lack of any acknowledgement of the situation from the captain, most of the crew had some idea of what might happen. Scuttlebutt took care of the rest.

That's why he was on his way to talk to the captain. He felt it would be better for morale if the captain were to speak with the men openly about their situation, their orders.

He knocked on the cabin door.

"Enter."

It took a few seconds for Captain Dunning to look up from whatever paperwork he was studying. Brett waited.

"Have a seat, Mr. Conyers. I'll be right with you."

Brett sat in the chair opposite the captain's small fold-down desk and waited. This was his first tour of duty aboard the *U.S.S. Savannah* under Captain Dunning, and he was still getting to know the man. Like most captains Brett had served under, he gave the impression of being a no-nonsense officer, who showed little emotion around his men. However, as the boat's executive officer, Brett should have been the one person the captain could open up to. Thus far he hadn't done so. Brett was hopeful that would change.

"What can I do for you?"

"Sir, I'm a little concerned about crew morale. Most were aware of the possible consequences of the comet before we sailed. Those who didn't have likely heard all sorts of wild things via rumor control. I thought maybe you should--"

"I'm not concerned with rumors. I'm only concerned the crew do their jobs."

"I'm sure they will, sir. I only thought if their captain would put the situation to them plainly, openly, it could go a long way towards ending all the speculation."

"And what *situation* is that, Mr. Conyers?"

Brett was sure the captain understood what he was talking about, but he replied, "The comet Smith-Kim, sir, and the likely catastrophic effect it could have on the entire planet."

The captain stared at him momentarily as if evaluating him--a disconcerting tendency Brett had noticed in the man.

"I know, as XO, it's your duty to keep tabs on morale, Mr. Conyers, but I have all the confidence in the world in this crew to fulfill our mission."

"Has there been in any adjustment to the mission due to the comet--any new orders?"

"There has been no deviation in our orders." He stared at Brett again, to see if he'd respond. "Look, Mr. Conyers, it's my understanding no one is sure what to expect. Scientific predictions have been all over the map. The only thing I've heard from command is that there's a possibility the ocean may become overheated, increasing the chance of hurricanes, and that there's the potential for undersea quakes."

"What if . . ." Brett paused, trying to frame his question just right. "What if the worst happens? What if this comet is as destructive on a planetary scale as many are predicting? What will we do then?"

"You said it yourself--*what if*. Right now it's all conjecture. But let me be clear about this. No matter what happens we'll go on."

"Go on with what, sir?"

"Our mission. Our mission to protect the United States of America."

It seemed, to Brett, like a pat military response for a situation that was anything *but* pat.

"Sir, what if there is no United States anymore?"

The captain looked at him as if it were a totally unexpected question. He didn't know if Dunning was going to answer or not when the boat's com sounded.

"Captain to control. Captain to control."

Ω

In response to the intercom summons, Dr. Virginia Freel made her way through the labyrinth she'd become all too familiar with over the last few weeks. She'd always been a touch claustrophobic, but she was finally getting used to the close quarters. Whenever she felt that old feeling creeping up on her, she would just laugh it off or try to think of something funny. The thought which occurred to her at that moment of unfettered whimsy was that her reaction was much like a lab rat, running a maze.

Despite her familiarity with the dim corridors and spiral stairs, she had yet to shed the disquieting sense of sterility pervading the Sanctuary. *Sanctuary*–the name itself seemed sterile. It was what their benefactor had called it, and now, by unspoken agreement, it was how they all referred to what could be their subterranean home for many years. She'd know in a few minutes, one way or the other.

In the face of everything, despite all the calculations, all the projections and probability factors, she hadn't really come to grips with the idea the world could be coming to an end. At least the world as she knew it. She felt that, somehow, she should be more emotional about it. There were times when she thought there was something wrong with her, that she didn't feel more.

Of course, it was a difficult thing to grasp. She'd studied the possible scenarios--they all had--but theoretical hypotheses were one thing, reality was another.

It wasn't as if she had anything or anyone to lose. Her parents were dead, there was no one special in her life. All she had was her work, and she'd still have that, though on a much more important scale. All she'd have to do--if the worst happened--was get past the death of billions of her fellow humans and the decimation of her planet.

Ω

Brett followed the captain's swift pace to the control room, more than once calling out "Make a hole" in the crowded passageways.

"Captain's in control," called out the chief of the boat when they arrived. "Captain, we have an incoming flash directive from COMSUBLANT."

On cue, the radioman rushed in with a printout and handed it to the captain. He read it and looked puzzled.

"What is this?" he asked the radioman. "Where's the rest of it?"

"I don't know, sir. It cut off mid-transmission and I wasn't able to regain contact. There's nothing on any frequency I've tried."

The captain handed the message to Brett.

"Confirm comet split, three fragments to impact within the hour, one fragment targeting mid-Atlantic coast, proceed to--"

Brett had read somewhere about the possibility of the comet splitting into pieces, though he didn't remember how or why. But this was the first time he'd heard anything about the location of impact. He wondered where the other fragments were landing, and what else the message might have said.

"Get back on it, sailor. Let me know as soon as you can reestablish radio contact."

"Yes, sir."

"Where do you suppose they want us to proceed to?" Brett asked the captain.

"Away from the impact would be logical."

Brett nodded.

"Is it the end of the world, Skipper?" asked the quartermaster.

"It's the end of days," responded the chief behind him.

"Belay that talk," barked the captain. "We're still here aren't we--we've still got orders, a mission to accomplish."

The captain looked around the control room as if to see if anyone would dispute him, and gave the order.

"All ahead standard. Diving officer, make your depth one-five-zero feet."

"Making depth one-five-zero feet, five degrees down bubble."

"Navigator, continue present course."

"Aye, sir."

"Raise radio buoy."

"Raising buoy."

To Brett the captain said, "I'm going to my cabin. Alert me when we establish radio contact again. Until otherwise ordered, we'll continue southeast to our patrol zone, away from the reported impact area."

"Yes, sir."

"XO has the conn," stated the captain abruptly as he exited.

"I have the conn."

The captain's voice was edgier than normal, and Brett was surprised he chose to leave the control room at a time like this. Of course his impression of the man could have been colored by his own emotions. He didn't believe in the chief's "end of days" dogma, but whether or not it was the end of the world, only time would tell. Apparently, that time would come soon.

Ω

The climb from the habitat level to the control room was relatively short, and when she arrived she found Michael and Eileen already there.

Eileen Pappas, the project's lead engineer, was monitoring communications from several sources. In the weeks she'd been actively involved in the project, Virginia had found the engineer to be a bit of a "cold fish," though an extremely intelligent and organized woman. She was one of those by-the-book types who shunned original thought as if it were a virus.

Michael Hanscom, on the other hand, was much harder for her to read. His boyish face belied the intellect simmering beneath. At times he seemed to have a sense of humor, but he was also prone to techno-babble. He was the "genius" behind the project's master computer, and he was never slow to sing the praises of the machine's hard-wired intelligence. Currently he was helping Eileen by establishing various links with outside sources, including governmental channels and public news reports.

"How's it going?" asked Virginia, realizing immediately how insipid the inquiry was, given the circumstances.

"At its current rate of speed, the lead fragment of Smith-Kim is 36 minutes out," replied Michael.

"Do we know yet whether--"

"What's happening?"

Her query was interrupted by the arrival of Kenji and the rest of the "inner circle"--as Virginia privately thought of them. Their real title, according to the manifesto of *Project Phoenix* they'd all read and signed allegiance to, was "Advisory Committee." The committee was made up of the department heads of each of the facility's main areas. Initially, the purpose of the committee was to, along with Michael's computer, advise the project's director on all major decisions. Unfortunately, the "director," who was also the creative and financial force behind the project and the construction of the Sanctuary, died nine days ago.

William Farkas was a man of rare insight and boundless wealth. Virginia was vaguely aware he'd made his fortune in the computer software and biotech industries. She'd only met him once, during her final interview for the project (she didn't mention her claustrophobia), but she'd immediately sensed the significant presence of the man. There wasn't an ounce of pretentiousness about him. He was interested in facts and results, and didn't seem to care for some of the niceties or political correctness that impeded others.

He established the groundwork for *Project Phoenix* years before anyone ever heard of Smith-Kim. At first she thought the title was a bit melodramatic, but the more she learned of its purpose, the more she realized how appropriate it was.

Whether it was luck or intuition, major construction of the Sanctuary was completed just days before the discovery of the comet. Of course, even then, no one knew how close to Earth its inconstant trajectory would take it.

Farkas, she was sure, would have continued with his plans even if Smith-Kim had stayed in the Oort Cloud where it belonged. He assembled his teams, completed final preparations, and when the odds of the comet missing Earth continued to decrease, he made the decision to leave his more mundane affairs in the hands of others and join his hand-picked scientists in their underground refuge. It was only two days after he announced his imminent arrival to the committee that a heart attack ended his life. Whether the fatal occurrence was connected to the excitement and stress surrounding the approaching comet, Virginia could only guess.

There were certainly contingency plans to ensure the project would go forward in the case of his death, but the chain of command was no longer as clear-cut. It hadn't really been an issue up until now--and wouldn't be unless Smith-Kim actually hit. But that hadn't stopped Virginia from laying odds as to who might try to usurp command if indeed they "locked down" the Sanctuary. One thing she knew though, it wouldn't be her. She had no interest in being in charge, beyond her own small group of biologists.

"So what's the latest? Is it going to hit or what?" asked Kenji. He was wearing what Virginia had come to realize was one of his trademark colorful shirts. This one was deep red with white and yellow flowers.

"According to Farkas' latest calculations," stated Michael, "the lead fragment, the largest of the three, will impact Eurasia. The second one mid-America. The third somewhere near the East Coast."

No one said anything at first. What do you say, how do you react, when you're told your world is about to undergo a cataclysmic upheaval?

"What do you mean *Farkas' calculations*?" asked Kenji, breaking the silence.

Michael suppressed a grin. "I named the master computer after our benefactor. Appropriate, don't you think?"

"I don't understand," said Fawn.

Fawn Mercer was the newest member of the advisory committee. She has been selected as the head of the zoological section only two weeks ago, after the original chief zoologist backed out of the project. She was a cute little thing--much younger looking than you would have thought from her credentials--but she'd already given Virginia the impression of being a bit mousy. Shy or not, the zoologist had a perfect button nose and long lashes that were like a siren's song to Virginia.

"What's this about three fragments?" continued Fawn.

Kenji, the lead botanist, was quick to explain. Virginia had already pegged him as a know-it-all.

"When it passed around the sun it *calved*," said Kenji as if subtly reproaching her ignorance. "The frozen gases that held together the mineral aspects of the comet began to thaw. That, combined with gravitational forces, pulled it apart. There are three main fragments, but likely dozens of smaller ones."

Virginia could tell from Fawn's reaction she didn't care for Kenji's condescending attitude. Coming in late to the project, it was probably all she could do to get her own department in order.

"Okay, I understand that. But how do you know where they're going to hit?"

"Farkas is linked with several computers worldwide," said Michael, "including NORAD and NASA. They use incoming data to continually revise their projections."

"That's it then, isn't it? It's the end of us," said Fawn.

"Not us," replied Eileen, "not unless it falls on top of us. But the rest of the world . . . when the impact ejecta reenters the atmosphere, everyone on the surface is going to be broiled alive. That's the theory anyway."

"Severe global warming," joked Kenji, though nobody so much as chuckled. However, Virginia noticed that Fawn's small frame shivered.

They'd all read the data--apparently except for Fawn--about the possible scenarios resulting from a major impact. Virginia knew if a large enough object, or objects, struck the Earth at the tremendous speed the comet was traveling, not only would there be devastation in the area of impact and massive earthquakes along regional seismic faults, but when the heat pulse Eileen referred to occurred, anything on the surface that *could* burn *would* burn. It would all go up like so much kindling.

Fawn disconcertedly fumbled with strands of her hair. Virginia sensed it wasn't so much she was completely ignorant of what could happen, but that she hadn't really had much time to contemplate it. By the expression on her face, reality had hit home.

The sixth member of their group, Dr. Joyce Finley, hadn't said a word. Of course they all had doctorates, but Joyce, being in charge of medical, was the only one Virginia thought of as being "a doctor." The wisps of gray in her hair, that marked her as the oldest of the bunch, also lent her an air of authority. However, she wasn't always so introspective--she and Virginia had already become good friends--but right now she seemed to be studying everyone, gauging their reactions to the impending crisis.

Virginia decided to sit, but noticed a little red ant wandering across the chair seat. She started to flick it off, then changed her mind. She wondered how it had found its way inside a sealed facility like the Sanctuary. Of course ants seemed to be able to find their way in just about anywhere. She supposed most of this little guy's friends would survive the coming catastrophe in their underground tunnels. Afterwards they'd do alright too. Ants were nature's scavengers weren't they?

"I guess it's time for this," said Michael, pulling a bottle of sparkling cider out of a bag on the conference table. Six plastic cups followed the bottle. Michael poured.

"What's this for?" wondered Eileen.

Michael didn't reply until he'd handed out the drinks. He raised his cup in the air and offered a toast.

"To William Farkas, who had the foresight to build this sanctuary, and to formulate a survival plan, not just for a few individuals, but for the planet itself. It's unfortunate he couldn't be here with us."

"Here, here," replied Kenji.

They all drank.

It was a somber toast, but one Virginia felt appropriate. Michael had known Farkas the longest. He'd worked for him for years before the Sanctuary became a reality. While Michael was the technical wizard behind their master computer, most of the concepts that went into its programming belonged to Farkas. They'd worked very closely together to design the most comprehensive and intelligent machine in the world. Within its memory core was the sum of mankind's knowledge--or at least the largest percentage of it ever stored in a single system. Virginia wondered what all that included . . . and what, by necessity, had been left out.

Before they could put their cups down, all the monitors, both video and audio, went static momentarily. In a few seconds they were back up again.

Michael answered what they were all wondering. "That was likely the comet passing through the atmosphere."

This was it then, thought Virginia. It really *was* the end of the world. Funny, even in her mind it sounded like such a cliché.

Eileen held up a hand for silence. "There's something coming in from NORAD."

Everyone waited while she listened to her earpiece.

"The lead fragment has struck somewhere south of Warsaw, Poland. Yes, they're confirming it. Wait a minute. The trajectory of the second fragment . . . Michael, I've lost them."

Michael reset his communications link. "Everything's fine on this end."

Eileen listened. "Nothing," she said.

"Switch to NASA."

"Can't you turn it up so we can all hear?" asked Kenji.

Eileen waved him off. "I've got them. There's some kind of problem.

They've lost contact with NORAD too." Eileen's concern was palpable as she listened in. "The final projection on the second fragment puts it somewhere near Colorado Springs. They think NORAD may have been affected. They're reporting the third fragment has struck along the mid-Atlantic coast, possibly near the Baltimore/D.C. area."

"Try NORAD again," urged Michael.

Eileen shook her head. "Nothing."

"They've got to be there," insisted Michael. "It would take a near direct hit to . . . ." He didn't finish. He turned from his console and looked at the others. "Of all the buzzard's luck."

"NASA's getting reports of nuclear detonations--unconfirmed though," said Eileen.

Kenji couldn't believe what he was hearing. "Someone's firing off nuclear missiles? Idiots! Did they think they could stop the comet? The U.S. government already tried that when it was much farther out . . . and failed, of course."

"It could be automated defense systems overriding human commands," said Michael. "Someone's anti-missile systems could think they're under attack."

"I can't believe anyone would be that stupid," said Eileen. "They should have been ready for this."

Michael, still working at his computer, shook his head. "Too many people didn't want to believe it--*refused* to believe it."

"Yeah," agreed Kenji. "And you know how many little Podunk countries have their own missile systems now? It wouldn't surprise me if they've lost control of their own weapons."

"Could it be terrorists?" wondered Fawn. "You know, just trying to take advantage of the opportunity."

"I wouldn't put it past some of those fanatics," said Kenji. "They're too stupid to realize their little nuclear bombs won't do a fraction of the damage the comet is going to do. It's like poking someone with a toothpick before you drop a grenade down their pants."

Ω

"Conn, sonar . . . reporting hurricane force winds and waves close to a hundred feet. There's one hell of a storm up there, sir."

Brett looked at Captain Dunning. "Just as you were warned, sir."

The captain nodded and flipped the intercom switch.

"Radio, conn. Anything at all coming through the buoy?"

"No, sir. Nothing at all."

"XO, come with me," said Dunning. "Mr. Maxey has the conn."

"I have the conn."

Brett followed the captain to a nearby passageway where they could speak in private.

"Don't you find it strange we've had no radio contact at all?"

"Yes, sir. But then, we don't know the extent of the damage on the mainland. From what I've read, worst case scenario, the comet could have caused a firestorm that's destroyed most of what's on the surface. That could include COMSUBLANT."

"Even so," said the captain, "I imagine the president and his staff have taken refuge in the White House's underground command center. I would have expected to have gotten some kind of a general message from there."

"The last communication said a comet fragment was headed for the mid-Atlantic coast area, sir. What if . . . ?" Brett didn't finish the thought. "It wouldn't even have to be a direct hit. Anything within several hundred miles is going to be devastated by major earthquakes. Even the White House bunker might not have been strong enough to withstand it."

Brett saw the captain didn't care for that scenario.

"I don't know where you got your information, but I find that highly unlikely. It could be they're just too damn busy to communicate with us. I guess we're on our own until they do."

"Sir, maybe we should return to Norfolk and see what's happened for ourselves. It could be that last message was telling us to proceed to Norfolk."

Dunning looked at him as though he'd just suggested they scuttle the boat.

"That message could have said anything. Without any contravening orders, we'll follow the orders in-hand. I'm not about to countermand them, mister. Not at this juncture."

"Yes, sir. I understand, sir."

What Brett understood was that the captain didn't seem to grasp the enormity of the situation. Or he was doing a good job of hiding it.

Ω

"That's it, all communications are down. I can't raise anyone--not even NASA," said Michael after several attempts. "The heat pulse must have begun. We're on our own."

The computer tech looked around, but no one had anything to say.

"I'll have Farkas run a systems check," he added quickly.

Sounding more serious than usual, Kenji said, "I guess that means right about now the world is on fire."

The finality of it began to sink in. Tears rolled down Fawn's cheeks and Joyce closed her eyes and turned away from the group for a moment. Virginia felt like she should cry too, but she didn't. Instead, her claustrophobia kicked up a notch with the idea now firmly implanted that she wouldn't be returning to the surface for many months, if not longer. She tried to ignore the feeling, but found she couldn't just shrug it off.

Reasoning with her inner voice she reminded herself she knew this is how it would play out. There was nothing to fear. They had plenty of air, both in storage and filtered from the surface. Sanctuary was a state-of-the-art facility. She was safe here. Everything was going to be okay. She should be more concerned about the people on the surface. The billions who would be incinerated.

"Someone had better inform the rest of the staff," said Joyce. "There are 50 people down there who've got to be wondering what's happened."

"Doc's right," said Kenji. "They must be going crazy with curiosity."

"I think we need to make some decisions first," suggested Eileen.

"Decisions about what?"

"Well, for one thing, who's going to be in charge."

Here it comes, thought Virginia.

"I guess we all are," responded Joyce thoughtfully. "That's why we're the Advisory Committee, right? We were going to advise Farkas."

"Yes," replied Eileen, "but Farkas was the decision maker. He was in charge. Now . . . ." She held up her hands, palms upward. "You can't have a committee in charge. One person needs, ultimately, to have the final say. You can't have six people making decisions."

"Why not?" wondered Joyce. "Sioux tribes were ruled by consensus."

Michael broke in. "Farkas reports the facility is stable. Power, water supply, cryo-vaults, everything is functioning normally."

"Maybe Farkas should be in charge," joked Virginia.

"Actually," responded Michael, "I was thinking of suggesting that."

"You're kidding, right?" Joyce thought he was. "Put a machine in charge?"

Michael shrugged. "It's been programmed with all the project parameters. It knows better than any of us what needs to be done to achieve our goals. Farkas, the original, had planned on running all major decisions through the computer. I'm just saying we defer to it whenever the six of us have trouble reaching a consensus. We use it to guide our decisions."

"That sounds sensible to me," agreed Fawn.

"I don't know," said Virginia. "The idea of letting a computer be the ultimate decision maker. I don't think I like that."

"Do *you* want to be in charge?" asked Michael.

"No, no," she said, gesturing emphatically.

"I don't either," said Michael, "not really. I don't think any of us do. Does anyone?"

"I do," spoke up Kenji so fast the others chuckled.

"Okay," said Michael, "no one except Kenji wants to be in charge."

"How many votes do I hear for Ken Nakajima?"

Everyone remained silent--even Kenji.

Michael went on. "How many vote for Farkas?"

Michael, Eileen, and even Kenji raised their hands. Fawn hesitated, then raised hers too.

The holdouts, Virginia and Joyce, looked at each other but said nothing.

"That's it then," said Michael. "For now at least, we'll defer all major decisions to the master computer, while each heading up our own departments. Agreed?"

Virginia reluctantly joined in the mutual assent.

"Alright," said Joyce, "let's go downstairs and gather everyone together."

"What do we tell them?" wondered Fawn.

"We tell them *Project Phoenix* is a go," said Michael.

Smoke, ash, and a mélange of chemical toxins were the spawn of the inferno that ravaged the world, blanketing it in darkness. Most of the plankton and swamp-based vegetation that survived the initial conflagration, eventually withered and died from lack of sunlight. Mega quakes rocked impact zones, leveled mountains, obliterated canyons, and propelled swarms of colossal tsunamis. Residual heat gave birth to hurricanes that lifted seas and battered coastlines, while cyclonic winds coalesced over the charred remains of terra firma, sweeping aside the untethered detritus of mankind.

ADRIFT

"CAPTAIN, WE'VE LOST THE RADIO BUOY."

"How could that happen?"

"The sea was churning pretty good up there," said Brett. "Sonar says it was rougher than any they've ever registered. The cable must have snapped."

Captain Dunning considered this. "Sonar, conn. What's the weather like up there now?"

"It's calmed down a bit, Skipper, but still rough. Winds are 30 knots, waves about 15 feet."

"XO, take her to periscope depth and we'll see if we can pick up any transmissions."

Brett gave the order. "Diving Officer, periscope depth."

"Periscope depth, aye."

Brett hoped they'd learn something--that someone was still out there to be contacted. He wasn't sure the captain would ever return to port unless ordered to, and crew morale was deteriorating every day. They wanted to know what had happened--they *needed* to know about their families. He'd already repeated his views about the crew to Dunning, but had been shut down again.

"Raising number one scope," called Maxey, the officer of the deck. "Breaking."

Maxey did a 360-degree check of the surface and reported, "No close contacts."

Brett moved up and peered through the eyepiece. He saw little but darkness. Strange, he was sure that . . . . "Chief, what's the local time?"

"14-30 hours, sir."

Brett stepped back from the periscope and looked at Dunning. "It's as black as night out there, sir."

Captain Dunning looked through the scope, spun it around checking all quadrants. When he backed away Brett saw a strange look on his face. It was as if he'd seen a ghost, but not so much an expression of fear as it was one of disbelief .

Brett wanted to know if there'd been any incoming messages. "Radio, conn. What have we got?"

"Nothing, sir. No UHF or VHF chatter. No radio contact on any frequency. The board's blank."

That wasn't the only thing that was blank. Captain Dunning had this thousand mile stare that suggested he was no longer present. The apocalypse had likely arrived, but Dunning didn't seem willing to acknowledge it.

Brett decided he had to say something, and he didn't care if the men heard it this time.

"Captain, we've been without contact for days now. I suggest we turn the boat around, head for Norfolk, and see if we can pick up any signals closer in. We can always--"

"Down scope," ordered the captain suddenly, interrupting his XO as if he'd never heard him. "Diving officer, make your depth one-zero-zero feet. Mr. Conyers, you have the conn."

"I have the conn," responded Brett, watching Dunning flee the control room as though the devil himself were on his tail.

He didn't know what was up with the captain, but he didn't like the way he was acting. To totally ignore his XO was bad enough, but his demeanor would only heighten the crew's anxiety. Word of it would spread and sink morale quicker than a torpedo.

Ω

It had been a week since the comet's arrival, and Brett was frustrated they didn't know any more about what had happened now than they did the day it hit. There had been no communications--not even with any other ships. They *had* detected a radiation cloud, but Brett surmised that didn't necessarily mean someone had fired off nuclear weapons. The heat produced by the

23

comet could have set off such weapons accidentally, or a nuclear power plant might have imploded. When he told Captain Dunning about the cloud, the captain refused to contemplate any explanation other than the nuclear attack option. He seemed certain someone must have launched an attack against the U.S.

Since then, Dunning had spent two days ensconced in his cabin. Brett had no idea what was going through the man's mind, but he knew right away something was wrong when the captain rushed into the control room with a fretful look on his face.

"I have the conn," announced Dunning abruptly.

"Captain has the conn."

"Chief of the watch, sound the general alarm."

The chief looked surprised by the order, but complied.

"Aye, sir, sounding the general alarm."

The klaxons sounded and all hands scurried to their battle stations. Brett hoped this was just an impromptu drill, but, looking at Dunning, he worried it was something else.

"Sonar, conn," called Dunning. "Anything? Any contact?"

"Conn, sonar . . . that's a negative, sir, I'm not reading any contact."

"Diving Officer, periscope depth."

"Periscope depth, aye."

"All stations report manned and ready, sir."

"Raising number one scope," called the officer of the deck.

Brett had no idea what was going on, and he should have. If it was a drill he should have been informed. But the wild look in the captain's eyes said it wasn't.

"No close contacts."

Dunning pressed up against the eyepiece and spent an abnormal amount of time looking in all directions.

"Take her down!" exclaimed the captain suddenly. "Down scope! Helm, all ahead flank! Make your depth five-zero-zero feet."

"What is it, Captain?" asked Brett.

Dunning ignored the question and called out, "Left full rudder."

"Left full rudder aye."

"Flood tubes one and two."

"Captain, we have no target."

Still Dunning ignored the XO.

"Open the outer doors," ordered the Captain. "Firing point procedures."

"Outer doors are open, sir. We're ready to fire."

"Sonar, conn. Do you have anything?"

"Conn, sonar . . . nothing sir."

"Right twenty degrees rudder," ordered Dunning. "Come to a new course, one-three-zero."

The crew was following his commands, but Brett saw they wondered what was up, and what he'd seen through the scope. Brett sidled up close to Dunning and asked in a low voice, "What is it, sir?"

"There's something out there." Dunning didn't bother to lower his voice.

"What did you see?"

"I didn't see anything. It's still dark as hell out there, but I can feel it. There's something out there . . . hunting us."

The captain's own words all but confirmed Brett's worst fear. The only question now was, what would he do about it?

Brett looked around the control room. Concern colored the faces of the crew--especially the senior members. The captain saw the stares too. Brett expected some kind of outburst, but Dunning didn't say a word. He walked away, out of the control room, without even turning over the conn. The men watched him go and a few began whispering.

"I have the conn," said Brett. "Chief of the watch, secure from general quarters. All ahead standard. Diving officer, make your depth two-zero-zero feet. Maintain course."

Ω

"What are you saying, XO? You think the old man's lost it?"

Brett had gathered some of the senior officers and chiefs in the wardroom to discuss the captain's unusual behavior. It wasn't something he'd done lightly, but he felt he had no choice.

"XO, I hope you're not suggesting what I think you're suggesting."

"I'm not suggesting anything. I'm only asking if any of you have noticed the same things I have."

"I uh . . . ."

"Speak up, Chief."

"I did see the captain talking to himself outside his cabin. But shit, I do that myself from time to time."

"What was he saying?"

"I didn't really catch enough to know."

"Look, we all want to go home and check on our families," said Mr. Maxey, "and I know the crew is a bit unsettled, but the captain gives the orders, and as far as I'm concerned--"

A knock on the wardroom door interrupted the discussion. Brett opened it. The petty officer standing there stuttered, "I heard this noise . . . in the captain's cabin . . . like a gunshot or I don't know . . . you'd better come look, sir."

Chief Roberts led the way, and all those in the wardroom followed. Several seamen were gathered outside the captain's cabin.

"Let's clear the area," ordered the chief. "You men return to your duties."

The chief stood aside once the area was clear and let the XO knock on the door. There was no answer, so he knocked again. Still no response, so Brett let himself in. What he found he half-expected, yet still couldn't believe his eyes.

The captain was slumped over on his bunk with a bullet through his brain. Brett motioned for the others to enter. No one said a word, until Chief Roberts looked at Brett and asked, "What are your orders, Captain?"

Ω

Brett had run several scenarios through his head since he'd learned Smith-Kim was on a collision course with Earth. He was prepared for a lot of things, but the captain's suicide wasn't one of them. Though the possibility he may have had to remove Dunning from command had crossed his mind, he hadn't really contemplated the ramifications of taking over that command. Now all eyes were on him as entered the control room. He met their gazes with a countenance he hoped radiated more confidence than he felt.

Brett picked up the handset and flipped on the intercom.

"This is Captain Conyers." Saying it out loud felt strange, but also made it feel real for the first time. "By now I'm sure you've all heard about the death of Captain Dunning. It's not something that can easily be understood, any more than we can understand what's happening to the world right now. I know many of you are concerned about the well-being of your families. The truth is, I don't know anymore about what's happened than you do. But we're going to do what we can to find out. We've lost all contact with command, so, in the absence of any further orders, we're going to return to Norfolk. We'll see if we can reestablish contact along the way. I expect everyone on board to do their jobs, and I promise to keep you informed."

Brett could tell by the faces of those in the control room that his little speech had accomplished its objective. They all wanted to know. They all needed a purpose.

Brett joined his XO, Mr. Maxey, at the navigation map.

"Where are we, Greg?"

"Right here, about 30 miles north of St. Johns."

Brett studied it a moment. "Plot a direct course to Miami. Let's cruise by there first and see what we can see before we head up to Norfolk."

"Aye, sir."

Ω

Almost two weeks had passed, and they still hadn't had any radio contact. He knew it couldn't be, but it felt as if they were last living souls on Earth.

"You'd better look at this, sir."

Maxey had called him to control after a routine surface check. The XO backed away from the periscope to let him look.

It was still dark out there, but marginally lighter than it had been. Light enough Brett was able to make out something. When he realized what it was, he was astonished. Yet it also filled him with hope.

Bobbing along the surface, about hundred yards away, was a hodgepodge flotilla consisting of several small boats, some inflatables, and various wooden platforms, all lashed together. But it wasn't what otherwise would have been floating refuse that gave him hope. It was the people who clung to it.

"Make all preparations for surfacing," ordered Brett.

As Maxey gave the orders, Brett speculated about who these people might be, and how they could have survived the maelstrom created by the comet's collision. He wondered, too, why they'd taken to the sea in such a dangerous manner.

"Ready to surface, sir."

"Let's take her up, Mr. Maxey."

The XO gave the order and the surfacing alarm sounded.

"Lookouts to the bridge."

"Order a rescue team to the bridge as well," said Brett. "It looks like we may be taking survivors aboard."

"Aye, sir."

Once they'd surfaced, Brett got to the bridge. The smoke wasn't as thick as the last time they'd surfaced, but the wind still carried ash. It was only light enough to discern the sun was up there somewhere. It was small comfort.

He maneuvered the *Savannah* as close as he dared to the ramshackle flotilla. At least 20 people were clinging to it. One of the women was obviously pregnant, and there were two small children as well. None of them looked to be in very good shape. There was no telling how long they'd been at sea.

Brett climbed down from the bridge and joined the rescue crew on the deck. They'd managed to get a grapple line on the framework and pull it close enough to secure it to the sub. They began helping the refugees climb aboard.

Brett knew from their appearance, and by the smatterings of language he heard, they were island people--most likely from nearby Cuba.

He pulled aside one of the deck crew, saying, "Go tell Mr. Maxey I need a Spanish speaker up here."

"I speak English."

Brett turned around to face one of the castaways. She was about his age, and might have been attractive if she hadn't been so disheveled.

"I'm Captain Conyers. You're aboard the United States submarine *Savannah*."

"I'm Vilma . . . Vilma Mendoza."

"Where are you from, Señora Mendoza?"

"I'm from Puerto Rico."

"Puerto Rico?" Brett was flabbergasted. Puerto Rico was a thousand miles away. "Surely you didn't float here all the way from there."

"No, no," she said shaking her head. "We came from Havana . . . Cuba."

That made more sense to Brett. Still they'd drifted 200 miles or more from where they'd started.

"What's it like there . . . since the comet?"

She turned her head as if remembering something painful. "Everything is . . . todo quemado   . . . fire burned it all."

"How did you all survive?"

She hesitated to respond, but did so looking him in the eye. "We were in prison--most of us. We were underground when it happened. We did not know anything. We heard explosions. We did not know . . . someone came and freed us. We went up, and then we saw . . . ."

Brett realized the memory was traumatic for her. He didn't want to question her any further. At least not right then.

"Let's get you and everyone into the boat and into some dry clothes." He tried to smile, but he felt it came off half-hearted. "I bet you're hungry."

"Yes, gracias--thank you."

Ω

The view from the bridge reminded him of pictures he'd seen of Hiroshima and Nagasaki. Only this holocaust wasn't man-made. Even without the binoculars he saw the devastation was almost complete. Very few buildings still stood. Those whose outer shells were impervious to fire were nonetheless gutted on the inside. Most of the grand tourist hotels lining Miami Beach looked like they'd been struck by massive hurricanes. Brett didn't know if that were the case, or if the turbulence from the firestorm that burned the city had created its own tornadoes. Even in the sea air he could smell the soot.

Maxey stood next to him. Both were searching for any signs of survivors. So far, they'd seen no one--no signs of movement. He knew Maxey had a wife and kids. They weren't in Miami, but he recognized the despondency on the man's face. He held it together though. Brett admired him for that.

He didn't see any reason to go ashore. Not yet--not here. He hoped other cities, other regions, might have fared better. He knew they'd have to return to their homeport, to Norfolk, where Maxey's family, and the families of many of his crew, lived.

"We're going to make for Norfolk," he told the XO. "But we'll remain on the surface for a ways, continue to hug the coastline, and keep looking for any signs of life."

"What if we see someone?" asked Maxey. Anticipating Brett's thoughts, he added, "We're pretty crowded as it is."

"I know," said Brett. He hoped for survivors, but he didn't know what he'd do if they found someone. "Just let me know if we spot anything."

Maxey nodded, but didn't reply. He was busy looking, searching. Brett knew the man hoped to find someone, anyone. Because one survivor could mean many, and that could mean Maxey's own family had a chance.

Ω

After less than a day on the surface, with no sign of survivors, the weather turned rough again, so the *U.S.S. Savannah* submerged. Brett knew he could make better time that way, and he wanted to see if Norfolk was in the same condition as Miami. They passed Charleston at night and he used the scope to look for lights but saw none.

If what they'd seen so far was any indication, the destruction was worse than he could have imagined. Civilization, as they knew it, had been annihilated. The implications of what that meant for his crew and their future was hard to grasp. He didn't want to contemplate it. It was too much. Maybe, he thought, that's what drove Captain Dunning off the deep end.

Yet he was certain there had to be survivors. The refugees from Cuba proved that. Sooner or later they'd have to go ashore and search. The men with families would certainly want to go. But what then? What if they found people alive? What if they found a large number of people? Their resources were limited. They could help some, but what if there were hundreds? He had to have a plan.

If Norfolk was, as he anticipated, burnt to the ground as well, then Brett saw no purpose in continuing up the coast. They'd been told at least one of the comet fragments had struck the East Coast, and he considered that maybe the destruction was worse here. He hoped the interior of the country might have fared better. At least they wouldn't have been hit by hurricanes, though he didn't know if climatic changes might have caused monster cyclones or worse inland. In the back of his mind he began developing a plan to turn south again, find the mouth of the Mississippi and travel up it as far as he could. Maybe there they'd find someplace untouched by the devastation.

Brett considered this option as he walked to where the refugees were bunked. He hadn't checked on them since they'd come aboard, so he thought it was time. He'd been told Señora Mendoza wasn't the only non-Cuban they'd rescued. The pregnant woman was from Haiti, another couple was Dominican, and three men were from Jamaica. The reasons for their imprisonment varied, but none, apparently, were hardened criminals. It was his understanding that Señora Mendoza had slapped a police officer who'd been too forward with her. The thought made him chuckle, though he also realized it was a slap that probably saved her life.

Chief Alvarez had been assigned to their guests because he spoke the language. The chief had informed him those in prison hadn't known about the comet. When they emerged they thought a bomb had been dropped on Havana, so they figured making their way to the U.S. was their best bet. They'd had no idea the destruction was global.

Brett found Alvarez with the two little kids who'd been brought aboard. They looked to be only four or five years old. How they'd survived he had no idea.

"How's it going, Chief?"

"Alright, sir. We gathered some extra clothes, but we don't have any that fit these two."

"Who do we have here?"

"Well, sir, I can't get either of them to speak yet, but I call the little girl Flo and the boy Jet--for Flotsam and Jetsam."

Though they seemed to have attached themselves to the chief, they looked fearfully at the captain. Brett smiled to try and put them at ease.

"Siblings?"

"I think so, sir."

"No parents?"

Alvarez shook his head.

Señora Mendoza made her way towards them and Brett realized he'd been correct. Cleaned up, she was an attractive woman. She'd gotten an American flag from someone and turned it into a skirt.

"Señora, you can't desecrate the flag like that," admonished the chief. "I'm sorry, sir, I'll find her something else."

"That's alright, Chief. I don't think that matters so much anymore." To her he said, "It looks wonderful on you, Señora--very colorful."

She curtsied in response and said, "Gracias, Capitán."

"Are you and the others doing alright?"

She shrugged. "As well as we can. Better than before you found us."

"Good. Chief Alvarez will see to your needs. Carry on, Chief."

He turned and walked away, but Señora Mendoza followed him.

"Excuse me, Capitán," she said, lightly taking hold of his arm.

Brett turned. "Yes?"

She lowered her voice to almost a whisper and asked, "Is it true what I have heard your men say? Is it true the whole world has burned like Havana?"

"I can't speak for the whole world, ma'am, but yes, Miami and the other areas we've seen so far appear to have been destroyed by fire."

"What will we do? Where will we go?"

"First we're going to return to our home base. Many of the crew have families there."

She nodded understandingly. "After that?"

"After that . . . I don't know for certain. We're going to have to figure that out."

"Entiendo . . . I understand. Wherever you decide to go, I am glad we have been rescued by such a wise and honorable man."

A little laugh escaped Brett's lips. "Well, let's hope I'm as wise as you say, Señora. I expect we're going to be facing many days where wisdom is needed."

Brett turned to leave again, but she said, "Capitán."

"Yes?"

"It's not señora . . . it's señorita."

Hours passed into weeks, weeks into months. Time became an abstract concept to those few who, by either forethought or happenstance, survived the cataclysm. There was no time because there were no days, only nights, only an endless dark winter. Frost seized hold of regions unfamiliar with its chilly touch. Acidic rainstorms poisoned soils, discouraging flora's attempted resurgence.

Slowly, as gradual as a glacier's dance, the darkness waned. Soon the remnants of humanity who sheltered in place or roamed the planet searching for sustenance noticed a discernible difference. The barest hint of sunlight made its way to the surface. The air warmed ever so slightly. The stygian night gave way to dank, overcast days. In the Northern Hemisphere the sun returned with the coming of spring, but the southern half of the world faced the onset of its natural winter, delaying its resurrection.

ADAPTATION

UNDER THE GUIDELINES OF *PROJECT PHOENIX*, and the timetable overseen by Farkas-the-computer, Virginia and her fellow biologists didn't have much to do the first few months. They kept watch over their cryogenically-preserved specimens and provided some assistance to the zoological team that had recently been given the go-ahead to begin inseminating the stock animals. Because of their longer gestation periods, the horses would be first. The bison, cattle, and sheep would follow weeks later.

The master plan was to release many of the animals to the surface soon after the first foals, calves, and lambs were born, while keeping plenty of breeding stock in the facility. It was hoped, by then, that natural growth and Kenji's botanical seeding project would have created enough vegetation to provide them sustenance. This would all take place approximately a year after "The End," as Virginia liked to think of it. A few months after that, in the early spring, turkeys, chickens, pheasants, and other selected fowl would be released into the wild.

Virginia, however, was anxious to get started with her phase of the plan.

Yet she knew from the project's timetable it wouldn't begin anytime soon. In the meantime she'd have to be content with helping others--until Farkas decided it was time.

She'd passed the weeks by developing relationships--two in particular. She'd discovered the best remedy for her occasional claustrophobia was sex. To that end she'd been spending quite a bit of time with Fawn Mercer, the cute but reticent little zoologist whom she discovered, to her delight, shared her appreciation of women. Fawn had become quite taken with her, and more than bit possessive. That was the one hitch that had developed. Because Virginia had also taken up a more casual affair with Joe Delancy, the fellow who'd been dubbed "The Zookeeper" because he tended to the animal pens. He was a rather muscular fellow with a great sense of humor--attributes Virginia appreciated.

Fawn, however, didn't care for men in that way, and couldn't seem to grasp why Virginia would.

"How could you do this?"

"I don't know why you're so upset, Fawn. I told you from the beginning I like men as well as women."

"Yes, but I thought we had something special."

"We do." Virginia attempted to put her arm around Fawn's shoulders, but the younger woman stepped away.

"Then why do you need *him*?"

"It's not so much a matter of need. I like Joe. He's a good guy. We have fun together, like you and I do, but different. I don't know. I guess, in a way, I do need him. But my relationship with you is different. Whatever you think, I *do* care about you."

Virginia put her arms around Fawn from behind, and, instead of moving away this time, she snuggled in.

"But why did you have to pick him? Someone on my staff."

"It's not a logical decision, Fawn. These things just happen."

"Maybe so, but I don't have to--"

"So what are you two arguing about?"

It was Eileen, who, along with Joyce, had chosen that moment to arrive for their Advisory Committee meeting.

"Men," responded Virginia.

"What else," snapped Eileen as if she had a few things to say on the subject herself.

Joyce flashed Virginia a knowing look. The doctor's sexual tastes didn't cross over to women, or their friendship might have been more. Still, Virginia had shared the state of her dual affairs with Joyce, so she likely guessed what the argument was about. She wondered if the doctor noted such things in the diary she was keeping, though she didn't really care one way or the other.

"Seeing as how Farkas decided Phoenix's staff should be 80 percent women," said Joyce, "it *is* a male's perfect scenario."

"Mathematically it does sort of render monogamy obsolete," added the engineer. "At least we don't have to worry about contraception."

"What do you mean?" asked Fawn.

"All the men here had to undergo vasectomies in order to qualify," Joyce explained. "The idea being, when the time comes to reproduce, only grade-A, genetically-approved, frozen sperm will be used to procreate."

"Oh."

"What I want to know is, when is that time going to arrive?" asked Virginia of no one in particular.

"I'm in no hurry," said Eileen. "I'm sure Farkas will let us know when the time is right."

"Yeah, it's all part of the *grand* scheme," said Joyce with a touch of sarcasm.

"I'm not so sure waiting on a computer is the best way to go," complained Virginia. "The next thing you know it'll be authorizing only certain sexual positions."

"Ginny!" exclaimed Fawn, embarrassed by her frankness.

"Well, it's true."

"What's true?" asked Michael as he and Kenji joined them.

"That with a ratio of 4-to-1 you guys are living in a male's paradise," said Eileen, poking Kenji with her finger.

"I do like the odds," responded Michael, smiling.

"The apocalypse is the best thing that ever happened to me," added Kenji.

"Okay, we're all here," said Fawn, wanting to change the subject. "What's the meeting about?"

"We've got video from the rover we sent out," said Michael. "I only glanced at it briefly. I thought we might want to watch it together."

"Let's see it."

Michael started the playback.

The uneven video revealed a desolate, scorched landscape, more akin to an alien planet than the Earth Virginia remembered. Much of the ash had been blown into ebony dunes, but the debris of civilization was evident too. Bits and pieces, metal and concrete--whatever endured the inferno.

Here and there were tiny signs of growth--plants whose underground root systems or dormant seeds had enabled them to survive the disaster. That was new. Two previous rover missions hadn't revealed life of any kind.

"Look at that weird plant," said Fawn. "What is that, Kenji?"

Virginia didn't recognize it either. Unlike the other growths, which had risen merely an inch or two above ground, this one was a full little plant, at least 18 inches tall. It was rather flimsy looking, almost ball-shaped, its scant spiral leaves a perfect vibrant green. She made out teardrop-size purple berries under the leaves.

"I don't know what that is," said Kenji. Virginia could tell by his voice he was perturbed he didn't recognize it. "It's very strange. The coloring, the shape . . . I've never seen anything quite like it."

"Well," said Fawn, "you can't know every species on the planet."

"Yes I can," insisted Kenji. "Especially anything native to this part of the world."

"Could it be a mutation caused by the comet strike?" asked Eileen.

"I don't see how that could be," Kenji muttered as the video moved on past the strange vegetation. "X-rays and other radiation are known to come from comets, but organisms don't mutate that fast."

"Maybe a space seed piggy-backed a ride on the comet," joked Virginia.

"Panspermia? I doubt it would have survived," replied Kenji seriously.

"What's panspermia?" wondered Fawn.

Before Kenji could answer her, Michael said, "It's a theory, never proven, that lifeforms, once part of other worlds and usually microscopic in nature, can survive within meteorites, comets, asteroids, traveling dormant through space until eventually landing somewhere. If that somewhere is conducive to the organism, it can revive from its dormant stage, become active, and begin to evolve."

"I've read there are some who think life on Earth began that way," added Joyce, "with microorganisms from another world."

"That's hard to believe," said Fawn.

"There have been documented cases of extraterrestrial bacteria and magnetite crystals found within meteorites," said Kenji. "The theory may not be proven, but it's very possible."

Suddenly there was something else they hadn't seen before.

"The sun's broke through!" blurted Kenji.

"Right on schedule," responded Eileen. "We estimated the 'impact winter' would last about six months. I can open the solar panels now."

"Perfect timing," said Kenji. "It's almost spring, if standard weather patterns haven't been disrupted. I can start planting." The botanist sounded as excited as a kid on Christmas. "My little farmers are all ready to go."

"We'll check with Farkas to be sure," said Michael, "but I would think so. That's how we formulated the master plan. Phase one, livestock insemination, phase two, botanical reseeding."

"What about the third phase--mine?" wondered Virginia.

"You know that's a ways off, Virginia," responded Michael.

"Why, because *Farkas* says so?"

"I know you're anxious," said Joyce, "but you know there's a good reason for waiting. Sanctuary can only support so many people, and until we're closer to resettling the surface we can't afford to increase our population. You knew that when you signed on, Virginia. You're just letting your impatience get the better of you."

"I know, I know. You're right. I guess it just rankles me that a computer is going to decide when we start making babies. The damn thing can't even talk so I can argue with it."

"Actually," said Michael, "I'm working on a vocalization program. You'll be able to have that debate with Farkas before you know it."

The sarcasm was as obvious on her face as in her tone. "I can't wait."

Ω

She relaxed, snug against Joe's chest, reveling in the passionate afterglow. He didn't say anything, but that wasn't unusual. She thought of him as the strong silent type. Not that he couldn't get going on a subject that interested him. He just didn't talk for talk's sake.

"If Fawn only knew what that was like," said Virginia, playing with the hairs on his chest, "maybe she'd understand."

"I'd be glad to help out."

"I'm sure you would." She yanked a clump of chest hair.

"Owww!" He started up but she pushed him back down.

"For someone with her credentials, she's led a pretty sheltered life," said Virginia. "Don't get me wrong, I'm very fond of her. Sometimes I just wish she wasn't so naive."

"Maybe we should try to hook her up with Lars. It'd probably be good for both them. Lars has been a little frayed around the edges ever since we went down under. I'm worried about him."

"I don't think she'd go for it, especially with Lars. For one thing, he's on her staff and she has a thing about that."

"She ever been with a man?"

"I don't think so. She says she hasn't. Who knows. Maybe she had a bad experience that turned her off men."

Joe shook his head. "I've been around her quite a bit. I don't get the impression she's a man-hater. More likely she's just wired differently--like a lot of people."

"Well, she's sure jealous of you," said Virginia, reaching down between his legs.

He responded quickly by rolling over on top of her. "And with good reason," he said.

"No, no. Get off, you beast," she said, playfully pounding his chest with her fists. "Really, Joe. I have to get up and go help Kenji with his little robotic tillers."

"Since when did Kenji need help with anything?"

"He doesn't really, but it gives me something useful to do. And I told him I'd be there."

Joe made no move to let her up. "I'll give you something useful to do." He gently grabbed hold of her wrists and slid them up the sheets above her head. "Kenji won't mind if you're a little late."

Ω

Kenji was so busy working with the other two botanists on their various projects, he didn't seem to notice Virginia showed up almost an hour late. When she asked about his robotic tillers--or, as he liked to call them, his "little farmers"--he began a lengthy oratory on how he was going to go about re-seeding the planet . . . or least the small part of it within his reach. He called it "terraforming Terra."

"The farmers are just the first part of a three-tiered approach, but the most reliable. They're designed with state-of-the-art technology, as sophisticated as Michael's rover, that is very similar to the ones NASA uses. Used," he amended. "When released on the surface, they travel in pre-set directions, stopping at intervals to conduct soil tests."

"They can do that?"

"Sure. It's their primary function. If the soil tests positive, then they go to work, planting a series of seeds, seedlings, rhizomes . . . . When they're finished, they return here to be re-stocked."

"How can you be sure anything will actually grow?"

Kenji's professorial expression clouded with concern.

"We can't. Once they're planted it's up to Mother Nature to provide enough sunlight, rain, and nutrients," he said as if having to leave the results to the whims of nature pained him.

"What are you planting?"

"Eventually, all kinds of things. We're starting with some hardy prairie grasses and grains, but we'll be trying fruits and selecting some vegetables once we get more data on soil conditions. Acid rains in the weeks immediately following the initial cataclysm were a definite possibility. They may continue dropping heavy metal poisons on and off for years. So we're uncertain what to expect until we get out there and test it."

"Wouldn't it be easier if you just went to the surface yourself?"

Kenji looked at her as if it were an odd thing to say. "Of course it would, but you know as well as I that goes against the procedures outlined by Farkas. None of us will be seeing the surface for quite some time," he added a bit wistfully.

"I know," replied Virginia. "It made sense when I read the project outline, you know, for the safety of the entire project and such, but now . . . ."

One of the other botanists approached them. Virginia remembered his name was Kirk.

"Control says the winds have picked up, Ken."

"Alright, let's get the first wave of balloons into the chute."

"Balloons?" wondered Virginia.

"That's the second phase," explained Kenji. "We release helium balloons into the atmosphere, with small loads of propagules--spores. They carry into the jet stream and fly much further away than the little farmers can travel. Speed and elevation determine when the loads are released. The same thing happens in nature, we're just giving it a little boost, trying to further our reach." Kenji shrugged. "It's a crapshoot though. I don't expect a high percentage of success with those."

Virginia thought about all the work he was putting into this, and what might really come of it.

"This is going to take years, isn't it?"

Kenji nodded. "The truth is we're only making a dent. We don't know everything that's already growing on its own out there. Hopefully quite a bit of flora has survived." He shrugged again. "In the long run what we're doing isn't much, but it's something."

Ω

Brett stopped to rest and looked around at his primitive but burgeoning colony. What shelters they'd erected were a hodgepodge of natural materials and elements they'd scavenged from the *Savannah*. It wasn't much, but they could always retreat to the sub when the weather turned bad.

Even so, they'd come a long way in the months since he'd chosen this spot. He'd selected it for no other reason than it had provided a good place to moor the *Savannah*, and because they couldn't go on much longer, crammed in the boat the way they were.

He'd known long before they couldn't roam the seas endlessly, and they could only travel up the Mississippi so far. He'd had only so much time to make a decision--to decide where his small band was going to settle. There didn't seem much to choose from. The same black devastation greeted them everywhere. The world was a burnt-out shell of its former self. Little had endured. At least life close to the river seemed to be coming back quicker than elsewhere. It wasn't much, but it revealed the world wasn't completely dead.

The search for family, friends, or comrades-in-arms in Norfolk had been fruitless. Not a single person related to the crew had survived the fiery maelstrom. Brett wondered if it were just bad luck or because of the military's ingrained code of secrecy. As far as he knew, his command structure never did admit to the coming cataclysm and how bad it would be. Did those families, who got most of their information from the Navy, who believed what they were told, not take adequate precautions? Would any precautions have even mattered?

The gloom of so many dismal discoveries had settled over his crew like an invisible fog--discernible by a palpable malaise. There had been two more suicides. Maxey hadn't found a trace of his family, which Brett considered a blessing, considering some of the remains they'd seen. But it had been a blow to him just the same. Yet he'd gone on, taken it in stride as if he'd expected it-- at least on outside. Brett had no idea how the man was handling it inside. And not only him, but all the other crew members who'd hope to find loved ones.

They *had* found a half dozen strangers they'd taken aboard. Some of his people took solace even in those few new faces. Most only kept going because following orders had become ingrained in them. Brett kept going because he had to--because his men depended upon him to--despite his fear he wasn't up to the task.

His plan to go inland to see if the Midwest had fared any better than the East Coast had been another disappointment, though they picked up a few more survivors in New Orleans, Baton Rouge, and St. Louis. His original crew of 130 had been supplemented by another 44 people. The boat had been much too crowded, and while they'd done their best to supplement their stores of food each time they went ashore, supplies were dwindling. All reasons he was forced to decide on a place to go ashore for good. A place where they could create some kind of settlement. The sub's nuclear reactor might last decades, but he knew his people wouldn't, crammed together like sardines.

His original crew had included only three women--officers who were among the first of their gender to serve aboard subs. Twenty-two of the survivors they found were women, and nine were children. That had helped, but he knew, even then, the imbalance in the sexes was going to be a problem once they established a settlement. He'd put it aside, thinking it was a problem for another day. He was right. It had been a struggle at first just to feed themselves. But now that they'd built their ramshackle shelters, begun their gardens, learned to fish and harvest what they could from the river, things were slowing down. Relationships were forming. An excess of young men were looking at a sparse pool of women.

Fortunately, Vilma had proved to be a take-charge kind of a woman. When it came to dealing with the imbalance of the sexes, she established firm rules. It had begun aboard the *Savannah*. With all the children and women sequestered in what had been officer country, she'd organized the civilian females and kept order among them. She was doing the same for the colony. She'd even taken charge of him, though nothing overt had happened between them. He got the feeling, though, it was only a matter of time.

Ω

Virginia had offered to help Fawn with the insemination of the horses, but then regretted it. It was a much more unpleasant process than with humans. Lars was there also, and Virginia could see he was still a bit edgy--at least as uncomfortable in the underground habitat as she was, though he didn't hide it as well.

Lars was doing most of the dirty work, which required, at one point, for him to sink his arm into the mare's vagina. First the horse had to be secured in what Lars called a "breeding stock," and her tail tied to the side to avoid contamination. Then the entire perineal area had to be scrubbed--disinfected. The insemination sample was drawn through a long pipette into a syringe. Like with human samples, the frozen sperm was preserved by cryoprotectants--substances that basically shield it from freezer burn.

Using a sterile, lubricated glove, Lars stuck his arm in to palpate the cervix. He would then guide the pipette into the uterus. He said this was the most delicate part of the procedure, as he had to be sure to avoid any internal damage. Finally, when he found his spot, the syringe introduced the semen into the mare.

Thankfully, they only asked Virginia to help keep the horses calm by talking to them and stroking their necks.

Despite her discomfort with the way the horses were inseminated, she was anxious to begin the procedure with human females--particularly herself. First, she had to convince the others in the advisory committee to move up the starting date for the process. That wasn't going to be easy, since most of them didn't want to deviate from Farkas' master plan.

Virginia already planned to be the first one inseminated. She didn't know why she was so anxious to have a child, but the feeling had intensified as the days and weeks passed. She theorized it might have something to do with the abortion she'd had when she was young. She'd been careless while still working on her bachelor's. It hadn't been the right time. It conflicted with all of her well-thought-out plans. So she'd terminated the pregnancy. She'd never doubted it was the right thing to do, but there were always lingering regrets of what might have been.

The horse she was stroking bucked a little, so she began talking to it in a quiet, soothing voice. It seemed to respond.

Though the horses would be the first animals impregnated and released, like with the humans in Sanctuary, there were only a few males. Females were more valued in this brave new world.

"Will you be releasing all the horses to surface?" asked Virginia.

"Eventually," said Fawn. "We impregnated half a dozen mares a few months ago. After those foal and have weaned their newborns, we'll release the six mares and one stallion to the surface. They should bond as a group--a starter herd--and then we'll do the same thing with the next batch. The foals will resupply our stock, and the adults, hopefully, will begin to repopulate the surface."

Joe showed up as they were finishing up with the third mare.

"Need some help?"

"Have the cattle been fed?" asked Fawn.

Virginia knew by her tone Fawn was still holding a grudge against Joe.

"The cattle, the sheep, the bison, the chickens, turkeys, pheasants--all fed and happy," replied Joe.

"Well then, take over for me here," said Fawn. "Farkas wants an update."

As soon as she was gone, Joe said, "She doesn't like me much."

"She's just jealous," replied Virginia.

"That's part of it, but not all of it," said Joe. "I think she even prefers the company of our grand computer to me."

Ω

On her way past the botany lab, Kenji called out to her.

"Virginia, come here. You've got to see this. It's new video from our rover. As a biologist you'll appreciate this. It's spectacular. Watch."

Kenji started the recording, but all Virginia saw was a close-up of that unusual plant they'd discovered several weeks ago. This one looked much bigger, much fuller, but without a point of reference, it was hard to tell how big it really was.

"*This* is spectacular?"

"Just watch," he insisted.

As she watched, the coiled chartreuse leaves of the little shrub spread open, billowing out like miniature sails unfurled by the wind. A gusty breeze suddenly raised the bush inches from the ground. Only the tether of its single root stem held it down. Then the stem broke apart, cleanly, easily, as if it were designed to, and the bush blew off out of the video frame.

"Did you see that?" asked Kenji excitedly. "I believe it's designed to catch the wind and blow away."

"Why?"

"To propagate, to distribute its seeds, just like our balloons. But that's not the spectacular part. In another video I've seen one of these roll into the picture, stop because the wind died, and then replant itself."

"What do you mean *replant itself*?"

"Exactly that. Its main stem actually inserts itself into the soil, like it's growing--growing at what for any botanical species is an incredible speed. Let me show you."

It happened just like he described. Within the space of less than 30 seconds after becoming immobile, the stem stretched down and burrowed into the earth.

"Have you identified it?"

"There's nothing like it in any records I could find. I've never heard of such a transplanting system. And I would have. I'm sure it's a new species."

"How could it be new?"

"It's got to have something to do with the comet," said Kenji, almost as if he didn't believe the words coming out of his mouth. "Rapid mutation, panspermia . . . I don't know. But it hasn't been catalogued."

"What are you going to call it?"

"I'm glad you asked. I call it *Nakajima amaranthus* . . . or just a naka bush for short."

"I can't say I'm surprised."

Ω

"Fawn, you called this unscheduled meeting," said Michael. "What's wrong?"

"One of my people, Lars Hansen, just blew up for some reason yesterday, and started acting crazy. I know he's been a bit claustrophobic, but I don't know what set him off. He stormed out and I haven't been able to locate him since."

Virginia had wondered who'd be the first to crack. She'd been worried it would be her.

"Lars Hansen, assigned to the Zoology Department, is deceased," announced Farkas.

Virginia still shuddered whenever she heard the computer's new voice. It sounded so real, so alive, so much like William Farkas returned from the grave. She wished Michael hadn't used the man's actual vocal patterns for the voice program.

"What do you mean he's deceased?" asked Joyce.

"He attempted to break out of the habitat and was electrocuted by the automated safeguards."

"Are you certain he's dead?"

"It is highly unlikely he survived contact with such extreme voltage. There are no signs of movement. The body will need to be removed and recycled immediately."

"Why was I not informed?" asked Joyce. "As lead physician I'm to be notified at once of any injury."

"Lars Hansen was not injured. He was killed."

"So you say. But you can't be certain," replied Joyce. "Where is he?"

"He is located at the terminus of Passage B."

"I'm getting a team and going out there," said Joyce. "In the future, Farkas, I need to know immediately of any injury *or* death. Is that understood?"

"Yes, Dr. Finley."

Ω

"How do we know Farkas didn't deliberately kill Lars to prevent him from escaping?" Joyce asked of the committee in-general.

"That's not possible," responded Michael. "That system is completely automated. It was meant to prevent intruders, but we were all warned not to attempt to leave Sanctuary--that such attempts could be fatal."

"Farkas could have turned it off in time," said Virginia.

"Farkas didn't kill him," said Eileen. "He killed himself."

"Alright, alright," said Virginia. "But I have another topic for discussion. I believe it's time to begin having babies--human babies."

"That's not scheduled for another year," said Kenji.

"I've been thinking about it, and I don't see any overriding logical reason to wait," said Virginia.

"The habitat's population must remain fixed," declared Farkas. *"We cannot overtax our resources and system requirements at this time. Our primary mission is to repopulate animal and plant species. Human offspring are not a priority. The planet's surface must be habitable before increasing your numbers."*

"But we already lost one of our numbers," argued Virginia. "I volunteer to give birth to a replacement."

"For organizational reasons, that is not possible. The master plan calls for all females to be impregnated at the same time, so the resulting offspring can be raised together with minimal disruption to other aspects of the habitat, and so they will mature together and be ready to procreate at the same time."

"Farkas is right," said Eileen. "We don't want to deviate from the master plan."

"Farkas is a computer, and he knows nothing about humans," said Joyce. "The grand *plan* was created by the real Farkas, and he's no longer here. We're the advisory committee for a reason. I think children would give our little population a real emotional boost. Caring for a child or children might prevent a reoccurrence of what happened with Lars."

"I'm against it," said Michael. "What about you, Kenji?"

"I can see the doctor's point. Maybe having some kids around wouldn't be such a bad idea. I don't think every woman should get pregnant at the same time. I can foresee problems with that. But a few more mouths to feed right now wouldn't harm anything."

"I disagree," said Eileen. "I say we don't deviate from the master plan. What about you, Fawn?"

"I don't know." Fawn looked at Virginia, then at Eileen. "I don't want to . . . change the plan."

Virginia gave her a dirty look. Fawn knew how much she wanted to have a baby now, but still she wouldn't go against Michael and Eileen.

"Well, we know where Joyce and Virginia stand, so it's three against three," said Michael. "That leaves it up to Farkas."

"I am programmed to follow the master plan."

Ω

It was fortunate for the little colony that life along the riverbanks returned at a quicker pace than it did elsewhere. Most of their forays inland found little but desolation. Here and there were signs of vegetation returning, and they'd even seen evidence of wildlife at times. Not that they had the skills to catch any and supplement their diet of mostly fish. Still, it provided a spark of hope that the Earth might stage a comeback. They had little else *but* hope, so every discovery was welcome.

The sub's provisions had been exhausted by the time they established their little village. They were fortunate the food aboard the *Savannah* had lasted long enough for them to get their land legs under them. Fortunately, there were hidden skills among their tiny populace. Fisherman, farmers, carpenters--abilities they now needed to survive.

Though Brett knew it flaunted convention, and ruffled more than a few feathers at first, the imbalance of the sexes eventually led to the formation of a few polyamorous associations. A few two men/one woman relationships developed, and one bonding between two women and five men. Given their situation, it seemed a natural progression of societal standards. Especially when the women began getting pregnant. It was hard enough to provide for everyone as it was, but it helped when a pair of men could provide for a woman and her child. Not that everyone didn't help everyone else. If there was one thing Brett was most proud of, it was the camaraderie of his little group. As tough as life had become, there was little grousing. With few exceptions, each person put their head down and did what was required of them. There was no other choice.

When it came to relationships, however, Vilma was more traditional. It took her a while to come around to the new lifestyles. Eventually she accepted them as necessary, but that didn't mean she was going to take part. She and Brett did end up together, and even held a brief wedding ceremony at one point because that's what she wanted. Brett was happy to oblige, because she made him happy, even in the face of all their hardships. It also created a pleasant distraction for everyone, and afterwards other such ceremonies were scheduled--even for one of the polyandrous alliances.

There came a time--Brett couldn't really pinpoint *when* it was--he began to think they might make it. Maybe it had been when his daughter, Savannah, was born. It made him happier than anything he could remember.

Once, shortly after her birth, he idly thought about how little Savannah would never know what it was like to live in the world before Smith-Kim. She'd never know the joys of shopping for a new dress with her mother, or deciding which kind of candy she wanted when her father took her to a movie theater. She'd never stare up at fireworks in wonder, or get a new bicycle for her birthday and ride it around the neighborhood. There were no more shopping malls, no more movie theaters, no fireworks, bicycles, or even neighborhoods. While that saddened him a little, it occurred to him she and the children to come might be better off than their parents--might do much better in this world without the past to hold them down.

Ω

On the way to the bio lab, Virginia passed Fawn in the corridor.

"Ginny, I--"

"Sorry, Fawn--in a hurry, can't talk now."

It wasn't very smooth, or polite, but Virginia wasn't about to get into any kind of discussion with her former lover. She'd broken it off the day Fawn sided with Farkas and the others to deny her the chance to impregnate herself immediately. She'd stewed over it for months, and now she'd decided to do something about it.

She wanted a baby. More than her desire to have a baby was that she needed something to keep her from going crazy in this place.

It was Christmas Eve, and she was going to give herself a present. One that would take nine months to unwrap, but would be well worth the wait.

Once it was done, there wasn't much they could do about it. She wasn't going to wait until some computer, basing its decisions on a dead man's schedule, allowed her to get pregnant. It was her choice, and she was choosing to do it now.

Ω

She didn't know what triggered the instinctual response or how its timing concurred with that of so many others of her caste. She only knew how to react. The programming was hereditary, wired into the circuitry of her nerves. The same sequence of actions had been followed, with minor fluctuations, for millions of years. All she knew, all her sense organs told her, was the time had come.

She made her way through the subterranean passages, following the chemical trail left by thousands of her sisters, leaving the shelter of her birthplace for the first time. The light was blinding. It took her several moments to orient herself to the expanse--the breadth of the world.

Once she'd overcome the sensory overload, she spread her four membranous wings and ascended into the infinite sky. There she joined a glorious swarm of flying males and other virgin queens in a frantic whirlwind of desperate recklessness. She flew this way and that, soaring to new heights, turning, twisting, diving. One of the frenzied males finally caught her and held fast until they spiraled awkwardly to the ground.

The act itself was straightforward, artless. Within minutes she had been inseminated with enough sperm to spawn thousands of eggs. Each of the stored spermatozoa had a lifespan equal to her own. She would never again need more. So she shook the male loose, ending the only mating she would experience in what could be three decades of life. His life, however, was over. His only purpose complete. Years of being fed and groomed by his female nurses all for a single moment of procreation. Unable to defend or feed himself, he would wander off to be consumed by predators or die alone of dehydration.

His mate was destined for greater things. She discarded her wings and began the search for an appropriate home, the place where she would give birth to an entire colony. What she found was a crevice between the roots of a small shrub. How that species of vegetation would come to influence her colony, and those that would succeed it, she had no concept. All she did was what she was programmed to do by her genetic code. She began to dig, and kept digging until she determined she was deep enough to lay the first of her eggs. If she were lucky, she'd be the one in ten thousand would-be queens to survive years of maturation, the mating process, predators, and natural disasters, to mother a thriving colony. But like the male who inseminated her, she'd have only one purpose in the years to follow--laying eggs. The proliferation of her colony would consume her every moment. Until it didn't.

Years after the last of the smoke and ash had dissipated, increased carbon dioxide and water vapor in the atmosphere left the world a much warmer place. Layers of ozone that had burned away resulted in intensified UV rays, and in some regions acid rains continued to salt water supplies with heavy metals and other poisons. Earth's comeback was ponderous and imperfect. While most of its aquatic lifeforms survived the devastation, many of the rest of its nearly nine million species would never walk, crawl, sprout, or fly across the face of the planet again. Evolution would begin anew, but with fewer pieces to move across the board of time.
Still among those pieces was man. Resourceful, tenacious, intelligent--mankind's children would survive, but not necessarily thrive in the desolate world they'd inherited.

LEGACY

HE DIDN'T KNOW WHY IT WAS HE STARTED REMEMBERING THINGS long forgotten. Maybe it was because he was truly alone for the first time in his life. Maybe it was the quiet desolation of the landscape--nothing but scraps of the archaic past from horizon to horizon.

Of course things weren't as bad as they were immediately after the comet set the world ablaze. In the years since, much of the plant life had regenerated, the way it does after any major fire. But barren, scorched areas where nothing flourished but a few hearty weeds still blemished the earth. In a sense, he was like those weeds, sprouting earnestly, unmolested, through the cracks of a bygone civilization.

His progress was slow. Navigating the Durango around countless derelict vehicles dotting the highways was always time-consuming, especially with the trailer he was pulling. Sometimes he was forced to detour completely off the road to make his way around. He had to proceed carefully each time because he had no real mechanical knowledge. If the Durango were damaged--when it ceased to function--he and his precious cargo would be stranded. Not that he knew where he was going--not specifically. He just knew he was headed north.

Before his dad had died, he'd suggested that if weather patterns held true, the rich forestlands of the north would grow back first. If Dad were right, it was there he'd best be able to live off the land, while avoiding the plague that had decimated erstwhile cities.

Dad was much on his mind as he drove. The memories of his death were as clear as they were frayed and sorrowful. But he tried not to think of how Dad was after he fell ill. Instead he did his best to remember what he was like before, at the beginning . . . at the beginning of the end.

Those memories were not so clear. They came to him piecemeal and in dim dreams. He'd only been seven and none of it made much sense to him at the time, even though Dad had tried to explain it. He hadn't really understood what was happening.

Two days before its arrival, Smith-Kim had become the brightest "star" in the sky. Of course it wasn't a star. He remembered looking up at it as Dad packed their brand new white Dodge Durango with food, water, books-- everything he could think of.

"Is it going to hit us?" he'd asked.

"It might, so we're going somewhere safe just in case."

"Is it going to hit Mommy?"

"No, she'll be okay."

What Dad didn't tell him then, was that he'd read all the scientific reports and knew it wasn't the collision, but the aftermath that would cause the most destruction. Incredible heat incinerating anything on the surface . . . dust thrown into the atmosphere blocking the sun for months . . . acid rain . . . nuclear fallout from damaged power plants and weapons set off by the heat. He didn't think, at the time, Dad really expected them to survive. But that didn't stop him from trying.

Fully packed, they'd driven off to the place Dad had found. He remembered, on the way, he saw thousands of people out along the streets, camped in parking lots, perched on rooftops, waiting for the comet's arrival. He didn't know if they thought it was going to bypass Earth and give them a show, or if they were just resigned to their fate.

Dad drove them to an underground parking garage, going as far down inside it as he could. A few other people had the same idea, but, at the time, he was too young to grasp why they were sitting down there, waiting, listening to the one radio station they could still get beneath several levels of concrete. At the time, he felt like he was missing out--that he wouldn't get to see what everyone else was waiting for.

He recalled the radio went static minutes before the chilly air of the garage grew so hot he burned himself when he touched the door handle.

When the heat got so intense he didn't think he could stand it, another family decided to drive out. Dad warned them not to go yet, but they left anyway.

He and his dad waited in the stifling heat for longer than he could keep track. He remembered crying at one point, and asking about his mother. Dad told him she was far away on a business trip, but that he'd warned her and told her to find a safe place like they did. What Dad didn't tell him was she believed less in what her own husband was telling her, and more in the assuaging news reports and adulterated government websites designed to lessen panic.

At one point he drifted off to sleep in the heat and woke with Dad putting a wet towel over his head. He fell back asleep and when he woke again it was much cooler, but the garage had gone dark--except for a few emergency exit lights.

When his dad finally decided to leave, it was as though they'd been transported to another world. They drove out onto a harsh, alien landscape--a hellish vista he still saw in his dreams. Fires were everywhere. Everything was burnt or burning--cars, buildings, bodies. There was no sky--only layers of smoke and ground fog. The smell filled the Durango and ash cascaded around them like black snow. It was so dark he didn't know if it was day or night.

He remembered being scared--so scared he turned away from the window and looked at his dad. Dad was silent, but tears rolled down his cheeks. He looked at his son, saw the fear on his face, and forced a smile.

"It's going to be okay, Adam," he said, wiping away his tears. "We're going to be okay."

That's when Adam had his first seizure. He didn't know what was happening, and neither did his dad.

He remembered crying out--whether in pain or confusion he didn't know. He remembered his head hurting, dizziness, and feeling like he was going to vomit. At some point he blacked out. When he finally woke he was soaked in urine, still lightheaded, and very scared. It didn't help that his father looked scared too.

Having never seen such a reaction before, Dad naturally assumed the seizure was in some way related to the comet. It wasn't until after many more such seizures, and years later when he began scouring library books and talking with other survivors, he realized he'd been struck by epilepsy.

Adam always felt more sorry for his dad than for himself. Not only had the world as he knew it come to an end, but he'd discovered his son was defective. At least that's how Adam used to think of himself. Now it was just one more thing he had to be wary of, in a world full of hazards.

Ω

The way ahead began to narrow. Adam hit the brakes, put it in park, and turned off the engine. He got out and climbed onto the hood for a better look. He had to shield his eyes from the glaring sun, but the clear air gave him a good range of visibility.

He noticed a trio of those strange windblown plants bouncing across the open plain to the East. He'd seen single plants being blown randomly about before, but never three together. Unlike dried out brown tumbleweeds, this strange bit of vegetation was garishly bright green. Up close he'd observed the plant's tiny purple berries and billowing spiral-shaped leaves. He'd also witnessed that whenever its lifecycle determined the time was right, the little shrub would bloom, catch the wind, uproot, and roll away. The unidentifiable plants were a post-cataclysmic mystery his dad never solved, no matter how many books he looked in.

The highway ahead was so clustered with derelicts, Adam knew he'd never be able to maneuver through. It had happened before, but he'd always been able to drive off the road, around the obstacles. This time that wouldn't be possible. He was approaching a stretch of highway cut out of a mountain, with no room either to the left or the right. He'd have to backtrack, take a smaller road he'd passed earlier, and hope to find a way around.

Impediments weren't anything new. He'd grown up among the vestiges of civilization. Some burnt out hulk of a building or rusted, corroded machine always stood somewhere nearby. Adam knew his dad found such sights depressing, but to him that's just the way the world was--a heritage of broken relics.

As time passed, he forgot the old world--for the most part. A seven-year-old doesn't know much anyway, but eventually he forgot all about video games, watching TV, and playing baseball. Those things didn't exist anymore. Such recollections faded with time. Yet some memories lingered--like how he used to laugh when Mom and Dad would put on their favorite music and dance.

That was the old world--their world. This was his world, the one he'd spent most of his life in, the one he had to live in. He didn't have a choice. But then he guessed no one did.

The first few months after Smith-Kim hit, were a struggle to survive. He remembered it was a long time before they saw the sun again. There was only dust and ash, tornados and hurricanes, earthquakes and ants. Ants were chief among the many insect species surviving the inferno. They not only survived, they flourished. It was a perfect world for scavengers. That's what he'd become--what all humans had become. They were scavengers, like the ants.

After the food Dad had packed was gone, they'd had to scrounge for everything. Most of it had been destroyed in the fiery aftermath, though they found canned and bottled food here and there. But there came a time when they nearly starved, and all they had to eat were mushrooms and various bits of meat Dad always told him was chicken. He realized later it must have been rat meat, or whatever kind of animal his dad could catch and kill.

Like the ants, the surviving rats thrived in the new world. For the first few years it seemed they might overrun the planet. But when the pickings grew slim, so did their numbers. Apparently, rats were dependent upon the leavings of mankind. A certain symbiosis existed between the two species. Of course they didn't disappear entirely. When he was older he became very good at hunting rats . . . even better at cooking them.

There were other human survivors as well. Not many--Dad once estimated less than 1 in 10,000 lived through the comet's impact. Of course, hunger, disease, and lawlessness would soon thin the herd even more.

Whether the survivors had been as smart as his dad or just lucky, Adam never knew till later. Some were friendly--as friendly as one could be in such circumstances--and some weren't. Mostly Dad tried to avoid others at first. He'd packed a gun with their supplies, and had to brandish it a couple of times to warn off some particularly nasty people. But the only time he ever fired it was to scare away a pack of hungry dogs that had caught their scent.

In time they met up with people they liked. Soon they had group of seven, then 13, then 20. Before long they had small community, eventually growing their own food, creating their own little patchwork society. Looking back, those seem like halcyon days now.

For years the group lived together on what had been the grounds of San

Diego State University. Thousands of books had survived in its underground library, so they had a wealth of knowledge to work with. Dad had a thing about books, so it was the perfect spot for him.

The community used the books as references for farming, first aid, water purification, sanitation--everything they needed to survive. They were also important for their sanity. There was little entertainment other than reading. Eventually Dad introduced him to such storytellers as Twain and Heinlein, Poe and Howard, Bear and Brin. He once told him fiction was as important as fact when it came to telling the story of mankind.

Adam didn't think any of it was very important at first, though Dad made sure he learned to read. The older he got, the less significant it seemed, until one day something finally clicked. It was a revelation of sorts. He came to understand all of mankind's accumulated knowledge, thousands of years of science and art, was still there in books, still available to the survivors so they wouldn't have to start all over again.

The point was driven home when they found a cache of gold coins someone had hidden away. Dad told him the coins once represented great wealth, but now gold was just another useful metal--if you had the knowledge to use it. He was right. Real wealth was knowledge, and that made books the most valuable things in the world.

He remembered, one day, walking with Dad to the hills overlooking an immense valley. He'd just finished reading *The Postman*, and they talked about whether such a scenario might come true some day. It was near sunset, and the clouds in the westward sky burned with a dozen autumnal hues. Down the middle of the valley, traveling in both directions as far was the eye could see, was a multi-lane highway. Dad called it a "freeway." North of this vast roadway was a concrete stadium that had survived the fires. The funny thing was, his Dad told him the old stadium had been scheduled for demolition. The comet had actually saved it. Saved it for what, he couldn't imagine.

Dad told him how he'd been in that stadium with his own father when the local baseball team had won its first championship. He said the noise of sixty thousand fans was so loud it hurt his ears. Adam believed him, but it was hard for him to imagine that many people, when his world consisted of less than sixty. At least until the plague came.

Ω

The detour he was forced to take led him up a coastal road with very few derelicts. It was a much more pleasant drive, seeing the ocean glistening off to his left instead of the scattered remnants of the past that usually garnished the scenery. They'd gone to the beach many times when he was younger, but he hadn't seen the ocean since the end of everything. The foam-flecked waves churning onto the sand, the retreating tide, the chill wind blowing off the water, gave it a sense of life compared to the bleak panorama he was used to.

Only once, late in the day, was he forced to slow and ease his way around an overturned truck. As he drove by he looked down. The driver had tried to crawl out of the wreck. He didn't make it far. Adam knew by the state of the corpse it wasn't the trauma of the accident that had killed him. It was the plague. He was familiar with those symptoms, and he knew the man hadn't been dead long.

He recalled when the disease had hit their community, it spread quickly. Within ten days most everyone was gone. Dad lived for twelve.

As soon as people started getting sick, they searched every medical journal and scientific text they could find to determine what it was and whether there was a cure. Those last four days Dad was too sick to help, but Adam kept at it . . . for all the good it did.

They were never able to determine whether the disease was something mankind had dealt with before, or a genetically engineered biological agent unleashed from some laboratory by the cataclysm. They had no doctors or real scientists in their community, and not enough understanding of cellular biology or virology.

Why he and a few others didn't contract the disease they never figured out. There seemed to be no reason why they were immune and so many weren't. They were all certainly in constant contact with those who were sick, but some dynamic of biology or whim of fate protected them. He considered that maybe it was the epilepsy that somehow made him resistant, but it was just another useless theory.

In those last few hours of his dad's life, Adam didn't want to be protected. He didn't want to be left alone. He railed against providence, cursed the universe, and tried to put his fist through a door. In the end, none of it mattered. All he could do was sit by Dad's side and watch him fade away.

He remembered him saying, "There's so much I wanted to teach you--tell you." Dad stretched his arm out, so weak Adam didn't think he could hold it up, and put his hand on the small stack of books by his bedside. "Don't let it all die, Adam. This is humanity's legacy. Don't let the words die."

He took his last breath less than an hour later.

At first, anger overwhelmed Adam. He was angry those same books his dad praised were no help in saving his life. He was angry at himself for not being smart enough to save him. He was angry that, for some reason unknown to him, he was still alive and healthy.

When his anger cooled and practicality returned, he hitched the small trailer he'd found to the Durango and packed them both with all the food and books he could fit inside. He attached his Honda scooter to the carrier on the vehicle's rear, said goodbye to the few others who'd survived the plague, and left, heading north as Dad suggested.

Ω

As the day grew long, Adam stopped to eat and watch the sun setting over the ocean. The colors streaming across the horizon, bouncing off the fringe of clouds and sinking into the sea were breathtaking. It was more beautiful than anything he remembered. But then he'd grown up in an ugly world.

At first, Dad had tried his best to hide the ugliness from him. But there were only so many ways he could turn, so many things he could do to protect Adam from the sight of seared bodies or the brutality of scavengers . . . animal, insect, human. It was a grim, unsparing existence he'd inherited. One that toughened him beyond his years.

Adam didn't like to travel at night. Even with headlights it was hard to see all the obstacles in the road. He didn't want to take a chance on damaging the Durango, so he decided to stay where he was for the night and see if he could find a way down to the beach.

Getting down wasn't hard, once he found what looked like a pathway cut into the cliffs. On the seashore he took off his shoes to feel the sand between his toes. The texture of the fine granules and the smell of the sea air brought back memories of being at the beach with his mom and dad, and how he used to dig a big hole in the sand, climb in, and wait for the tide to roll in and create his own little pool.

The sand on this stretch was near-white, but it wasn't a pristine beach. Rocky outcroppings protruded here and there--dwindling fortresses of stone battered by centuries of surf. Tide pools formed in the shallow depressions of the rocks, giving shelter to a variety of crustaceans.

Adam rolled up his pant legs and walked across the damp sand. The water was cold--too cold to think about going in any further. He strolled through the shallow surf, lost in thought but careful to avoid the sporadic mounds of seaweed until he saw something else. It was bouncing around near the edge of the water, repeatedly grazing the shore before being tugged back by the tide.

It was a bottle--a singular glass container. As soon as he saw it he remembered something he'd read somewhere--a phrase about "a message in a bottle." He plucked it from the surf and looked through its dark glass exterior. No message lay inside, no great insight as to where it came from or what human hands might last have touched it. Churning within were only grains of sand and foaming sea water. He thought about putting his own message inside, but had no writing implements at hand. So he reached back and threw it seaward as far as he could.

When he turned around he saw something small move behind one of the rock formations. He was certain it was an animal of some sort, but the glimpse he had was too quick to be sure exactly what it was.

It didn't matter. Drawn by the sight of another living creature, he walked quickly as he dared, not wanting to scare whatever it was. He looked behind the rock. There was nothing there. So he stepped up onto it to get a better view. There, down the beach a short ways, was a cat.

It was a striking animal, with a snow-white face, a golden sheath around one ear, black around the other. Its lower torso was all white, but its back was a patchwork of gold and black running down to the tip of its tail. It was so out of place, so unreal, that he considered, for just a moment, he was imagining it--seeing things. Not many cats had survived Smith-Kim. Those that did, like the rats and the dogs, often became someone's dinner.

Adam began walking towards it, slowly, saying, "Here, kitty, kitty."

It was unimpressed with his cat call and sat there on its haunches for a moment. As he drew closer, it walked away--not like it was scared, but nonchalantly, like it had better things to do.

He quit calling it, but kept moving forward. After a moment it sat back down and waited.

When he was close enough he squatted and reached out to pet it. He was afraid it would run off again, but it stood its ground, and wallowed in his touch. It even began to purr.

"Where did you come from? Are you by yourself out here?"

It accepted his attention for a bit, then sauntered off.

"Wait," he said, getting to his feet. "Where you going?"

It wasn't running, but it was moving steadily down the beach. He followed it quite a ways, sure it was leading him somewhere and not just out for a stroll. The further they walked, the higher the shoreline cliffs rose, and the rockier they got. It wasn't long before he spotted more cats up ahead. When he got closer he saw a large opening in the cliffs--the mouth of a cave. The cliffs were dotted with smaller such crevices, and he didn't think anything of it until he saw the chair. It was right there, just inside the opening. A large wicker affair with a faded red cushion. He had only seconds to contemplate the misplaced furniture, when a man rounded the section of cliffs jutting seaward All around the fellow, following him, were cats. A half-dozen at least--all scampering to avoid the surf.

At this point the feline that had led him here pranced over and began rubbing against his legs as though they were old friends. Adam bent down to scratch its head. That's when the other fellow saw him.

"Go away!" he shouted, walking towards him and waving his arms. "Shove off! Get! Go away!"

Adam stood.

"I don't mean any harm. I saw this cat and followed it down the beach."

The stranger looked at the cat, still rubbing against Adam, and slowed his walk. He stopped waving his arms but continued to draw near. His cats still trailed him, though haphazardly. A couple of small kittens paused to play. Another, larger one, took a moment to scratch and lick its coat.

The man who approached him was an old fellow for sure. Both his hair and beard were gray, in sharp contrast to his sun-darkened skin, and he walked with a slight limp. Adam was no judge of age, but this fellow had to be least 60--probably older. His feet were bare and he wore one of those rolled up woolen head covers. His clothes were as tattered as Adam imagined Robinson Crusoe's must have been. That's the image which came to mind anyway.

"My name's Adam," he said, hoping to break the tension.

The stranger didn't respond at first. He looked Adam over with a suspicious eye. Adam didn't particularly like the way he was being sized up. A part of him wanted to turn around and go back the way he came. Another part was just plain curious, even though he expected the old fellow to start screaming at him again. Instead the stranger said rather mildly, "Well, I guess Kimber likes you." He half-gestured at the cat between Adam's legs. "Come on up if you want."

With that he turned and headed for the cave.

Ω

Up close the stranger looked even older. The backs of his withered hands were a maze of wrinkles, veins, and bony ridges, crisscrossed by long, thin scars. Judging by his companions, Adam guessed the scars were cat scratches. But there was something not quite right about the fellow's eyes--something askew--as if there were times he was somewhere else, seeing something no one else could see.

He had an eclectic array of old furniture inside the cave, including a small bed, that rested under a mottled wooden sign reading "Home is wherever I drop anchor." A large cast iron pot hung over a fire pit, and something was cooking. It smelled good, but Adam didn't ask what it was.

"Do you live here?" Adam inquired, gesturing at the cave.

"Course I do."

"All alone?"

"Do I look alone?"

His sarcasm was justified. With all the cats he was hardly alone.

Cats were everywhere. The longer they sat, the more that appeared. Black cats, white cats, gray cats, orange/gold cats, tabbies, calicos, Siamese, and combinations thereof.

"I've never seen so many cats. I thought most of them died in the cataclysm."

"Cat-what?"

"You know, when the comet Smith-Kim hit."

He didn't respond, and his blank look made it seem he didn't know what Adam was talking about. Adam guessed it was a memory he didn't want dredged up.

Two playful kittens diverted his attention, taking center stage when one pounced on the other. The resulting ball of fur rolled over and over, their high-spirited battle compounded by tiny snarls and hisses. They separated and faced off, each with a paw poised to strike the other, their tails whipping back and forth like crazed pendulums. One of them growled menacingly and pounced again.

While this was going on, the cat who'd found Adam jumped onto the old man's lap. It spoke to him in a half cry, half purr, punctuating and accenting its sounds as though forming the words of some ancient feline language.

"I catch your drift, Kimber. I was thinking the same thing."

The cat settled on his lap and Adam asked, "Do all your cats have names?"

"Course they do," he snapped. "Cats are people too."

Adam ignored the inanity of that. "How many cats do you have?"

"Too many," he said with a short, wheezy laugh. "More than a shark's got teeth."

Paying no heed to the cat on his lap, he stood. Kimber landed easily and walked away as though the affront were nothing new. The old man walked to the side of the cave entrance and lit a lantern.

Adam hadn't noticed how dark it had become--maybe because a full moon was already shining down on them.

"How do you remember all their names?"

"Each one's an individual," he said with authority as he stirred whatever was in his pot."Each has got his own mind, his own disposition, his own voice. Hell's bells, they even walk different." He sat back down. "If you give a cat a unique name, it'll be a unique cat--that's just common sense."

"How do you feed them all? How do you feed yourself?"

"The sea is bountiful."

"You mean fish?"

"Fish, kelp, crabs, sea spinach, sea beets . . . whatever it brings. You go ashore a ways there's licorice fern, crowberries, cotton grass, mushrooms. There's cures too. Irish moss is good for fevers you know . . . and laver prevents scurvy."

Adam had read about edible plants, but most of those mentioned he was ignorant of.

"Is that why you live here?"

"I like the sea. Used to be seaman, a navigator, long before you were born. There ain't no crowds out in the deep, no long lines to wait in, no noisy highways and byways and gizmos. Just quiet. I sailed the seas in more than dozen different ships. Freighters, tankers, tuna trawlers . . . you know what I'm talking about?"

"I've seen pictures in books."

"Psssss . . . pictures in books," he said with contempt. "You have to see a ship up close, smell the rust of its gunwales, hear the groan of its engine as it turns into the wind, feel its deck roll under your feet. You can't see that in a book. Hell's bells, you could even navigate by the stars if you knew what you was doing--and I did."

Adam felt chastised by his lack of experience in such matters. His only real experience was post-apocalyptic. The only things he knew about the world before *came* from books. So, somewhat defensively, he said, "Did you know the light from the stars you navigate from is billions of years old? It takes so long for the light to get here, some of the stars we see might not even be there anymore. I read that in a book."

"That so," he said, apparently unimpressed by Adam's factoid. But he turned and looked up at the night sky as if contemplating the essence of it. Or maybe he was just remembering another time, another place.

It occurred to Adam he was likely the first person the old man had talked to in years. He wondered how the fellow went on, day after day, this ancient mariner, this cat man. How he faced each day alone. Of course he wasn't alone--not to his way of thinking. But if all he had to talk to were cats . . . .

It only took a moment for Adam to realize the real question wasn't about the old sailor. It was the one he'd been asking himself. Not out loud, but deep in the recesses of his thoughts.

What's the point? Why go on? For what reason? To end up like this wretched fellow?

He didn't have an answer. He didn't know if he ever would . . . even if his dad did.

Adam remembered asking his dad once, when he was older, why he didn't just let them die--how he kept going in those first, dark, desperate years. Dad told him he didn't believe in giving up--whether you were playing cards, baseball or board games--you did your best until it was over, no matter how badly you were losing. You competed until the end. He said the human race needed to compete now more than ever. Winning was surviving.

An ebony tomcat with yellow eyes and a torn ear stalked in from the darkness. Adults and kittens alike moved aside, leaving no question as to his dominant status. He sauntered close to Kimber, the she-cat that had taken a liking to Adam, paused and snarled at her. She responded with a warning of her own, but the male ignored her and casually settled next to the old man.

He chuckled. "That was just a shot across the bow. Reefer here doesn't get along with Kimber--never has. She usually gives him a wide berth. Like some people--oil and water--they never mix."

A mewing sounded from deeper in the cave. His host looked back, concerned, and Adam followed when he went to investigate. There, on an old blanket, lay an exhausted mother and four newborn kittens. Fatigued as she must have been, she raised up and began cleaning one of the babies.

The old fellow turned to him and said, "Nature keeps marching on, doesn't she?"

That's when Adam was hit by a familiar feeling, one almost always accompanied by dizziness and the smell of burnt toast. They were the first signs of an oncoming seizure. He tried to sit, but was blinded by flashing lights and muscles that wouldn't respond. He felt himself falling just before he blacked out.

Ω

When Adam woke, he was covered with a blanket. He was confused, thirsty, and his head hurt. But he wasn't so confused he didn't know what had happened. He'd experienced too many seizures not to know. He waited while the nausea and fuzziness dissipated. When he finally sat up, Adam saw the old man sitting close by.

"Those were some rough seas you sailing on there," he said. "You alright?"

"Yeah, I'm okay."

"Happen often?"

Adam shrugged. "Once in a while."

"What's wrong with you?"

"It's epilepsy."

"I've heard of that," he said. "but don't rightly know what it is."

"A seizure's kind of a disruption of the communication between neurons." Adam realized, by his expression, the old fellow had no idea what he was talking about. "It's kind of an electrical storm in the brain."

He nodded. "Seemed like you were riding out quite a squall. You okay now?"

"Yeah, I'll be fine."

The old guy looked at him as if he wasn't so sure, then walked back out into the open and looked up at the moon for some time. Adam was about to break the silence when he said, "It's almost time."

"Time for what?"

He didn't respond. It was like he was somewhere else again. He started down the beach. Slowly, but eventually en masse, the cats followed him. What Adam thought was maybe a score of felines became dozens. Some came down from the cliffs, others out of the darkness. It was startling to see them all moving as one, avoiding the murky fingers of the tide, but definitely following the old fellow.

Adam also followed, not asking any more questions. When the old sailor reached a stretch of beach meeting with his approval, he turned and walked straight into the surf. Adam was afraid he'd be swept out to sea, but he stood there, knee-deep in water, holding his ground against the surge, waiting. Waiting for what Adam didn't know. But each of the cats, and there must have been half a hundred, kept vigil at the tide's edge.

The sound of the waves was gradually infiltrated by a growing number of deep-throated cries--a scattered chorus coming from the waiting felines.

"What's happening?" Adam finally called out.

He got no answer.

The waves crashed, the tide rushed forward, then retreated, and suddenly, magically, the lifeless wet sand was swarming with activity. Hundreds of tiny fish, glistening silver in the moonlight, squirmed and wriggled in the sand. The cats silenced as abruptly as the fish appeared, but a grunting sound emanated from the sea creatures.

It was an astonishing sight, spellbindingly surreal--except it *was* real. Just as amazing were the cats. Each and every one held its ground, watching, waiting, as many of the fish struggled to burrow into the sand.

The old man returned to shore, walking among the fish.

"What are they doing?"

"Propagating," he responded as he knelt and grabbed hold of one fish. "Life goes on." He tossed the single fish towards his waiting friends. It was a signal. As it dropped the cats raced down into the mud and shallow water and began to feast.

Ω

Adam woke near the mouth the beach cave with Kimber curled up next to him. He didn't see the old man anywhere, so he started down the beach in the direction of the Durango, followed by his feline friend. Doubt crept into his head. He worried about the car. Not only was it his transportation, but it contained all his supplies and worldly possessions, as meager as they were. He didn't usually sleep so far away from it. He wanted to check on it, and get back on the road. He hoped to be able to say goodbye and thanks to the old sailor, but he had no idea where the fellow had gone.

As he walked he glanced seaward and saw something odd. Far out, almost at the horizon, was a mountain of blue-white ice, floating with the current. He thought of what he'd read about ice, about the expression "tip of the iceberg," and considered how large it must be under the surface. He wondered, too, how enormous it must have been before it began its voyage to this warmer clime--wherever it came from.

Before he reached the lower cliffs where he'd descended the previous day, he came across the old man--along with a small contingent of cats. Adam figured he never went anywhere alone.

"I wanted to thank you for letting me spend the night . . . and for the soup." The old fellow responded with a slight nod. "I'm going to have to be on my way now. My car's up the hill."

"Time and tide," he responded, shrugging. "Well, if you gotta weigh anchor, I'll walk with you."

It was more of a climb than a walk, and Adam was worried the grizzled fellow might not make it. But he did, with more grace than Adam managed.

Kimber and many of the other cats followed them up. She hadn't left his side since he'd first happened on her--except for the fish feast. Adam didn't know why, but the thought sparked a memory of his mother, who, when he was little, followed him everywhere when she took him to the park or the playground. She was afraid to lose sight of him even for an instant.

At some point, after the world went to hell, he asked his dad, "Is Mommy dead?"

Dad had looked at him with a forlorn expression and said, "I don't know." For a moment he thought his dad might cry, but he contained his emotions and added, "I know she'll never be dead as long as we remember her."

From then on, he always tried hard to remember his mom. But over the years those memories dissipated, like wisps of smoke in the wind, until all he could picture was her dark, wavy hair. It saddened him he couldn't see her face anymore.

Kimber followed him all the way to the Durango, even though the old man and the rest of his tiny entourage paused at the cliff's edge.

"Go on," Adam said to her with a shooing gesture, "go on, go back with the others."

"I think she wants to go with you."

Adam picked her up and scratched her head as he carried her over and set her down with the other cats. But when he walked away, she followed him again.

"She likes you--no getting around it. She's always been kind of a loner, fighting with Reefer all the time. I think she's decided you should take her."

"I can't do that--she's yours."

"She's not mine. You don't own a cat."

"But how will I . . . how will I take care of her?"

"Cats pretty much take care of themselves. And they pretty much go where they want."

Adam didn't know what to do. All he knew was he didn't want the responsibility, not for another life, not when he'd seen so many lives extinguished while he stood by helplessly. Not even a cat's life.

"They say cats have nine lives," the old man remarked as if privy to his thoughts. "They're healers too. She'll take care of you as much as you will her. Help you keep an even keel."

"I don't know . . . ."

"You don't always get the post you want," the strange old sailor admonished him. "You can tread water for a long time, but eventually it's sink or swim. Life's funny that way."

Adam wasn't sure what he meant, but he gave in. "Okay. I guess she can come with me." He wouldn't have admitted then, but deep down he was lonely. Part of him liked the idea of a companion--even a feline one.

He unlocked the door, picked up Kimber, and made space for her on the passenger seat. The old fellow turned to leave. "Wait a minute," said Adam. "There's something I want to give you."

It took him a minute to search through the books stacked on the floorboard, but he found the one he was looking for.

"Here, you take this. I've got as many books as you have cats. Call it a trade."

The stranger walked over--almost cautiously--and took the book from him.

"I'm not sure I need a book," he said. "Haven't read one in a whale's age."

"Books can be good companions--like cats," said Adam, not knowing if he'd take offense. "I once read books are lighthouses erected in the great sea of time." Adam thought he might appreciate the metaphor.

He looked at the cover and slowly read the title as if rediscovering each word, "The Old Man and the Sea." He smiled at the words, revealing a glint of silver in his teeth.

As quickly as it was born, the grin faded and his countenance grew thoughtful.

"We had a saying when we were at sea and things got bad--storms and such. We'd say we're closer to what's ahead than what's behind. You'd do good to remember that."

With that he turned and headed for the cliff's edge, followed by his feline honor guard. He stopped short of the drop-off, looked at Adam and raised his hand to his forehead. Adam couldn't tell if he was saluting or just shading his eyes from the sun.

"You keep her trim and true and you'll be fine."

Adam didn't know exactly what the old sailor meant by that, but he had an inexplicable feeling he was right.

Both man and beast did what they could to cling to life. But it was no longer just a matter of surviving day-to-day. If the living were to thrive, they must transform, alter old ways of thinking, obsolete ways of doing things. To persevere they must evolve along with a world reborn. A world often unrecognizable to those who came before.

RESOLUTION

SHE LIKED TO SPEND HER TIME AROUND THE PENS AND STABLES, where Uncle Joe let her help feed the animals. But what she liked most was riding Pegasus. She thought he was the most beautiful horse in the world, because he was all white. Uncle Joe told her Pegasus was born in Sanctuary just like she was, but that she was older than the horse, even though he was so much bigger.

"He's just a yearling now," said Joe, walking alongside to make sure the girl didn't fall from Pegasus' back. "But some day--oh, probably in ten years or so, we'll take Pegasus to the surface and let him run free."

She held on tight to the horse's mane and considered this. She knew the "surface" was a place she wasn't allowed to go. No people were allowed up there, but she also knew many of the animals in Sanctuary were taken there and set free.

"Will Pegasus grow his wings when he's on the surface?" she asked.

"Wings?" Joe laughed. "No, that's just a story about another Pegasus. But he'll run so fast it'll seem like he's flying."

She continued to ride as Joe guided Pegasus in his usual circular route.

"Uncle Joe, are you my father?"

"What?" The question caught Joe off guard. "Well, in a way, all the men in Sanctuary are your fathers, and all the women are your mothers."

"That's what Dr. Joyce says, but Fawn says my real father is Farkas. How can a machine be my father?"

Joe wasn't sure how to respond. "That's right. Farkas isn't your real father. But in a way, he's a father to all of us, because he tells us what we should do.

That's why so many of your mothers have babies now, because Farkas said it was time. He's sort of your grandfather."

She thought about this, but it was a puzzle, and she wasn't sure all the pieces fit.

"Okay, Erica, it's time to let Pegasus rest."

Joe grabbed her under her arms and set her on the ground.

"Will I have a baby some day?"

"Sure you will. Whenever Farkas says it's time."

Ω

The further north he traveled, the smaller the highways became. Fortunately, in those days, there was always a lot of fallow land on either side to ease his detours. Only once did he have to use the Durango to push a small car out of the way. The going was often slow, but he was in no hurry. A by-product of having no particular destination.

Occasionally he would detour off the main highway to look for anything that might have survived the destruction--food, fresh water, people. That usually ended in disappointment. Very little food suitable for eating remained from before the cataclysm, and even fewer people.

Except when she was asleep, which was often, Kimber liked to jump onto the perch he'd made for her on the passenger seat, and see what she could see. There wasn't much in the way of scenery, though once he spotted a quartet of horses standing atop a hill, watching him go by. He wondered where they came from and how they survived the cataclysm. That got him to thinking about what other kinds of creatures endured--and what kinds were probably extinct. One kind that apparently hadn't survived, were birds. He figured somewhere there were probably chickens or other farm fowl that had somehow been protected. But he hadn't seen a single bird in flight all the years since Smith-Kim. He guessed when all the trees burned, so did the birds and their nests, though he'd read some birds lived in burrows under the ground. He knew birds were the natural prey of cats, and felt bad Kimber might never know the feline thrill of such a hunt.

Though she'd never caught a bird, she'd captured, and eaten, a few lizards and a couple of mice. He'd also seen her eat several kinds of bugs. She had a feast one day when a swarm of grasshoppers enveloped them. He'd ran for the shelter of the Durango, but Kimber just kept swatting them down.

When he stopped at night, she would run off--hunting he presumed. But she'd always come back, often making him a present of some dead creature.

He would thank her, but leave it for her to eat. Occasionally, when he came across any canned meat that still seemed good, he'd share some with her. It was a rare treat, and he figured that was a good thing. He didn't want her to become dependent on him for food . . . for anything.

Whenever he spotted a building that hadn't been burned too badly, he'd stop and search it. He knew he had to keep trying to replenish his rapidly vanishing provisions. Most of the time he wouldn't find anything still good after all those years, but he wasn't picky with what he did find. Anything still sealed in a can he assumed was good, though sometimes the smell and the taste test said otherwise. Often he discovered signs other survivors had been there before him. There was never any way to tell how long it had been since the ransacking had taken place, but the idea other people existed always roused his curiosity . . . and made him more cautious at the same time.

There were times when traveling through the ruins of some small town that shadows played tricks on him. Signposts would dart with movement, black shapes would peer out of empty windows, and long-abandoned cars would come alive with passengers. A couple of times he stopped to look, only to find nothing but the scraps of his imagination.

Fuel was no problem--not yet anyway. When he ran low, he'd simply siphon more gas from vehicles that were still intact, just like Dad had showed him. Most car gas tanks were airtight, and the fuel had yet to deteriorate.

He discovered, much to his surprise, in some places water still ran through the pipes. The pipes had run dry early on in San Diego, but he guessed gravity must be keeping them filled elsewhere, depending upon where the local reservoirs were located.

Dad had been right about the northern part of the state. Much of the foliage had grown back over the years, and it was much greener than the landscape he was used to. He had a couple of books on edible plants, but he hadn't discovered anything he found appetizing. He wasn't that desperate yet, but he knew the day would come. He did discover a lone peach tree in one spot. It wasn't large, but the fruit was sweet and juicy. He gorged on peaches for a couple of days.

They'd been on the road together for a week or so when he noticed Kimber's stomach swelling. A week later it was definitely larger, and he worried she'd eaten something infectious. But she seemed alright--not in any distress--so he figured maybe she was just getting more than enough to eat. That got him to thinking about the old cat man, and how he hadn't seen anyone else since leaving San Diego.

It was strange how, just when he was thinking about how alone he was, he spotted her. At first he thought she was just another figment of his imagination. Especially since her image wavered mirage-like through the heat vapors rising off the asphalt. He slowed his approach, wondering if she'd vanish. She didn't.

His first thought was one of caution--a reflex ingrained in him by his dad. She didn't look dangerous. She was wearing a pink backpack, and when he approached she casually stuck out her fist, thumb upraised. Was she telling him everything was okay--that she was okay? He slowed as he neared her, seeing no reason he shouldn't stop.

She was older. Not like the old hermit--not even as old as his dad--but older than him. Her hair was long, blonde, and looked remarkably well-kept. She wore a frayed purple and blue sweatsuit that would have made her stand out even in a crowd of people. But there were no more crowds. She was all alone. He had to stop.

She opened the passenger door, pushed back a lock of windblown hair, smiled and said, "Give a girl a ride?"

It wasn't like they were the last two people in the world, but her comment seemed rather nonchalant, considering.

He didn't respond, but instead began moving Kimber's perch to the back seat to make room. As soon as he finished, she took off her backpack, hopped in, and closed the door.

"Thanks for stopping," she said, still smiling. "I thought I was seeing things when your car came over the rise. I haven't seen one running in years. Oh, sorry--I'm Johnnie."

"Adam," he said.

The first thing he noticed up close were her eyes--her sage-green eyes. He didn't know what word he would use to describe them--winsome, alluring, otherworldly--but he could feel their pull. She offered her hand in greeting and he gripped it briefly. A warm, tingling sensation from that fleeting contact ran up his arm. Whether it was just the touch of another human being or something else, he couldn't say.

As he started the car forward, he considered the sensation might be a sexual one. Not that he had any experience in such matters at the time. He certainly knew what sex was, had even stumbled upon others in the act, but most of what he knew of love and lust came, of course, from books. There were no girls his age in their little community, and he'd never experienced anything other than his own self-gratification. But, like any male his age, he had stirrings.

"Your name is Johnnie?" he said, to distract himself. "Isn't that a boy's name?"

"Yeah, usually. My parents named me Janelle, but no one's called me that in a long, long time. I'm just Johnnie now."

She turned and reached behind the seat to pick up Kimber.

"What a doll. What's her name?"

"Kimber."

Kimber settled in her lap beneath a steady stream of petting.

"You're sure a pretty kitty, and a pretty pregnant one too."

"Pregnant?"

"You didn't know?"

He shook his head.

"I'm no expert, but I've seen pregnant cats before. I'm fairly sure you'll be having some more mouths to feed in a couple of weeks."

He looked at Kimber and realized she must be right. He hadn't even wanted one cat, now . . . .

"Where you from?" she asked.

"San Diego."

"Yeah? I was there once. Real nice place . . . at least it used to be. Any people still there?"

"Some. We had a small community, but the plague killed most everyone. I was one of a few that didn't get sick."

"I've seen that. That's why I stay away from cities." She smiled. "I'd hate to get taken down by a bug after all these years."

"What about you? Where are you from?"

"I'm from all over. And I mean *alllll* over. I traveled around a lot, even before . . . before it happened."

"How'd you survive the comet?"

She sighed and looked out the window as though she wasn't going to respond.

"I ran away from home when I was 15, moved around for a few years. I didn't know much about the comet, and cared less. I was just living from one place to the other--one meal to the next. I broke into this house one day, and when the owners came home I hid in the basement. There was an old fridge

72

there with some food, some beer, and no one came down, so I stayed there a few days. When I finally snuck back up, I found the roof and most of the furniture had burned away. The brick walls were still standing, but outside I found the bodies of whoever must have lived there--burnt to a crisp. I guess they went outside to see the comet." She paused as though the memory took a moment to shake. "At the time, I had no idea what had happened. It was dark, everything had burned, and the sky . . . the sky was full of ashes."

"I remember."

Her expression transformed and she asked, "Does this thing work?" She reached over and turned on the radio.

"It works, but you won't find anything."

Apparently it didn't occur to her that no more radio stations were broadcasting. She fiddled with it, but each frequency was blanketed with static. She gave up, turned it off, and sighed.

"I miss music," she said, looking out the window. "For a while I followed this band around. Those were fun times." She looked at him and smiled. "I was a real wild child back then."

"Wild child, full of grace, savior of the human race . . . ."

"What's that?" she asked.

"Something I remember reading from a book of poetry and song lyrics. It just popped into my head."

"I wouldn't have thought you'd had a chance to read many books. What were you, five or six when it happened?"

"Seven. But my dad made sure I learned to read, and then kept on reading. He used to say 'The man who does not read has no advantage over the man who cannot read.' That was actually a quote from Mark Twain."

"Is your dad back in San Diego?"

"He died."

"Sorry."

He shrugged. "After he died I wasn't sure what to do. I didn't even know if wanted to go on without him. But his last wish was that I protect the wisdom, the knowledge, he found in books. I've got dozens of them back there," he said, motioning at the trailer.

She turned and saw some other books stacked behind his seat. She picked up several of the paperbacks and began reading the titles.

"*A Canticle for Leibowitz, The Right Stuff, The Lords and the New Creatures, Red Sky Blue Moon, Time Enough for Love*--I've heard of this one. Some rocker I used to be with was really into this Robert Heinlein guy and his books."

"You can have that--read it if you want."

"Okay, sure, I'll check it out." She stuffed it into her backpack. "What are you going to do with all these books?"

"Save them--I guess--for posterity. For whoever comes after us."

"That's cool." She leaned back and put her feet up on the dash. Her shoes were so worn he was surprised they didn't fall apart. "Everyone should have a mission in life. I've got my own mission."

"What kind of a mission?"

"To plant as many bobbin seeds as I can."

"Bobbin seeds?"

"Yeah, you know . . ." She started singing, "*The answer my friend, is blowin' in the wind . . . .*"

She saw the blank look on his face. "Didn't you read those lyrics in your book?"

He shook his head.

"Bob Dylan, 'Blowin' in the Wind'--the song?"

"I don't understand."

"Have you seen those bright green plants with the purple berries? The ones that blow with the wind?

"Oh yeah, I've seen them. They were one of first things to grow after the comet hit. My dad tried to find pictures of them in the library but never could. He thought they might be some kind of mutation."

"I don't know what they're really called, but I call them bobbins--for Bob Dylan--and because they kind of bob up and down, bouncing as the wind blows them around."

"We couldn't find a name for them, but I guess that's as good as any. Why are you planting those?"

"I was sick once, hadn't eaten in days. I don't know if it was the plague or some kind of flu or that I was just hungry, but I was feeling pretty bad. So I when I came across a bobbin rooted by the side of the road, I started eating the berries. I didn't know if they were poison or not, and, at that point, I didn't care. Well, it wasn't long before I was totally wasted. I mean I was trippin' through wonderland." She looked at him and realized he didn't have any idea what she was talking about? "Have you ever been stoned? No, of course you haven't. Well, I'll tell you, I've done just about every drug there is, and this was totally different. Not only did my sick feeling go away, my mind kind of woke up in a strange way. It was like smoking weed, but to the tenth power."

"You smoke weeds?"

"Weed, you know, grass, ganja, cannabis . . . marijuana."

"Oh, yeah."

"Anyway, once the high wore off, I felt fine--great in fact. I wasn't sick anymore, though I was still hungry. Bobbin berries aren't very filling."

"So you decided to spread the seeds because you think the berries healed you?"

"I don't think--*I know*. Later on I cut my leg pretty bad and smashed some berries over the cut. It totally healed in like two days.

"But I'm not just planting them because it's some miracle cure. If man ever rises from the trash heap of this shitty world to build something again, he's going to need to get high. Because man doesn't live by bread alone."

"I understand," he said, even though it still seemed strange to him.

"I've got a big bag of seeds, and I plant some wherever I go. Someday there'll be fields and fields of it. Bobbins as far as the eye can see."

She laughed as if the image were absurd even to her, and he caught himself staring at the swell of her breasts beneath her clothes. When she turned he quickly averted his eyes. He didn't know why he felt the need to turn away. But he felt his face grow flush as another strange sensation coursed through him.

She looked at him and smiled. "Everyone's got to have something to keep them going." Her smile faded as she turned to look at the road ahead. "Some reason to *want* to keep going. That's mine."

She reflected for a moment, then asked, "Where *are* you going?"

"I . . . uhh . . . I don't know exactly. I guess I won't know until I get there."

"That's cool," she said, staring out the side window again.

They drove in silence for some time, on a single lane highway, away from any old towns or inhabited areas until he looked at his gauge and decided it was time to find more gas. He hadn't seen any vehicles recently, but he soon spotted a scorched truck ahead. It was attached to a small trailer, the kind someone might have used for camping.

"I'm going to see if there's any fuel in that truck."

"Good. I need to stretch my legs."

A gully caused by torrential rains had formed alongside the road, partially undermining the truck so that it rested lopsided. The only safe place to pull off the road was some 20 yards ahead of it.

Kimber was asleep in the back, so he decided to leave her there until he was done. He took his gas can and siphoning tube to the truck and got to work while Johnnie stretched her legs.

He didn't know how Smith-Kim might have affected the planet's overall weather patterns, but the vegetation in this area had grown back with a vengeance. None of the trees were that high, but not far from the road the brush was thick and green. It was a nice change from the barren wastelands of the south.

There was indeed some gas in the old truck, and when his can was full he walked back to the trailer. Its door was closed and the inside was still pristine. Its aluminum shell had protected it.

Nothing inside had burned, though the glass in one of its windows looked partially melted. There was a little sleeping area in the rear, and a small table with seats on either side. He looked for any salvageable food, but he all he found was a box of crackers and a can of sardines. Experience told him, though unopened, the crackers would be stale but edible, and the sardines would probably be okay. He hated sardines, but, as Dad often said when they were foraging, "beggars can't be choosers." Kimber would love them anyway.

He left everything there and went to find Johnnie. She wasn't anywhere near the road but there was an obvious gap in the brush, so he figured that's where she had gone. He didn't want to come upon her unexpectedly, in case she was looking for privacy, so he called out.

"Johnnie . . . Johnnie."

"Over here."

He found her on the ground, spreading a patch of soil with her hands. She'd left her backpack in the car, but she had a small pouch with her.

"This is a good place. The soil is rich and it looks like it gets plenty of sun and rain. It should grow well here."

"I found some gas, so we can go when you're ready."

She stood and brushed the dirt from her hands.

"I'm ready now."

They started back, and that's when he saw them, slinking out of the brush behind them. A half dozen dogs of various breeds and sizes. They were low to the ground, moving slow like hunters. He'd seen this before, in the city. He knew they had only seconds before they attacked.

He judged the distance. They'd never make to the Durango in time.

He pointed them out to Johnnie. "Look."

At that instant the dogs broke into a run, snarling and barking with intent as they did.

"Run!" he yelled. "For the trailer!"

The lead dog, a Doberman whose ribs looked like they were going to pop out of its skin, was a short leap away when he pushed Johnnie into the trailer and slammed the door shut. The dogs went crazy--barking, howling, scratching their nails against the door.

"Omigod," said Johnnie, still catching her breath. "That was close."

"Too close."

"What about Kimber?" she asked frantically.

"She's okay. She's in the car and I closed the door."

He looked out the window at the dogs. He didn't think they'd be going away anytime soon. They were hungry and they knew food was inside. He had no idea how they were going to get back to the Durango.

"We could have been eaten alive out there," said Johnnie, still a bit frantic. She plopped down on one side of the table and set her pouch on it. "I need to bob."

Before he could ask, she pulled something tiny out of the pouch. It smelled like lavender, but Adam knew it must be one of the bobbin berries she'd talked about. It looked dried, like a purple raisin.

"Here, have one," she said, offering it to him.

He'd never used any kind of drug in his life, though he had drunk some wine once. He hadn't liked it. He was curious, but also apprehensive. He had no idea how it might affect him.

"Go ahead," she said, chewing her own berry, "it'll be good for you."

"I don't think I should, with those dogs out there."

"Those dogs aren't getting in, and we're not going anywhere. I think we're going to be here for a while. Try it. It'll lighten your load--smooth out the rough edges."

Despite her logic he hesitated.

"You know, sometimes it's better *not* to think . . . to worry. Sometimes it's better just to relax, feel good, and not fret about all the what-ifs and whys--you know?"

It seemed flawed advice for the world they inhabited, but he took the berry and popped it in his mouth. Maybe it was the spark in those lovely eyes of hers that convinced him. Or maybe he realized she was right. They were going to be there a while.

After he finished chewing the dried berry he swallowed and said, "I don't feel anything."

She chuckled. "You will."

She was right. It crept up on him slowly, but he soon realized things weren't normal. It wasn't bad . . . he wasn't in pain or anything. But his perception was off. It was like his brain was floating inside his skull. Like she said, he *was* relaxed.

He wondered what the dogs outside were doing. He listened, but didn't hear a thing. He got up and looked out the window. They were still there. Most of them lay on the ground--waiting.

Standing there he felt out of balance. Nothing was spinning, but he had the sense it could happen any second.

"I feel a little dizzy."

"Lay down," she suggested.

He made his way to the trailer's bed and did just that. Laying there he felt much better. In fact, he felt great.

It wasn't long before he realized she was crawling onto the tiny bed next to him. He scooted over to make room.

"Are you okay?" she asked.

"I'm fine. I'm good."

"That's good."

He felt fine, but his mouth felt dry. He decided to see if it was really dry, or just his imagination. He started to whistle.

"Don't do that!" squealed Johnnie.

"Why not?"

"Don't you know it's bad luck to whistle indoors? It'll call forth demons . . . evil spirits."

"That's a silly superstition. Besides we've already got a pack of demons outside waiting for us."

"I guess you're right. Still, no whistling. Better safe than sorry."

"Okay."

They laid there for a time, resting, relaxing. For some reason he started thinking about the crackers and sardines. They were sounding better, but he didn't feel like getting up. He was ready to fall asleep when she said, "Have you ever . . . done it . . . with a woman I mean?"

He was still adrift in a haze as he tried to decipher her question.

"You mean sex?"

"Yes, I mean sex."

He shook his head.

She leaned over and kissed him, but he was so relaxed he barely responded. That didn't seem to deter her. Her hands began caressing him, so he responded in-kind, touching her, hesitantly at first. The tingling feelings that had run through him before soon converged and solidified in one very determined spot. But it wasn't until she grabbed hold of him there that he realized how hard he was.

Soon they were both naked, and a flood of sensations he couldn't begin to categorize or keep track of followed. But it wasn't long before he knew what all those poems, and all those stories he'd read, were talking about. He finally understood why so many writers had been so obsessed with the subject.

Ω

He was woken by a shrill cry. He sat up so quickly he banged his head on the low ceiling above the trailer's bed. Johnnie still lay next to him, naked as they both were. He briefly devoured the vision of her, recalling the marvelous sensations they'd shared. He heard the cry again and looked out the window. It was Kimber, still trapped in the Durango, and howling for attention. She'd gotten it. All the dogs now surrounded the car, attracted by her noise. Once she saw them her caterwaul took on a more threatening--or threatened--tenor. The dogs barked and circled, trying to find a way in.

He got dressed in a hurry.

"What's going on?" asked Johnnie. "Are you going outside?"

"The dogs are all around the Durango. They know Kimber's in there."

"But they can't get to her--right?"

"No, but I got an idea last night after I ate that berry, and I think this is a good time to give it a try."

He pulled down the curtain rods inside the trailer, and wrapped them with old towels he'd found.

"What are you going to do?"

"You need to get dressed," he said. "I'm going to get the car and drive it over as close as I can to get you."

"You can't go out there," said Johnnie, putting her clothes on.

"Don't worry."

Once the rods were wrapped, he picked up a lighter he'd found, handed it to her, and opened the trailer door as quietly as he could. He grabbed the gas can he'd left outside and soaked the towels in gas.

"Be careful," she said.

"When I get the car over here, make sure you bring the gas with you--alright? Grab those crackers and sardines too, if you can."

She nodded.

He opened the door wide and looked outside. All the dogs were still at the Durango. He stepped down.

"Okay, light them."

As soon as his two torches burst into flame he started running straight at the dogs. He yelled at the top of his lungs and waved the torches all around.

They scattered. His screams alone probably freaked them out momentarily. He doubted anyone or anything had ever charged at them before.

He tossed the flaming rods at the retreating canines, opened the Durango's door, and jumped into the driver's seat. Kimber was hiding somewhere, but he didn't worry about her. He started it up and pulled over to where Johnnie was able to get inside. The dogs still hadn't regrouped.

They drove off and Johnnie exhaled with relief.

"You saved me. You're my hero."

He thought she was making fun of him. "Don't exaggerate."

"No, no, you saved my life," she insisted without any hint of derision. But her relief transformed to melancholy in a disjointed heartbeat. "What kind of life it's going to be in this crappy world . . . ." She didn't finish the thought, but began crying.

He didn't know what to do--what to say.

"It's not all that bad," he stammered.

"Bad? It's worse than bad," she countered almost angrily, still crying. "Look at it. There's nothing--there's nothing left. It's all gone to hell . . . even the dogs. I used to love dogs."

He didn't know what had suddenly happened to the strong, independent woman he'd picked up beside the highway, or what dark memory had suddenly emerged, but her intrepid facade had withered away. He stayed quiet until she calmed down.

"I know things aren't like they used to be," he said when she seemed composed. "But at least you remember what it was like. You have memories of your travels, your music, the people you knew . . . I don't have any of that. Even when I read about it, it seems like ancient history. Stories of how the world used to be, might as well be fairy tales to me. All I have is *this* world--

today's world."

"You're right. I'm sorry I lost it there for a moment. My hormones must be out of joint. I'm not usually so weepy."

"I guess we all have our moments." He cleared his throat. "Speaking of which, I wanted to thank you for last night."

"For what?"

"You know."

"You mean the bobbin?"

"No. Well, that was good--certainly different. No, I mean thanks for the other thing."

She shook her head. "You don't ever thank a woman for sex," she said adamantly. "It's not a present--it's not something you give. It's something you share. It's a two-way street. You both give, you both take--if you're doing it right anyway."

"Were we doing it right?" he asked, only half in jest.

She laughed. "You silly boy. Of course we were. I only do it right."

"Well, thanks anyway."

He looked at her and smiled.

She smiled back and said with a strange accent, "It was nothing, dahling."

Ω

They did it again that night--outside. He remembered lying there, exhausted, looking up at the stars. He still hadn't caught his breath when he glanced at Johnnie and said, "I love you." He thought it was the right thing to say.

It wasn't.

Even in the dark he saw her frown.

"Don't say that."

"Why?"

"Because you don't know what it means."

"Do you?"

"No," she admitted. "But I'm pretty sure it takes years to really know if you love someone . . . or at least a very long time."

"Have you ever loved anyone?"

"There were a couple of times when I was very young that I thought I did. But I didn't."

"But if you're not sure what it is, what it means, how do you know you didn't?"

"Because it didn't last. I think real love lasts a long, long time."

He thought he'd read enough about the subject to understand it, but he guessed love was one of those things you couldn't just read about. You had to experience it. He didn't know how he would ever know for sure.

"Well, for tonight anyway, I love you."

That made her laugh, which made him feel better. He lay back, relaxed, looking up and trying to find Venus in the sky. He knew Venus was the Roman goddess of love, and figured she might be up there watching over them. Without meaning to, he fell asleep.

The next morning Johnnie was gone.

At first he thought she'd wandered off to pee or something. But then he saw the note, written on the inside cover of his copy of *Time Enough For Love*. She'd propped it open with a rock.

Before he read it, he jumped up and desperately scanned the horizon for any sign of her. But she was gone, and he had no idea what direction she'd taken.

Resigned, he picked up the book and read her note. He gathered from the mistakes that writing wasn't something she'd done much.

> *"Deerest Adam*
> *Its time to say good by. Dont think I left because of any thing you did.*
> *Its just well were worlds a part you and me. You got places to go and*
> *things to disscover and I have seeds to plant. I will allways remember*
> *you and hope you will never forget me. Take care of Kimber and her*
> *kittens. Life goes on much the same some times better.*
> *Luv, Johnnie"*

At the time, he was very upset--mad she'd left without saying goodbye-- angry she'd want to leave at all. But he wasn't being totally honest with himself. He shouldn't have been so surprised. He hadn't known her long, but even in the short while he knew Johnnie, he felt she had this unexplainable ephemeral quality about her, as if she might vanish any second. Not that she wasn't real. She was no figment of his imagination. Of that he was absolutely sure. But as time wore on, he found it more and more difficult to picture her-- to recall her face. He didn't know why. Maybe because he always visualized her naked, doing what she wanted, planting seeds for posterity.

Ω

Directives went out, passed methodically from worker to worker, using a vocabulary of taste and smell. Chemical messages as an exchange of information or a mandate for specific undertakings--a variety of pheromones, each with its own distinctive command to attendants, foragers, soldiers, nurses. Day by day, routine after routine, the colony thrived. Everyone to a task--a specialized task for everyone.

One day, a day like any other, the foragers carried something new to the queen--something with an unusual shape and texture. Her attendants examined the offering, determined it wasn't a threat, and submitted it to the queen along with a dead spider, a bit of caterpillar skin, and a grasshopper leg.

The queen tasted the purplish berry, unaware of either its color or its origin. It wasn't carnal but sweet. She'd consumed sugared sustenance before, but not exactly like this. It was unique. Even its aroma was tantalizingly different. A chemical signal of pleasure emanated from the queen. She was pleased with this new offering. A royal proclamation was issued. Her attendants passed the signal on to the foragers. Something new was on the menu. More would be brought.

While the unfamiliar taste satisfied the queen, she had no idea this new fare was more than just nourishment. There was no way for her to grasp the concept that the juices from this food would have a side effect on her reservoir of sperm--changes at a genetic level that would ultimately alter her eggs when fertilized. All she knew was her continued survival meant the colony would endure. And that was her prime ancestral directive.

Much of the planet was still a barren wasteland, deserts of sand and scrub. But, in time, sea-drenched clouds swept over the empty territories. Here and there life sprung from the ground with new hope and vitality. Trees sprouted into burgeoning forests, prairie grass and sagebrush covered the plains, while weeds of boundless variety poked diligently through layers of cracked pavement.

While some survivors looked to the past, others eyed the future with a certain sense of freedom. They could go wherever they wanted, live however they chose, build whatever they desired or forsake planting roots and just roam from place to place. At least until the inevitable day they were cultivated, penned-in, and regimented by a power greater than their own--the inherent drive of a species to endure.

DERIVATION

ERICA ENJOYED HELPING TAKE CARE OF THE CHILDREN, no matter who she was working with. What she didn't like, was all the rules. There were too many rules, and she thought most of them were stupid. She liked Fawn, but Fawn was a stickler for the rules, always reminding her she couldn't take any of the kids outside the nursery, she couldn't go straight from the pens to the nursery without a thorough cleaning, she couldn't do this, she couldn't do that.

Like any teenager, she was curious--always asking the adults questions. Of course, she'd always been curious--even when she was little.

"Why are all the children so much younger than me?" she asked Fawn.

Fawn frowned, as she often did, and considered her answer before speaking.

"You were . . . special," she said. "You were a test, to see how we would handle a new baby."

"But why wait so long before any more babies were made?"

"Because Farkas said so. We were waiting until the proper time, according to his schedule."

"But there's no one my age. I don't have any friends."

"That's silly," replied Fawn, taking something out of the mouth of one of the toddlers. "We're all your friends--your family."

Erica knew that. She'd been told so many times. But she still had questions. "Which one of the children is yours?"

"They're all mine," said Fawn, frowning. "I've told you that before."

"But one of them came out of your belly," said Erica. "You must know which one is yours."

"Of course I do, but that's not important," said Fawn. "Farkas has said we must raise the children as part of the community. That we all must take turns raising all the children together, and not treat anyone differently. I think that's a good idea."

"Will you have more children?"

"Yes, of course. Many of the women in Sanctuary are already pregnant for the second time. My turn will come soon. And soon--very soon--you'll be old enough to carry a baby of your own. When it's born, it will be cared for in the nursery just like the others. Maybe we'll be pregnant together. That would be fun, wouldn't it?"

Erica didn't know. From what she'd heard from many of the women, being pregnant wasn't fun at all. It was a burden.

"I don't know if I want to be pregnant."

"Shush," said Fawn. "Don't say such a thing. Of course you want to be pregnant. It's up to us to begin to repopulate the world. It's our duty as women."

"Who says it's our duty?"

"Farkas says, and not just Farkas, *I* say it is. Everyone knows it is. You know the story of how those on the surface were killed. You know it's important everyone do their part to bring life back to the world. That's why Sanctuary is here. That's why *we're* here."

"I don't know," said Erica hesitantly. "I'm not sure I want to have a baby."

"Don't talk like that," said Fawn angrily. "You mustn't talk like that. You sound like your mother."

"What do you mean? Do you mean the woman who carried me?"

"Yes, yes. Your birth mother was too contrary, and she got in trouble for not following the rules."

"You never talk about my birth mother," said Erica. "Even when I ask you."

"I told you she's dead, so it doesn't matter," responded Fawn. "We're all your mothers now. You have more mothers than you need. Come now, we need to check the little ones. Joshua needs to be changed."

"What was her name?"

"Whose name?"

"My birth mother."

"You don't need to know her name," said Fawn, gathering up a little girl in her arms.

"I want to know her name," said Erica, raising her voice enough it startled Fawn.

"It was Virginia, alright? Now, can we get back to work?"

Virginia thought Erica. *My mother's name was Virginia.* She wanted to ask more, to ask how her mother died, but she knew Fawn wouldn't tell her. Dr. Joyce might, if she pressed her, but she knew another way to find out what she wanted to know.

Ω

Erica snuck into the conference room when most everyone else was eating dinner. She'd told Fawn she didn't feel well, and was going to rest.

She knew she could ask Farkas questions and he would answer, because she'd seen others do it. Until now, she'd been too afraid to sneak in, too young to be brave enough to talk to the great Farkas who was her father and grandfather and the rule-maker of Sanctuary. She figured he knew everything, so he'd know about her mother.

"Farkas?" she timidly asked the electronic unit set in the wall. "Farkas, are you there?"

"I am here."

"Can you tell me about my birth mother?"

"Who are you?"

"Erica," she said. "I'm Erica."

"Yes, Erica, derivative of America, first child born in Sanctuary."

"What do you mean *America*?"

"The name you were given by your birth mother, Dr. Virginia Freel, was America."

"I didn't know that. Everyone calls me Erica."

"It has been explained to me Erica is a nickname, a diminutive, a derivation of America."

Erica found it strange no one had ever called her by that name. She knew America was a place, a place on the surface before Smith-Kim, before the end of everything. She'd learned that in her studies. So it was odd to discover it was also her name.

"Can you tell me how my birth mother died?"

"Dr. Virginia Freel was banished to the surface for a number of infractions of Sanctuary regulations, the most severe of which was impregnating herself in violation of the timetable."

"Banished to the surface?"

"Yes."

"Was I the baby she impregnated herself with--against the rules?"

"Yes."

The revelation left her unsettled. She felt a little sick to her stomach. She moved aimlessly out of the conference room, lost in dazed contemplation. It had been the secret no one had told her. A dark secret that outraged her the more she thought about it. Her mother had been sent to the surface, had been sentenced to certain death, for giving her life.

Ω

The day finally arrived when they told her the time had come for her to be impregnated. But Erica didn't want to become a birth mother. Not yet. Not just because Farkas said it was time. She hated Farkas. Hated that he controlled all their lives. Hated that he had banished her mother.

Yet everyone did whatever Farkas told them to--everyone but her. She knew they would force her if they had to, just like they'd forced her mother to leave. Erica wasn't going to let them. She had a plan.

They were going to use the main tunnel to release some of the animals today, including Pegasus. She'd cried and pleaded with Joe to let her be there to say goodbye to her favorite horse, and he'd given in. Only she wasn't going to say goodbye. Not to Pegasus anyway.

In preparation for their release, Erica had helped feed the horses Kenji's seed packets, which Joe explained were biodegradable. The packets protected the seeds from the animals' digestive systems. He said when the horses excreted them, the packets would slowly dissolve and they'd become little pre-fertilized gardens, growing everything from corn to oats to cotton. But seeds weren't the only thing they'd carry to the surface.

She met Joe and two of the other zoologists at the tunnel entrance. They'd already set loose a number of turkeys and pheasants that morning.

"What you got in the sack?" asked Joe, referring to the large shoulder bag strapped across her chest and snug under her arm.

"Just some stuff I have to take to Dr. Joyce when we're done," she lied.

She didn't like lying to Joe. She would miss him the most. He'd been more like a father to her than anyone else--certainly more than Farkas. She thought about telling him what she was going to do--wanted to tell him--but was certain he'd try to stop her.

What she really had in the bag was all the food she could hide and fit inside, along with some water. It wasn't much, but she hoped it would be enough until she could find more. She knew Kenji and his staff had been planting produce on the surface for years, so she was counting on those plants to sustain her.

As much as she was certain she had to do was she was doing, she was afraid. Joe must have seen the distress in her eyes and mistaken it for sadness.

"I know you're upset about Pegasus," said Joe, putting his arm around her, "but just think about all the room he's going to have to roam now. He'll be able to run as far as his legs will take him. He'll mate with the females--he's always liked Epona over there--and he'll be a father to a whole new herd of horses."

Erica was too choked up with thoughts of leaving the only place she'd ever known to respond. She nodded.

Joe handed her Pegasus' lead rope and stayed with her and the horses while the other men herded a group of bison up the tunnel. When they returned, they took some of the leads and helped Joe move the horses up. Erica stayed close to Pegasus, holding the rope that was wrapped loosely around his neck. She'd never been allowed to venture up the tunnel before, and when she saw the light ahead of her she had to shield her eyes. It was so unnaturally bright she hesitated.

"Come on," said Joe. "It's time to say goodbye."

She led Pegasus up to where Joe stood. He reached out for the rope. Instead of handing it over, Erica pulled herself onto the horse's back and looked down at Joe. He had a bewildered look on his face. That look became one of realization, but he wasn't quick enough.

"Goodbye, Joe," she said through tears, urging Pegasus forward with a kick in the flanks.

Ω

The sun was so bright, she was blinded. It was so hot, sweat seeped from her skin. Tiny creatures landed on her and bit her. But she didn't let Pegasus stop until she was certain she was far enough away from Sanctuary they couldn't come after her. Not that she imagined they would. They wouldn't dare to violate the rules of Farkas.

The females had followed Pegasus in his mad dash, and now all the horses grazed on a small patch of sparse prairie grass. They looked as content as they could be. Not at all apprehensive over being thrust into a strange new world.

Erica, however, was overcome by the spatial differences between the Sanctuary and the outside world. Everything was so open, so large. The land stretched on and on for what must be miles--a distance of measurement she'd learned but always found hard to grasp. The sky spread out forever. She had no idea how high it was, but certainly it went further up than the clouds she saw floating above her.

She felt anxious, lightheaded, and a little shaky. She turned her eyes to the ground and narrowed her focus. After a time she felt a little better and looked up at the horses. Yet as she watched them graze, Erica began to have doubts. Her fears magnified. She had no idea how she'd survive, or if she would. She had to remind herself she wasn't just fleeing Farkas and the idea of pregnancy being forced upon her. She was going to find her mother. No matter how far she had to travel. No matter how long it took.

Ω

John stood in front of the little shrine, staring at the clay statue, wondering if it stared back.

That's what the padres called it, a *shrine*--a shrine to his mother. A holy thing that never quite made him whole. He stared at it, wondering what she must have looked like. He always wondered.

Did she look like that figurine? She must have, or why would the padres have made it like that and put it there? Did she watch over him like the padres said? Did she watch over them all?

He often asked himself the same questions, but never got an answer. He wasn't sure if he believed the answers would suddenly pop into his head like some new idea or just gradually come to him as the night comes to day.

"Are you thinking about your mother, El Carrito?" He was so caught up in his contemplation, he hadn't heard Father Diego draw near. "Are you praying?"

John didn't answer.

"Maybe it's time for me to tell you about your mother. I think you're old enough now to understand. Sit down here, and I will tell you the story of your mother, and how you were born."

John knew he was eight, but he didn't know that was the magical age where he'd finally learn more about his mother. He didn't know that anyone would ever tell him.

He joined Father Diego on the bench opposite the little courtyard shrine, and listened intently as the padre told him the tale--the tale he'd waited so long to hear.

"I was tending the vegetable garden outside the abbey one day when a man from the village approached me. He was very agitated. He said to me . . ."

> "Father Diego, you must come, quickly."
> "What is it, Manuel?"
> "Una mujer, esta inferma--she is ill. Dying I think."
> "Dónde?"
> "Cerca--not far. I take you."
> "We'd better get the horse and cart," said Diego.
> Not far turned out to be the edge of the wastelands, almost a mile away. The woman was lying naked in the shade of a saguaro. As they drew closer, Diego saw she was unconscious and, apparently, with child.
> He took water to her, raised her head, and tried to pour it into her mouth. She barely stirred.
> "You must drink," he said, patting her face with the water. "Drink."
> He tried again. This time she swallowed, but more out of reflex than conscious effort. Diego laid her back down.
> "Help me get her in the cart, Manuel. We must take her to the abbey."

"You must understand, John, your mother was very sick when we found her. Already she was close to death. How she survived even that long was a miracle. A miracle that gave us you."

John tried to imagine his mother lying in the wastelands. He tried to imagine the figurine in front of him being *with child*. He'd seen women in the village described as such. He knew he was the child his mother was with, but he wondered where she could have come from.

"We took your mother to the abbey and did our best to care for her," said Father Diego, continuing the story. "We tried to speak with her when she regained consciousness, but she was still delirious . . . not in her right mind."

"What is your name, child?"

She opened her eyes, but did not respond.

"Your name, what is your name?" Father Diego asked again.

"Janelle," she said, closing her eyes again. Without opening them, she added, "Johnnie."

"Is Johnnie your husband? Is he the baby's father?" wondered Father Josiah, who'd come in from the fields when he heard about the woman.

"We found no one with you," said Father Diego. "Where is the baby's father?"

She opened her eyes once more, stared at the two friars, then closed them again as if the effort to keep them open was too much. "There is no father," she said.

Diego and Josiah looked at each other. They were both thinking the same thing.

Father Josiah said it first. "Do you think she's . . . El Uno? Is the niño she carries the--?"

Father Diego put up his hand for silence before his fellow friar could finish.

"She's delirious. She doesn't know what she's saying," said Father Diego. "Besides, you know the talk of El Uno is only allegory, not gospel."

Father Josiah nodded reluctantly and asked, "Are these the only possessions she had with her?"

"Yes. A bag of seeds and a book."

"Should I put the book in the kindling with the others?"

"No. There might be a reason she's carrying it."

"A reason?" asked Father Josiah as if he could think of none.

"Yes. Maybe the same reason she is here--the same reason God sent her to us. Let me see the book.

"*The Teachings of Don Juan: A Yaqui Way of Knowledge*," he said, reading the title. "I will examine it before making a decision.

"Examine it?" A hint of shock colored Father Josiah's voice.

"You mean read it?"

"Possibly," responded Father Diego.

"But that's . . . that's blasphemy. There is only one good book."

Father Diego didn't reply. Instead he examined the book's front and back covers.

Father Josiah turned his head slowly side-to-side as if he believed his brother was contemplating a dangerous course of action. One that might require penance self-delivered. He looked down at the sickly woman.

"Could Johnnie be the name she's given to the child?"

"Possibly. But I don't think she has long. The child won't live unless it is born before . . . ."

"Birthing the baby will surely kill her," said Father Josiah.

"And if God sent her to us to deliver this child . . . ?" Father Diego hesitated, then said, "Go get the village midwife."

"So you were born that day," said Father Diego, patting John on the head. "And that is how you got your name--your mother gave it to you."

"But you always call me El Carrito."

Father Diego laughed. "Yes, El Carrito is your apodo de niñez, my pet name for you because when you were younger you were always pulling that little wagon behind you. But you know your real name is John--the name your mother gave you."

"She said Johnnie."

"Yes, that's a version of the name John--like John the Baptist."

John vaguely remembered the story of John the Baptist he had heard in the chapel.

"Is that all of the story of my mother?"

"I'm afraid so. She died as you were born. But you must know it was all a part of God's plan. God sent us your mother as surely as He sent the comet from heaven to cleanse the Earth. You were an immaculate conception. That means your life has special purpose. Like the seeds your mother carried with her."

"The Mescalito seeds?"

"Yes, the same seeds which have grown to produce our Mescalito berries."

John thought about it. He knew the berries were special, holy, and that no one was allowed to eat them without permission. Even with permission he would be afraid to try them. He'd heard enough tales about the berries to believe they were enchanted in some way. They healed wounds, cured the sick, and, at times the Mescalito allowed the padres to speak to God. If his mother brought the seeds, she must have been special too. Maybe that's why they called her St. Janelle.

"Why didn't the Mescalito cure my mother's sickness?"

Father Diego thought about it before answering. "I don't know. But it must have been part of God's great plan. Only He can answer that question. Maybe someday He will tell you."

The idea that God would someday speak to him was frightening. He quickly asked another question.

"What about my father? Who was he?"

"I've told you, John, all of the padres of the abbey are your fathers. And God is your father . . . He is father to us all."

John knew the children in the village had only one father, so he wondered why he had so many. Was it because his mother was special? He didn't really understand how it all worked. He also didn't understand something else Father Diego had said.

"Father Diego, what is *'maculate 'ception*?"

"Ah, that, El Carrito, is a story for another day."

Ω

She was cold--cold like she'd never known. She was hungry--hungrier than she'd ever been. And she was alone.

She'd never been alone before--not really alone. Where she was born, where she grew up, there were so many people living in such close quarters. You couldn't take more than ten steps without crossing paths with someone else. She never knew the world above was such an immense place. When she first burst forth, fleeing the protective womb of the Sanctuary, she'd been overcome with anxiety. So much space--a vast open plain of nothingness. It was all she could do to close her eyes and hold on tight to Pegasus' mane.

She hadn't seen another human since that day. How many days that had been, she wasn't certain. But she hadn't really felt so totally alone until Pegasus had run off. She'd known him, fed him, groomed him, since she was a little girl. Yet he deserted her without a thought . . . or did he? Like her, he'd never seen the open sky or run any further than his exercise track. She wondered what he must have thought when he was finally released upon the world above. What did he think when they encountered a herd of horses who called to him in their own language? He'd resisted at first, but when she dismounted to search for food, he'd succumbed to his wild urges and abandoned her. Now she lay huddled in the dark, in the hollow of a rock formation, feeling more alone than ever.

The search for her mother had quickly morphed into a desperate struggle to survive. She soon came to realize how naive she'd been--how unprepared she was to endure the hardships of the outside world.

Each day was another quest to find food and water. She'd tasted nearly every growing thing she'd come across, but most were bitter, and many were rejected by her stomach. She'd even come across a naka bush--named by her Uncle Kenji Nakamura after himself. She never understood why he was so excited about the plant, even though he explained his theory that it had come from outer space. To her, outer space was just another name for somewhere outside of Sanctuary.

Though she'd never shared his enthusiasm, she was thrilled to find one of the plants--especially because of its purple berries. She ate a handful, but soon regretted it. They made her feel so strange she couldn't see straight, much less walk. Everything was distorted and uneven. All she could do was curl up and go to sleep. She felt okay the next day, but never ate any more of the berries.

At times she'd seen some of the birds released from the Sanctuary-- chickens, turkeys, pheasants--but they were hard to catch. When she finally did capture one of the chickens she cornered in a rusted-out automobile hulk, she'd tried to eat it raw, because she didn't know how to make a fire and cook it. It made her sicker than any of the plants had.

The sickness had left her weak. She hadn't been able to travel any distance for some time. It had been days since she'd eaten anything substantial, and the only water she'd had came from the morning dew. She needed to move on, to find a new place to forage, somewhere with a regular source of water. But she no longer had the strength. She'd long since wished she could return to the Sanctuary, to feel its artificial warmth, to see Uncle Joe's friendly smile, and even to submit to the dispassionate machine logic of Farkas. She didn't even care anymore that if she went back, Farkas and Mother Fawn and Dr. Joyce, and probably even Uncle Joe, would tell her she had to fulfill her duty as a woman. Certainly having a baby couldn't be as bad as she felt now. But she no longer knew where Sanctuary was. She'd gone too far.

She wrapped her arms around herself, curled into the womb of the stony alcove, and tried to sleep. At first she was too cold to even sleep. But she knew sleep, like her impending death, was just a matter of time.

Ω

A sharp ridge loomed in the distance, high above the plain. She had to shield her eyes from the sun to look at it. At first she wasn't certain, then the hazy tableau rounded into focus. Four men on horseback stood atop the ridge, unmoving. She was too far away to see any details, she couldn't even be sure they were men, but it appeared they were looking down at her.

She thought she must be dreaming. *But if I were dreaming*, she pondered, *then I wouldn't know that, would I? Was it a memory? Have I seen those horsemen before?*

She felt movement, a rising consciousness. Somehow she was being bundled into a blanket and carried away. "No one touches her." It was strange voice with an even stranger accent. "The nomads will pay more."

She was laid onto a hard surface and, after a while, it began to move. It was a bumpy ride, one that eventually woke her. She opened her eyes against the sun's glare just enough to see she was in some kind of wooden vehicle. A couple of men on horseback trailed the conveyance, but that was all she could see. She was too weak to sit up, so she closed her eyes again and pulled the blanket tight around her. The chill in her bones was slowly dissipating, needles of pain poking and prodding her limbs.

She briefly wondered who these men were that had found her. They didn't look like they were from the Sanctuary. They were ragged and dirty and all had bearded faces. But she didn't wonder long. Despite the rough ride, she soon gave in to sleep again.

Ω

Unconsciousness was a boon for her debilitated body. Awareness came and went, but by the time she was fully awake she had no idea where she was, or how long it had been since her rescue. She'd been propped up against cold cement and an old woman was trying to feed her some warm soup. She swallowed it and tried to inspect her surroundings between spoonfuls.

She was in a small triangular clearing. Cracked slabs of concrete were piled behind her, a thicket of scrub walled off one side, and a manmade enclosure of rusty metal and dead brush covered the other. The sky above her was clear, though it looked like the sun was going down.

She swallowed once again and tried to ask, "Where am I?"

The woman didn't answer. She just offered another spoonful until it was accepted.

95

When the soup was gone, the woman got up, looked down at her and asked, "You a virgin?"

She thought she knew what the word meant, but the oddity of the question stalled her. When she didn't reply right away, the old woman asked in a tone of aggravation, "You ever been with a man?"

She shook her head, thinking it to be the right response.

"I didn't think so," said the woman, who turned and opened a portion of the enclosure. She stepped out, closed it back and fastened something.

The warmth of the soup had revived her. She felt alive again, though confused and still wondering about the old woman's strange questions. She also wondered why she was in this space all alone. It felt almost like a cage.

Cage or not, she felt safe--safe enough to fall back asleep until the old woman came again the next morning to feed her some mush that didn't taste nearly as good as the soup. Famished as she was, she ate it just the same. Like the previous day, the woman wouldn't answer any of her questions. She just told her to be quiet and eat.

When the woman left her again, she got up and tested her legs. They were still weak, but not so much she couldn't make it to the ostensible door of her prison. She pulled on it. It gave a little, but it wouldn't open. With enough time and energy she could have easily kicked a portion of the haphazard structure down, but she had neither. She heard voices outside, but not what they were saying. Being on her feet for just a minute had exhausted her, so she sat back down, propping herself against the concrete.

Sunlight shone in from above, splashing a portion of her prison with blinding light. A four-legged reptile--some kind of lizard if she remembered correctly--basked in the warmth of the sun, its head cocked as if to keep an eye on her. She, in turn, watched the little creature, until she grew drowsy.

Her eyes had closed when her cage opened again. This time it wasn't the old woman. It was a young man. Not as young as her, but definitely younger than her Uncle Joe had been. He wasn't as tall as Joe, but he was muscular like him. And, unlike those that had found her, he was clean-shaven, though his black hair was long and his skin was dark. He wore a band of red cloth around his head--she guessed to keep the hair out of his eyes. Dark brown eyes that were staring at her now.

She found she didn't like the way he was looking at her, though there was no malice in his gaze. It was more of an appraisal. He stood there for only a handful of seconds, then stepped out and was talking with another man. She couldn't hear what they were saying, but after a brief exchange, he reentered her cage and held out his hand to her.

"Come," he said matter-of-factly. "You're leaving this place."

She didn't move.

"What place is this, and who are you? Where are we going?"

"You are going with me. I am Oh'hut Nahgo. Also known as Jim Standing Bear. What's your name?"

She wasn't sure she wanted to answer him, but couldn't think of a good reason why not. She started to say "Erica," but decided to use her full name.

She stood and said, "My name's America."

He smiled and responded, "That's a good name."

"My mother gave it to me. I'm looking for her," she said hopefully. "Do you know anyone named Virginia? Dr. Virginia Freel?"

He shook his head. "I know no one by that name."

She hadn't really expected a positive response, but the disappointment was still obvious on her face.

"Come now. We must go," he said, waving his hand towards the opening.

"Go where?" she asked again. "Why am I going with you?"

She couldn't tell if he sighed or grunted. "Because I just traded three horses and a load of buffalo meat for you. I bought you."

"You . . . bought me?" Having never bought anything in her life, she struggled with the concept, even though she knew the meaning of the word. Nothing was bought or sold in the Sanctuary, though she did recall reading something in a history text about people being bought and sold. They were called slaves. But that was ages ago.

"I don't understand. Why would you . . . buy me?"

She saw he hesitated. But when he spoke he was clear. There was a strength and finality to his words.

"Because you're going to be my wife."

Ω

Erica resisted at first--refused to go with this man who said he had bought her. The very notion of it confounded her, while at the same time fostering her anger. She stood her ground, refusing to move, balking at the very idea, until her would-be husband, as calmly but directly as possible, explained how the men she'd been "rescued by" would use her if she refused to come with him.

Slowly, stubbornly, she gave in. Going with this strange man seemed the lesser of two repugnant fates. It was the only choice she could make, though it outraged her she was forced to make any.

Standing Bear had ridden into this encampment with comrades. When he ushered her out of her cage, they whooped and hollered like their friend had won some kind of prize. Standing Bear and his companions mounted their horses and he held his arm down to her. Once again Erica hesitated. She looked around at the people in the encampment, then made her decision. She took hold of Standing Bear's arm. He pulled her up behind him, and said, "Put your arms around me and hold tight." She almost hesitated again, but when she felt his horse bolt forward she grabbed hold of him, throwing her arms around his waist.

The wind felt fresh against her face, reminding her of the days she spent riding Pegasus. But it was a long hard ride, and when they finally stopped to rest and eat, they still hadn't reached their destination.

Erica was still weak and tired, but not too tired to ask more questions of this man who had purchased her . . . yet also, possibly, rescued her. Despite the barbaric circumstances of her situation, she saw a kindness in her new captor's eyes. He answered all her questions--all except for the ones she was afraid to ask.

She learned he had been a young boy when the comet known as Smith-Kim devastated the world. He and his family, part of a group of Native Americans known as the Cheyenne, had hidden in some mountain caves. The rest of his family were all dead now, but their small group had grown to more than two dozen, and would grow still if he had his way.

Not everyone in the group was Cheyenne, but their "tribe," as he called it, had adopted many of the old ways of the Native Americans to survive. Using bows and arrows and spears, they hunted buffalo, following the herds wherever they ranged. He didn't know how the buffalo had managed to survive the firestorm of the comet, and she wouldn't even think of trying to explain to him until much later how it was the work of the Sanctuary that brought them back from the brink of extinction.

He admitted to her that, despite his name, he'd never even seen a bear--except in picture books. But his great grandfather, whom he was named after, had gotten the name as a boy when he actually confronted a bear who raised up on his hind legs and scared his ancestor right back to his village.

He explained one reason he wanted to increase the size of his group was that they needed new bloodlines to grow, to thrive. They could only intermarry for so long. That was why he'd bought her, and why he was always looking to find others to join them.

After hearing his story, Erica understood. She'd been taught all about breeding in the lessons she'd been given in the Sanctuary--both about animals and humans. It was the destiny of the Sanctuary's livestock, and the duty of its people to breed and populate the future. That had been ingrained in her since she was very young. It was also one of the reasons she'd fled the Sanctuary. Yet it seemed, in this barren new world, she couldn't escape being someone's brood mare.

Ω

Awareness came slowly, gradually, without warning. Perception swarmed instinct, comprehension overcame reflex and apprehension. The concepts were alien, but the dawning was the difference between light and dark, cold and warmth. New imperatives were realized--new methods discerned and developed. She had no understanding of mutation, no concept that the primal drive of her ancestors was no longer hers, because it had been altered at the genetic level. She had no inkling her exoskeleton was larger than her mother's, as was her brain--no clue her pheromones were even stronger or that she was impervious to most bacteria. She had no idea nor cared she might be different from her sisters.

When the day came, she flew into the mating swarm, danced the brief dance, excavated her nest, and began laying eggs--eggs larger than her predecessor's, as would be the generations of workers that would follow. Size wasn't the only difference between her colony and the one she matured in. The number and variety of chemical signals that passed through the colony increased and became more complex. The queen's pheromones no longer only concerned foraging, defense, and propagation of the colony. New directives involved the clearing of land, a more vigorous search for water sources, and the transportation of a particular kind of seed far beyond the borders of the colony's territory.

The seeds were the residue of the berries the queen and other members of the colony fed upon. The berries had become a staple part of their diets as the symbiotic nature of the relationship between neighboring vegetation and colony grew. For the chemically-transferred signals were not only emanating from the queen outward, they were being carried *to* the queen from the associate plant life. Through biochemistry they'd become a conjoined mind-set--nearly, but not quite, a single entity.

At some point in the midst of this symbiosis, the vegetal consciousness developed new cravings--sent signals for new sustenance. It no longer needed only soil and water. It wanted meat--protein to sustain its burgeoning intellect.

The tribes of mankind roamed the barren wilderness, seeking shelter and a place to till the soil. But disease and despondency still infected the survivors, who found their lives as hard as the parched earth. Eventually, the time came when survival alone was not enough. Humanity endeavored to pass on its history, its cultures, its knowledge, its faiths. Not always successful, but always striving, mankind marched forward to the beat of archaic drums, even as a new cadence was pulsating all around it.

REVELATION

ERICA CRADLED LITTLE JOE AGAINST HER BREAST and let him suckle. She thought it funny how it all seemed worth it now--now that she held him in her arms. The months of ungainly discomfort, the pain of delivery, the fear neither of them would survive. But they did survive, and now she was a mother. It was partly her resistance to motherhood that had brought her here. Yet, at that moment, with her baby in her arms, she didn't think she could be happier.

At first she'd resisted Jim Standing Bear, but she'd come to admire and respect him. Though they were wedded in what she was told was a Cheyenne ceremony, he never forced himself on her. He waited until she was ready, until she'd come to care for him. It didn't take long. He was a good man, a smart, sensible man she thought--especially for his age. He provided for her, protected her, genuinely cherished her. How could she not love a man like that?

In private he called her Erica--she endearingly called him Jim. Outside their tent, she was known by her full name, America, and to everyone in the group, their tribe, he was Standing Bear, their strong, fearless, wise leader. In public she only called him Jim when she was trying to get his goat.

Their band had grown in the year she'd been with them. They now numbered more than 60, counting the children. They never stayed in one place for too long--always following the herd of buffalo that provided for most of their needs--no matter whose territory they had to cross. Sometimes that led to hostilities. For they weren't the only group that had formed. Besides various outlaw bands, there were other clans, tiny city-states setting down roots here and there--even if there weren't any real cities. Whether they were a congregation of farmers or a pack of ruthless marauders, people tended to band together. Leaders emerged--some selfless, some more predatory. Erica believed with all her heart Jim was the former. As for their wayfaring nature, he was always saying he never wanted stay anywhere long enough for the dust to settle on his dreams.

Jim liked to pretend he was mysterious, talking in riddles and then laughing about it later. Whenever Erica asked him where they were going next, his answer was always, "Where the clouds go to die." By which he meant the horizon. Which also meant he didn't really know where they were going next.

Once, when the entire tribe uprooted in pursuit of the herd, they traveled around an enormous mountain. On the other side the tribe stopped, each member staring up in awe at the four giant faces carved into the white rock of the mountain top. Jim said the four men must have been gods to the people of an earlier age. Erica guessed they were kings or princes, or some kind of royalty.

At times, excursions for trade and exploration took Jim and others away from their encampment for days. They always came back--often with word of new discoveries--sometimes with new tribe members. There were other groups, pockets of people here and there. Some were friendly, some weren't. How they or their ancestors had survived the great holocaust, she didn't know. Everyone she asked, who was old enough to have been alive at that time, had a different tale.

She remembered how, when she told Jim she'd been born underground, about the workings of the Sanctuary, and how she'd never even seen the sun and the moon until she was 16, he thought it was just a story she made up--a fable like the ones his grandfather used to tell him. At first she argued it was true. Then she decided to let him believe what he wanted. It became a running joke between them.

At one time she considered telling her husband how the scientists in Sanctuary were responsible for repopulating the plain with the horses and buffalo and so many other species. But what was the point? After all, it didn't matter anymore. She was here now. That was another world, another life.

Not that their life on the plain was easy. Her time in Sanctuary seemed a luxurious dream in comparison. The surface was a dusty, hardscrabble world, and like all the animals, all the plants, all the life reemerging in it, they scratched and fought and worked hard to endure, to persist. Yet she was happy. She was content. Never did she wish she was back under the ground, obeying the cold logic of some machine.

Once, Jim and the party of men he'd gone out with came home with a trio of turkeys they'd killed. It was such a treat to have something other than buffalo meat, she suggested they have a celebration. So they did, with such a feast people were still talking about it weeks later. Jim said it had done wonders for the morale of the tribe, and they'd try to do it more often in the future.

But the future was as uncertain as the path of the buffalo. It was all they could do to follow the beasts and hope for the best. Jim and some of the other members of their group had learned many things from their grandparents, who'd passed on the traditions and bygone wisdom they'd absorbed from their own grandparents. That knowledge aided them in getting almost everything they needed from the herd. Their food, their clothes, their tools and cooking utensils, their tents, ropes, bow strings, blankets, water bags-- even a glue made from their hooves and their excrement that fueled the tribe's fires. Almost no part of the animals went unused. So wherever the herd's migration took them, they followed.

Erica was always optimistic that during their travels she might find her mother, who'd been banished to the surface by Farkas. She asked everyone she met if they knew a Virginia. Though no one ever did, she always held out hope--always reminded Jim to ask those he met about her. But now she had a son, and he was the most important thing in her life. She'd wanted to name him after the man she'd known as Uncle Joe, and Jim had added *Vo'omo Nizi*, making him Joe White Eagle. He'd chosen that name because when little Joe was born, the first thing Jim had said was, "He's so white."

It was a private joke of theirs. It didn't matter to Jim what color his son was. He was as proud as a father could be.

Mother Fawn and Doctor Joyce and Farkas the computer had been right about one thing. It *was* their duty to repopulate the world. Now she'd done her part. At least she'd begun to do her part. She figured little Joe wouldn't be her only contribution.

Ω

She came, as all the pregnant women from the village did from time to time, to kneel and pray at the foot of St. Janelle's shrine. John assumed she, like all the others, prayed for a healthy, blessed baby. He should have been proud. He should have been imbued with feelings of contentment and honor. But his emotions were mixed. Because Saint Janelle, the Blesséd Virgin Janelle, was his mother. The mother he'd never known. The mother who died upon his birth. The mother who abandoned him.

He knew, logically, his mother didn't choose to abandon him. It wasn't her fault. Yet he still felt a touch of shame--of unworthiness. He knew he was supposed to be proud. All the padres said he should--they said he was special because of who his mother was . . . though they couldn't seem to explain, to his satisfaction, why. Some whispered to him privately that they believed his mother was El Uno--*The One*--the special one foretold to be the mother of the new messiah. Foretold by whom John didn't know or care. Such talk was frowned upon, and he never heard Father Diego utter a word about it. John was glad of that. He didn't like to think about his place in such a fanciful tale.

Despite it all, despite everything he was told, he felt no connection to his mother. It seemed to him he didn't deserve to be special, no matter what his mother might have done or could have been.

"El Carrito, there you are." It was Father Diego. "I should have known you'd be here. Saying adiós to your mother?"

Though he wasn't really, John nodded. He wasn't sure if the nod was a small lie or a bigger truth. Either way, he didn't think God would mind.

"I've got your seeds," said Father Diego, holding the small pouch out to him. "Are you ready? Ready for your romería?"

"Yes, Father."

Father Diego put his arm around him as they walked outside. "When you return, you'll no longer call me 'father.' I'll be your brother then. You'll be one of us. You'll be Father John."

John couldn't quite wrap his mind around such an idea. Father Diego, who'd raised him along with the other padres would be "Brother Diego"? It didn't seem right. He knew it would take some getting used to. Even harder would be to think of himself as "Father John."

"I'll no longer be your El Carrito?"

Father Diego laughed and replied, "You'll always be my little El Carrito, even though you're not so little anymore . . . even after you become Father John."

Walking out of the abbey, John was briefly blinded by the glare of the sun.

Though it was still early morning, it was hot already.

"Now let's see--do you have your water? Of course you do. Remember, the water is for you. God will provide for his seeds."

John nodded.

"It won't be easy--it never is. But remember, though we carry the sins of mankind's trespasses on our backs, our faces are forever turned towards God and His forgiveness."

Father Diego seemed more nervous about his romería than he was. He wondered why. It wouldn't be the first time he'd gone out into the desert to commune with God and plant the seeds of His blossoms. It was just the first time he'd be doing it alone, and the first time he would commune with the Mescalito. He wasn't worried, so he wondered why Father Diego was so apprehensive.

"Come back to us, El Carrito."

It seemed a strange thing for him to say. As if for some reason he wouldn't.

"Of course, Father Diego."

"Then off with you, and remember what you've learned--God is your ally."

John nodded and started off, with a vague heading that would lead him into the open desert. It was a vast, endless wilderness, where ominous sunsets faded into obscurity over a realm painted with the brush of enigmatic legends. Yet he wasn't afraid, just anxious to be done with it.

"Vaya con Dios," called out Father Diego behind him.

John didn't turn to acknowledge the blessing. but after a short distance he did look back at the monastery. Its mishmash of stone and brick and adobe was a familiar sight, though it had never appeared so small to him. It was an ancient structure, or so he was told. Its construction supposedly went back many decades before the great end. How it had survived the cataclysm, he didn't know. The padres liked to say God preserved it for a reason--so they could continue to do their work. John didn't know if that were true or not, or if it was only because its walls were fireproof. All he knew is that it was the only home he'd ever known.

He turned back toward the wastelands, stared out into the raw distance, and began reciting the mantra of the romería in his head. *One foot after the other*.

Ω

He was hot, his feet were sore, and he was thirsty. But he remembered what he'd been taught. *Don't drink until you have to* had been the admonition.

So he waited, walking alone, accompanied only by his shadow. He'd already gone a great distance when he came to a deep, jagged ravine. The way the earth's crust was split open reminded him of the grimace he'd once seen on the face of a dead man. After that thought passed through his head, he tried not to look at it again. He skirted the chasm, giving it a wide berth.

How far he'd gone from the abbey he couldn't say, but certainly he'd traveled further than he'd ever been before. That was one of the tenets of his romería, to go further than he'd ever gone. He said a prayer and looked out across the expanse of desert that lay before him. It was nearly barren, but to his mind beautiful. Certainly a harsh beauty--one requiring an observer to see more than sand and rock. But God had created this, so he knew there was beauty in it, even if he couldn't define it. God knew what He was doing, even if mankind felt lost and neglected and parched with guilt.

He searched the expanse for signs of growth--for anything green. There was very little. But that was one reason he was there. He took out his pouch full of seeds and set off to find just the right spot. He didn't know what that spot would look like, but Father Diego had told him he would know it when he found it. He would feel it in the pit of his stomach.

John walked and walked, round and round, staring at the dry sand beneath his feet, looking for that perfect spot. All the while, the sun crept toward the horizon. Finally he felt something in his stomach. Whether it was a signal from Mescalito or just hunger, he wasn't certain. But he knelt down and dug into the sandy soil. The seeds were not supposed to be planted too deep, so he didn't dig far. He took his seeds out of the pouch, put them in the tiny hole, and lovingly covered them over. Then he said the prayer of fecundity.

When he was finished he found a place to build a fire nearby. The sun was setting and it would grow cold soon. Unfortunately, he was never very good at fire-making. He gathered dry brush and formed a little nest just as he'd been taught. He found some larger twigs and dry branches to have on hand. He pulled out his flint and steel and began trying to spark the dry nest into flame. It worked on his second attempt, which surprised him. He shielded the nest with his hands and blew on it gently. This was the hard part--keeping the spark alive with your breath, but not so hard you extinguished it. As the flames grew he felt a sense of pride. It was the quickest fire he'd ever made. Once it was going good, he fed the larger sticks into it.

With the fire going strong, it was time. He couldn't put it off now if he wanted to. Part of him *did* want to, but a bigger part of him was consumed by curiosity. He pulled out the three dried Mescalito berries he'd brought with him. They represented the Father, the Son, and the Holy Ghost. He chewed slowly. They had surprisingly little taste. Then he sat back, cross-legged, and stared out into the desert.

It wasn't long before he no longer felt thirsty or hot or hungry. Instead a sort of drowsiness came over him. It wasn't a need to sleep, but a sort of haze that settled over his mind. His heart began to beat--beating as if he'd just run a great distance--pounding at the walls of his chest. He grew certain he could hear each heartbeat, just as he could feel the blood coursing through his body.

His eyes sharpened and he stared at the setting sun through the desert shimmer. The sky looked more colorful than normal. It seemed he could see further across the landscape than before, and when he looked down he could see each individual grain of sand. They weren't all the same color as he would have imagined. Each one was made distinct by its hue, by its striations.

He saw an ant traversing the grains. It too appeared larger than life. Suddenly the ant was sucked away in a red flash. A long, florid tentacle had snatched the ant. It all happened too fast for John to follow, but he saw the nearby lizard and knew it was the creature's tongue that had captured the insect.

He'd seen lizards before, but this was an odd one. It sat on a rock not five feet from him, pale gold in color, its skin more velvet than leathery. It turned its head sidewise, staring at him with its left eye. Then it began to wobble. The wobble became a sway, and the sway became a dance. Not on two legs like a person, but on all four legs--five if you counted its tail. It shifted its weight to and fro, back and forth, occasionally raising one limb completely from its rocky dance floor.

John couldn't help but think the reptile was dancing for him. What this absurd spectacle was supposed to mean, he had no idea. He stared in fascination until an upsurge in the wind caused him to blink and rub his eyes. When he looked again, the little creature was gone . . . if it had ever truly been there.

The wind roused again and again as he sat there, almost in a stop and go pattern. He listened to it as it came and went. Soon he heard music. It was as if the notes were carried on the breezy gusts. Whether it was the singing of voices or some unfamiliar instrument, he wasn't sure. He was only sure he heard it.

107

He closed his eyes to try and hear the music more clearly. The sound didn't change, but the blackness in his mind's eye focused with more clarity. Something was coming towards him, out of the void, out of the dusky pitch. It was a large, enclosed wagon, drawn by a pair of horses. A solitary man sat aboard the wagon, holding the reins. He kept getting closer. John heard the wagon wheels and the horse's hooves coming up close to him. It sounded so real he opened his eyes.

There was nothing there. Nothing but the desert, now fading into night.

Quickly he closed his eyes again, but the wagon didn't reappear. He waited--waited so long he could no longer judge time. Then, in the darkness of his mind he saw a person on foot, walking towards him. It was a woman. She grew closer, more familiar, before he realized . . . it was his mother. She was as he'd always thought of her--a cross between the statue in the abbey and the features he'd given the blank canvas he'd painted with his imagination as a child. She had long primrose hair, a sun-bright smile, and playful green eyes. She was right in front of him, looking as if she were speaking to him, but he couldn't hear her over the oscillating sounds of wind and music.

"Mother!" he shouted involuntarily, opening his eyes at the same time.

She wasn't there in the dwindling twilight, so he quickly closed his eyes once more. But she was gone. He kept them shut, hoping she would return. She never did.

Ω

" . . . grows inside the mother, right here," she paused to place her hands on her belly, "where it gets all of its food and water and even its air from its mother. The egg grows for nine moons before it becomes a baby ready to come out and see the world."

She watched their eyes as she delivered the lesson. Fourteen pairs of eyes--each pair a different shape, a different color, a different attitude. The younger children, like her own Virginia, had wide eyes and open mouths. They were wonderstruck to learn how they each had come into existence. The older ones, like her son Joe, had heard it all before. Joe sat in the back of the class, his arms folded, his face unable to disguise his impatience for school to finish for the day. He would soon be 12. When that day came, his schooling would be over and he would leave behind his camp chores to join the men in their hunts and expeditions. Waiting for that day, he was like a wild pony, pulling at the restraints that held him, anxious for the freedom he was so certain he desired.

Erica was just as certain she didn't want him to go. Not yet. Not her little boy--even though he'd grown almost as tall as her. She knew the dangers he would face, and thought him too young, too eager. She feared for his safety, but knew in her heart nowhere was truly safe. It was a dangerous world they lived in. Even in their own encampments.

Just days ago a dust devil had invaded their camp, consumed their fire pit, and become a flaming whirlwind that shot dozens of feet into the air. No one was hurt, but a pair of tents had burned and several horses had scattered. It had been a terrifying few moments, but the small dusters were relatively harmless compared with the sandstorms that raged for miles, or the gigantic tornadoes that changed landscapes and stampeded the buffalo. Even decades later, the earth was still suffering from the devastation of Smith-Kim. It was not the relatively docile place it had been before--at least not the place she'd read about as a young girl.

"What about horses?" asked her son James. He was several years younger than Joe, but with a curiosity wider than the sky. "How are horses born?"

"Horses are born in exactly the same way as people," she replied. "The only difference is that a baby horse stays inside its mother for more than 11 moons. Sometimes for a whole year."

She saw the incredulous looks coming from some of her students, and remembered she'd reacted much the same when her Uncle Joe had explained it to her.

"Alright. That's enough for today. Everyone go finish your chores. Tomorrow we'll get back to studying our letters . . . " Hearty groans greeted this, as most saw little use for learning to read or write. " . . . and I'll tell you the story of Smith-Kim." This announcement was followed by several *oohs* and *ahhs,* as most of them knew what the comet was, even if they thought of it as a great monster.

Jim was waiting for her when she returned to their tent. He'd only been gone for a day this time, but she'd missed him. She always did. No matter how many times he went away, she always worried he wouldn't return.

She embraced him and then saw the blood on his arm.

"What happened?" she asked, doing a poor job of keeping the concern out of her voice.

"We came across some river people."

"What were you doing close to their village? You know they're not friendly."

She'd already gotten a cloth and some water to clean the wound.

"We weren't. They had a scouting party out, and we just happened to run into them. I recognized one of them from our last run-in. They have guns. We never saw guns before."

"What? They shot you?"

"No, I think they just fired a warning shot to scare us off, but the sound frightened Blade and he reared up." He smiled. "He went up and I went down . . . right into an ocotillo."

"That must have given the men a laugh," she said, cleaning the wound she could now see was actually several small punctures.

"Not right away, but I heard about it on the way back. I believe there was some mention of Jim Sitting Bear, Jim Falling Bear, and, oh yeah, Jim Flying Bear."

She laughed at that, but grew serious again.

"Why do you think the river folk are so unfriendly?"

"They're probably just afraid of strangers. With all the bandits roaming the land, it's hard to be trusting. We know."

She nodded her head. They'd had their own run-ins with wild marauders, strange religious orders, irrational and demented vagabonds. You had to very careful when you encountered outsiders. The river people had warned them away from their encampment before, but no guns had been seen.

"There," she said, tying a clean bit of cloth around his arm. "You'll be fine. You're lucky you didn't break anything."

"Only my pride." He smiled and swept her up in his powerful arms.

"Be careful," she squealed. "You're injured."

"Not so much I can't do this."

He kissed her and she returned the affection.

When she broke away to catch her breath, she said, "Are you sure you're alright?"

"Let's find out."

Ω

Brett sat in the shade of the smokehouse, watching the children play as he worked on the flute he was whittling. They were kicking around a ball made of river grass and reeds, and making that joyful, high-pitched noise children made when they were having fun. He was especially watching his granddaughter, Vera. He had several grandchildren now, but she had been the first. He'd never admit it to anyone, but she was his favorite. She had just celebrated her eleventh birthday, which had only served to remind Brett what an old man he was now. He would have loved to have gotten up and kicked the ball around himself, but his knees didn't work as well as they used to.

Vera could run rings around him now. From his slightly skewed viewpoint, she was the fastest one out there. She wasn't a bad ball-handler either. He figured it was time to organize another soccer game. Vilma would like that. She was a big soccer fan long before they met. Maybe after Jet and his scouting party returned from their expedition north she could plan a post-game fiesta, and they could make an event out of it. His people worked so hard, it was good for them to have something to look forward to.

Vera stole the ball from little Gregor Maxey and Brett clapped with approval. He'd have to remember to needle his former XO about it. Maxey's grandson wasn't the most athletic of the bunch, but he knew Vera and Gregor were good friends. They'd grown up together, and who knew, maybe someday they'd be more than that.

The mid-day fun ended when his daughter, Savannah, showed up. She snatched up the ball to the groans of the children.

"Alright, everyone, time for afternoon lessons," she said.

The children, didn't argue, but ran off towards the clearing where school was held.

"You're a spoilsport, Daughter."

She looked at him and stuck out her tongue, just like she used to do when she was little. But it was even funnier because she was pregnant again.

Brett tested his flute, making a discordantly shrill sound. He and Savannah both laughed, and then she followed the children to their outdoor school.

Many of his people didn't think learning to read and write was important in this new world, but he knew it was . . . or that it would be someday. He'd insisted they start a school as soon as they had children old enough. It had been a tradition for more than 30 years now. Their "library"--whatever books they happened to have onboard the *Savannah* when they came up the Mississippi--were now all dog-eared, faded, and falling apart. He'd personally read them all at least twice. Unfortunately, they were almost all fiction. He wished they had more technical how-to books that would help them going forward with their community. The only one they had was *How to Plan for your Financial Future*, and that wasn't particularly helpful. His fondest wish was to find a cache of undamaged books buried in some undiscovered junk pile. But he never had.

One idea he'd come up with some years ago was to have people with particularly helpful skills write down what they knew for future generations. Chief Alvarez knew about construction, Maxey had some expertise in welding and woodworking, Vilma and some of the other women got together to write down cooking tips and recipes using what foodstuffs they had access to. Others had expertise in gardening, chemistry, fishing, hunting. All those skills had been put to use over the years, but Brett wanted them written down for posterity. Of course they had run out of blank paper before they'd run out of knowledge, so he had them write in the margins of some of their books. Now you could pick up a copy of *Huckleberry Finn* and also read about how to best grow corn or make gunpowder. *Stranger in a Strange Land* had tips on cooking, carpentry, and first aid. Even though these skills were being passed on daily by example, by actually doing the work, Brett felt it was important to have it all recorded somewhere. He wasn't the only one getting old, and his original crew wouldn't live forever. What they really needed now, was someone who knew how to make paper.

His left knee cracked as he stood and flexed his legs. He thought he should probably go down to the river and see how the fishing was coming. But before he got too far, he saw his scouts returning from upriver. They'd been gone for almost a week now, and most peeled off to find their families. Jet saw Brett and came straight for him.

Jet had been his right-hand man for many years. He'd kept the name Chief Alvarez had given him when they'd first fished him out of the ocean--just shortened Jetsam to Jet. He was steady, smart, and fearless. But mostly, Brett trusted him to make sound decisions when Brett wasn't around. It didn't hurt that he was also his son-in-law. Considering the state of the population, Savannah could have done much worse.

"Find anything worthwhile?" asked Brett.

"Not much, Captain. Hardly anything at all."

Brett had long ago given up trying get them to use his first name. He'd been "Captain" for so long, it was what everyone except his family members called him.

They clasped hands in greeting and Jet said, "We came across one place that somehow weathered the end, but all we found inside that was still good was some salt and sugar, and a small quantity of rice."

"Well that's something," replied Brett. "Hell, we haven't had any sugar in two decades. We'll have to make sure the ladies whip up something special with it. Anything else--anything up there we should know about?"

"The land's starting to come back near the river. The further we traveled, the greener it got."

"That's good," said Brett.

"We saw another sandstorm far to the West--a big one--a real monster."

"There have sure been a lot of them, but as long as they stay to the West, we'll be fine. What about the ants?"

"Didn't see any this time out."

Brett remembered, years ago when he was leading a scouting party, they'd run across a trail of red ants that seemed to go on forever. They were the biggest ants he'd ever seen--the size of honeybees. Some were hauling small rodents back to their nests as if they were weightless. Using his binoculars, Brett had seen they were headed towards these giant mounds in the distance--oversized anthills nestled in a grove of vegetation he wasn't familiar with. Others were outbound, marching away from the anthills, carrying purple berries. Where and why they were taking them he had no clue. Fortunately, the ants showed no interest in the human observers, but it was still a fearsome sight.

"Any other trouble?" he asked.

Jet hesitated. "We ran into those horse men again."

Brett didn't care for Jet's tone in the way he said "horse men," but he knew Jet's opinions of the nomads were milder than some. He realized fear of strangers was somewhat normal, especially when they seemed so different from his own people.

"I was hoping to avoid any conflict and just talk with them," said Jet," but when young Roberts brought his rifle to bear, it went off."

"It went off?" Brett flashed a look of disbelief.

"He didn't mean to shoot," said Jet. "He's a little on the nervous side, and his finger slipped."

Brett shook his head. "Anybody hurt?"

"No, but the shot spooked the horses, and one of the nomads was thrown. He was okay, but it put an end to any chance of a parley."

"Damn it! It would be nice if we could form an alliance with someone out there, maybe trade, get some new blood in here."

"You're still worried about inbreeding?"

Brett nodded. "We had a pretty shallow gene pool to start with, and we've only added a few stragglers over the years. A little new blood would be good."

"I agree, but, so far, the only groups we've encountered were pretty unfriendly. And I can't imagine us and them, well . . . you know, those nomads never stay in one place for very long."

Brett sighed. "I guess I'd better have a word with Roberts about weapon safety."

"I, uh, wish you wouldn't, Captain. I already spoke to him, and he feels bad enough."

"Okay. If you've got it handled, I won't mention it. I think Savannah's at the school. You should let her know you're back."

"I will, straightaway."

Ω

It was no longer just a colony, but a super colony. The matriarch who dug the first hole and laid the first egg was no longer the sole queen. As she aged, a new social structure developed around her in conjunction with the colony's vegetal ally. A collective mind now linked each of the queens through their pheromones and ruled over colony decisions.

The newest directive was migration. The colony would no longer stay in one place, rule one territory. It would venture out, search for new lands in warmer, moister climes. Exactly where the directive had originated, no single queen could identify. But the decree had gone out. Marching orders had been delivered.

Woe to any alien colony or beast that stood in its way.

Ω

The brotherhood was his life. He owed them everything. Yet his conviction wasn't as strong as that of Brother Diego and the others. They raised him on nothing but their beliefs, their creed, their faith, but still he had doubts. He didn't understand why he had to suffer for the transgressions of his forbears. He hadn't done anything to anger God. He had committed no great sins. Yet he and his equally blameless brothers had to endure the callous ruin of a world God's great destruction had left them. Had mankind been so evil, so degenerate that God had been forced to cleanse the world in fire? Now the only thing they cleansed with fire were the dead--those who died of unknown diseases. And there were many of them.

John didn't understand everything in his world, and he was ashamed of his ignorance, his doubts. He tried to ignore them, but, nevertheless, they haunted him. His lack of comprehension led him down new paths of supposition, prodded him towards new philosophical postulations, led him to the subliminal formulation of new doctrines. Beliefs he kept to himself.

However, just because his faith wasn't as strong as theirs, didn't mean he didn't love his brothers. He did--with all his heart. He loved his work as well, whether it was in the fields growing sustenance, or in the village where he was now, caring for the people, blessing the mothers-to-be.

All the villagers knew who his mother was, and every woman who was expecting a baby wanted him to bless them and their child. John had come to accept this as his duty, though he still doubted whether his blessing was more powerful than any of his brothers. But he felt it was an honor to do what he could for any woman about to bear a child. For children were the future of mankind, and prized above all else.

"Muchas gracias, Padre," said the woman he'd just blessed. She looked ready to burst--to give birth at any moment. Despite her condition, she tried to give a little bow, but John held her up.

"Vaya con Dios, mi hija."

She was the last in line, so it was time to return to the abbey. On his way, Brother Josiah approached him.

"If you are finished, Brother, I could use your help with some repairs," said Brother Josiah.

"Certainly, Brother."

They started back together.

"What needs repair now?"

"The last storm damaged the windmill. If we don't fix it, we'll be grinding the corn by hand again."

"The corn grows well this year."

"Yes, God has blessed us with a bounty."

"If only the tomatoes had fared as well."

Brother Josiah shrugged. "He giveth and He taketh away. As always, we are thankful for what we have."

"Of course."

On their return to the abbey, Brother Josiah spotted something that furrowed his wrinkled brow more than usual.

"What's that there?" he said more than asked, pointing at a child sitting off by himself.

The boy looked filthy, and had obviously been digging somewhere, probably in the nearby ruins where the children liked to play despite warnings from the padres. John saw a variety of items spread out in front of the boy, none of them very noteworthy--broken bits and little indefinable items. But Brother Josiah's eyes were sharper.

"What have you got there?" demanded Brother Josiah in a tone of reprimand. "What is this?"

The boy shrugged as Brother Josiah picked up a pair of books that were off to the side of the boy's found treasures. How the printed paper had managed to survive the fiery holocaust of the great end, John had no idea. However, every once in a while a book or two would surface in the village, much to the displeasure of the padres, and particularly igniting the ire of Brother Josiah. He picked up the two books, looking at them more closely.

"*The Day of the Triffids . . . Monster Town*. Fiction, fabrication and falsehoods," declared Brother Josiah. "Monsters indeed. The devil's work."

John knew the abbey's cellar contained a small cache of books other than the one good book they were allowed to read, but they were all books on farming and building and such. Even so, their pages were opened only by specific padres when the need was great. The fantasy of fiction and drama and poetry was heretical because it espoused false beliefs. It was a basic tenet of their faith John had never questioned, though once, as a youngster, he'd surreptitiously read a book of fiction. He'd seen no signs of Satan in it, but neither had he read anything worthwhile.

"Show him what must be done," Brother Josiah told John, handing him the books.

John took the books and led the boy to the nearest cooking fire. The boy obviously had no interest in the books he'd found, other than maybe the pictures on their covers. He didn't even know how to read. But John figured it was a good lesson for him regardless.

"Quema los libros, mi hijo."

The boy looked up at him as if he didn't understand why he was being told to do such a thing--to throw the books into the fire.

"Ellos son la obra del diablo. Quema ellos ahora."

The boy shrugged as if he didn't care one way or the other, and tossed the books into the flames.

Fear, violence, superstition, greed, conflict, lust, territorialism, are not only the purviews of man, but humanity has always had the ability, the willful proclivity, to elevate these pursuits to new heights--to transform war into an art form. So it was inevitable, that even in the aftermath of near total annihilation, mankind would revert to form, forego forbearance, and thrust its fist into the face of tranquility.

CONFRONTATION

WHENEVER THE HERD REACHED THE RIVER on its annual migration, it always turned to the north. North was where the better grazing lands were. But Joe always wondered what lay to the south. Since he'd been old enough to join the scouting parties, they'd never gone very far south. So the next time the tribe camped by the river, before they turned north, he convinced his friend Akeem to go with him on a brief expedition south. Akeem was a couple of years younger, so it was easy to goad him into doing things, even when he didn't particularly want to.

Joe didn't tell his father or his mother where he was going. They would have said it wasn't safe. Even though he was a man now, they were always worried about him. They tried not to show it openly, not to embarrass him, but he knew it. It was all the more reason he felt he had to get away on his own at times--to feel like the man they said he was.

Joe knew the river people lived somewhere to the south, though his people had not had any contact with them in years. He'd never seen them himself, but he'd heard about them. But, for all he knew, they'd moved on or died out due to disease or bandits. It didn't matter. He figured they were much further south than he was planning on going.

Of course, judging distances wasn't always easy, though the location of the sun helped gauge time. By the stretch of the shadows, it had hardly moved at all since they'd begun their ride through the gentle slopes meandering along the river. Before long they spotted a group of pheasants. Joe figured it would be good to come home with supper hanging from his horse. Then no one

117

would question where he'd been.

"Whoever gets the most birds takes the other's watch for a week," shouted Joe, turning the hunt into a contest.

He and Akeem dismounted, tied their horses to a cluster of manzanita, and grabbed their bows. The birds scattered in all directions. Joe went right-- Akeem went left.

Joe knew it wouldn't be easy without another hunter flushing the birds towards you. Tracking pheasant took time and patience, especially now that the birds had been spooked by their horses.

He followed them into the brush, moving as quickly and quietly as he could. The terrain was hilly, and he was moving up, bow at the ready for any bird that decided to take flight. It was a difficult shot to hit a bird in mid-flight, but Joe White Eagle was known for his marksmanship. As it turned out, the first pheasant he encountered was still grounded, making it an easy target.

After the kill, he tied the bird's legs with buffalo gut and slung it over his shoulder so he could continue hunting. He was still moving up the hill when he spotted what looked like an entrance to a cave. The opening was taller than he was, and wider, though partly concealed by undergrowth. At once his curiosity overcame his competitive spirit. He cleared some brush out of his way and walked inside.

He wasn't stupid enough to go far into a cave without light, and was about to turn back from the blackness when he spotted what looked like an exit. A faint illumination shimmered from deep inside. He carefully made his way towards it. Whereas he'd gone up to reach the cave, he was now traveling downward. It didn't take him long to reach the other end. Coming out, he saw he was very close to the river. Pheasants liked to stay near water, so it was possible he could find more birds where he was.

He followed the river looking for signs of his prey. He even tried calling out like a pheasant, but there was no response and no sign of any birds. He was about to turn back when he spied something in the water. It was still some distance away, and he wouldn't have even seen it except for a bend in the river. It was . . . he didn't know what it was, but it was gigantic.

He worked his way closer to the thing, though with all the brush and tall reeds along the river's shore it wasn't always within sight. He'd almost convinced himself he hadn't really seen it, or that it was a trick of the light, when a break along the riverbank brought it into a view again. He ducked down.

It was some kind of massive black monster. He stayed down momentarily before daring to raise his head again. Whatever it was, it was half in, half out of the water, and longer than 20 horses set nose to tail. It didn't move at all. It just sat there along the riverbank, as if waiting silently for some unimaginable quarry.

Joe continued moving closer, but still cautious. When he was near enough to get a good look, he realized, despite its size, it wasn't some gigantic creature at all. It wasn't even alive. It was a monster of metal construction-- something manmade. He'd seen metallic remnants of things the ancients had built, but those relics were almost always rusting and corroded, and never as huge as this thing. He didn't understand why it didn't sink like rock, unless it was so huge it was already resting on the mud of the river bottom.

"I bet you've never seen anything like that."

Startled by the sound of a voice, Joe ducked flat onto the ground.

"I can still see you," said the voice.

Joe lifted his head and looked around. Behind him, up a slope just a bit, was a woman. A second look told him she wasn't as old as he first thought-- possibly his own age, maybe a year or two younger.

She laughed. "You should get up--really. You look silly lying there."

Joe stood, asking as he brushed himself off, "Who are you?"

She hesitated, then responded, "My name's Vera. Who are you?"

"White Eagle," he said, puffing up his chest just a bit.

She giggled at hearing his name. "What's your real name?"

"That is my real name," he replied, somewhat deflated. "Joe White Eagle."

"Where did you come from, Joe White Eagle?"

He pointed north.

"No, I mean where do your people live? How'd you get here by yourself?"

He didn't answer right away, but gave her a closer look. She wasn't as tall as him, but her dark hair was even longer than his own. Her green eyes sparked with curiosity, but no malevolence. He couldn't identify the material her sack-like dress was made of, but he saw enough of her to tell she was of childbearing years.

"I came with a friend," he replied. "We were exploring. My tribe lives everywhere--anywhere we go. We don't stay in one place."

"Are you with the nomads?" she asked, both excited and apprehensive. "Are you one of the horse people?"

He'd never heard his people described like that, but he knew what she meant.

"Yes," he said.

"Then where's your horse?"

He motioned again. "I left it back there."

"Can I see it?"

He shrugged and said, "First, tell me if you know what that thing in the river is."

"That? That's just an old submarine."

"Sub--marine? What is it? What does it do?"

"It doesn't really do anything. When I was little, it gave us electricity, but it doesn't work anymore. It's a boat. Do you know what a boat is? My grandfather and all the other seniors used it to travel up the river a long time ago. It's how they got here."

"A boat? For traveling on the water?"

Vera nodded.

"It looks like it would sink to the bottom."

"Well, it didn't. It could travel on top of the water or underneath it. That's why it's called a submarine. Sub means under, and marine means water . . . I think."

He shook his head slowly, not sure he believed her.

"What are you doing out here, so far from your village?"

"I was following the ants."

"Ants? Why would you follow ants?"

She chuckled at his perplexed look, then got serious.

"I find ants very interesting," she said. "Especially the big ones. Did you know they work with the indigo tree?"

"Bugs working with trees? That's loco talk."

Vera put her hands on her hips and declared indignantly, "No it's not. I've seen them. I've watched them."

"What have you seen?"

"The ants clear out areas the indigo grows in. They get rid of all the other plants there. They also bring water to the plant."

Joe laughed. "How can an ant carry water?"

"They use leaves," she said, countering his disbelief. "One ant can't carry much water, but a thousand can."

"Why would they do that--help these trees I mean?" asked Joe, still skeptical.

"I think because they eat the indigo berries. At least I've seen them carrying the berries back to their mounds."

"Show me," said Joe.

"Okay. Follow me," she said with assurance.

Vera started up the hill and Joe followed. He admired the way she moved-- quick and agile. He also admired her posterior, of which he had a good view.

As they neared the top of the rise, there was a small clearing. At one spot on the perimeter of the clearing was a large mound. Joe recognized it as an ant nest. He'd been warned at an early age to avoid them.

"Be careful where you step," said Vera. "They won't bother us unless you start smashing them."

"I'm not stupid," Joe responded defensively. "I once saw a wild horse caught up in an ant nest. His leg broke in a hole and they swarmed him. Next day there wasn't much left of him."

"Stop it. I don't want to hear about that."

"I'm just saying, I--"

"There," she said, pointing. "See?"

Joe saw it for himself. A line of scarlet ants carrying purple berries to their nest. Their march originated from the center of the clearing, where a dense hedge had taken root.

"That's not a tree, it's a naka bush," said Joe.

"Well, we call it an indigo tree because of the purple berries," replied Vera. "I've studied them. The ants cultivate the indigo like we grow vegetables, and they eat the berries. It's a . . . symbiotic relationship. That's what my papa calls it. Everywhere the ants go, the indigo grows."

Not wanting to admit she was right about everything, Joe asked, "How do you know it's not the other way around? Maybe everywhere the naka grows, the big ants follow."

He saw she was thinking about it, but she just shrugged.

"So where's this horse of yours?" she finally asked.

"I can show you. Come on."

They started down the slope, then she slipped and tumbled, rolling several feet through the brush.

Joe moved to stop her fall and tried to help her up.

"Let go of me! I'm all--owww!"

"What's wrong?"

121

"I think I twisted my ankle. I can't put any weight on it."

"Sit down," said Joe. "Rest it a while."

She sat and Joe did the same across from her. They were both silent for a bit, but Joe noticed she wasn't comfortable with the quiet. It seemed a chore for her to hold her tongue.

"So why do you ride horses?" she finally asked, breaking the silence.

Joe thought it a foolish question, but answered. "It's how we travel--how we go from one place to another."

"Why don't you just stay in one place?"

"Because we must follow the buffalo herd. The herd is everything."

"I've never seen a buffalo, but I've read about them in a book."

"I've never seen a book."

"You've never seen a book?" she said, astonished. "You can't read?"

"I can read," he said defensively. "A little bit. My mother taught me."

"But if you don't have any books, what do you read?"

"Whatever she writes with the charcoal." While Vera pondered this, Joe asked, "Where are your people? Where do you live?"

"Over there--just past the *Savannah*."

"The what?"

"The *Savannah*. It's the name of the submarine. The *U.S.S. Savannah*. My mother was named after it by my papa--my grandfather."

"You must live with the river people."

"Is that what you call us?"

Joe nodded.

"I guess that's as good as us calling you the horse people."

She laughed and Joe smiled.

"Do you want to see if you can walk now?"

She started to get up and Joe reached out to help her. She took his hand, but when she tried to put weight on her right ankle she cried out in pain again.

"I'm not going to be able walk," she said has he helped her down again.

Joe thought for a second. "I'll go get my horse. It can carry you back to your tribe."

"Really?" The thought intrigued her. "I've never been on a horse before. That would be cool."

"No, it won't be too cool. I'll have to ride around the way I came here before, but I'll be back before dark--before it gets too cold."

"Not cold, dummy, *cool*. That's what my papa says when he really likes something."

"Okay," said Joe, a bit confused. "You be cool, and I'll get back as soon as I can."

"Okay, Joe White Eagle," she said with a smile. "I'll be cool until you get back."

Ω

"Where's Joe?"

Erica looked up from the hide she was scraping to see her husband standing over her.

"I don't know. I haven't seen him since this morning."

"His horse is gone, and so is Akeem's."

"I'm sure they're just out doing what young men do," said Erica.

"What is that?"

"I don't know," she replied. "Weren't you a young man once?"

She chuckled but he didn't.

"When I was a young man, I had responsibilities. Family to care for. I didn't just go off for no reason."

"Maybe he had a reason. Maybe they're hunting."

Jim's responding grunt brimmed with skepticism.

"If you've got nothing better to do than be annoyed, why don't you sit down and help me with this?"

"That's woman's work," he said, turning away so she wouldn't see his smile.

"You!" She reached out and punched him in the leg. "It's not woman's work if you get your lazy ass down here and scrape."

"I can't," he said. "I see Akeem."

Erica stood and shielded her eyes to look in the direction her husband was staring. She saw Akeem riding in, a pheasant lying across his horse, but no sign of Joe.

"See, they were hunting," she said.

Jim flashed her a frown.

Akeem guided his horse up to them, but didn't dismount. Erica could see he'd ridden hard and fast to get there.

"Joe," he said, catching his breath, "I don't know where Joe went."

"Slow down," said Jim. "Tell me what happened."

"We rode to the river, saw some pheasant and separated to hunt them.

When I got back, Joe's horse was gone. I looked for him, I called out, but I couldn't find him. Then I saw some of those people."

"River people?"

Akeem nodded. "I think so."

Jim stood there for a few seconds, then told Akeem, "Get yourself some water and a fresh horse. You're going to take us back to where you last saw Joe."

"What are you going to do?" asked Erica.

"I'm going to get the men and find my son," he said with as stern a determined look she'd ever seen on him.

"I'm going too."

"No you're not."

"You've got a hot head, Jim Standing Bear. I'm going to make sure you don't lose it."

"You're not going."

"Try and stop me."

Ω

Brett and Vilma, along with Flo and her husband Gary, were sitting outside enjoying the sunset and a bit of Gary's latest brew. He'd built a still some years back and kept refining it until its byproduct became somewhat tolerable. However, at his age, Brett had only a taste. Just walking without being inebriated was hard enough on his bad knees. He'd taken to using a cane to get around. It was a tree branch one of his grandson's had found and fixed up for him, but it was just the right length.

"The sunsets are probably the only thing good that came out of that comet," said Vilma. "They're so much more colorful now--más magnífico."

"It's definitely impressive," agreed Brett. "Though I'm guessing you two don't remember sunsets before the comet very well, do you?"

"Not really," replied Flo. "Though it's hard to imagine they could be any more spectacular."

"It's probably all the dust particles and ash in the atmosphere reflecting the sunlight," said Gary.

"You think so? You think there's still that much up there after all these years?" wondered Brett.

Gary shrugged.

"Don't ruin the moment with that scientific talk," scolded Vilma. "Just let it be beautiful."

Brett looked up again. The last of the sun's corona was sinking in juxtaposition to a nearby stand of indigo trees. The radiant green of the tall shrubs stood out, even in the glare.

When they'd first discovered the indigo berries, he'd hoped they'd be another food source. Unfortunately the berries had psychoactive properties, which precluded them from use in their normal diets. However, they'd proved to have several important medicinal uses.

Flo, who'd kept her foundling name like her brother Jet, had become their doctor/chemist after the *Savannah's* doctor died. She'd studied the berries and the indigo trees with their spiral leaves, but was never able to identify them. The connection between the unusual vegetation and the oversized red ants was one of several conundrums yet to be puzzled out in this new world, despite a variety of theories.

Brett turned his attention from the sunset back to his homemade flute. It was only a hollowed-out indigo branch, but he'd gotten pretty good with it. He was working on a tune he'd come up with himself. He liked what he had so far, but it was still a work in progress. He played a little bit of it.

When he stopped and fiddled with his fingering, he thought he could still hear music in the distance. There were no hills large enough to cause an echo, so he figured it was just a combination of his imagination and the wind. He started up again and his companions were able to enjoy the music and the glorious view for a few more minutes before Flo's brother clambered up to their hillside spot with an air of panic.

"There are riders headed this way, Captain. At least a couple of dozen, and they're coming fast."

Brett was out of his chair and leaning on his cane before Jet finished his report.

"Arm the men and get them all to the barrier," ordered Brett. "Double the outlying guards." When Jet hesitated, Brett bellowed, "Go, man, go. Get it done. It'll take me a couple of minutes to get there. Vilma, Flo, gather all the children--count heads. Gary, help me navigate this hill."

Ω

Brett took his position at the defensive barrier they'd constructed out of rock and brush. It wouldn't stop a determined band of marauders, but it would slow them down, and provide cover for his men. They'd had trouble before with strangers. Even though the population of the Earth had been decimated, or maybe because it, there were still those who insisted upon picking a fight. He knew it had been that way throughout history. There was always someone, or some group, who wanted to take someone else's land, or didn't like the cut of their jib, the philosophy of their god, the tint of their melatonin.

Facing north, he raised his binoculars and got a good look at the oncoming enemy. Nomads by the look of them--horse people--some 25 to 30 of them, armed only with bows and arrows. At least that was something, though his scouts had reported in the past just how efficient they were with the crude weapons. He had more men, but fewer weapons and limited ammunition due to previous skirmishes with bandits. To make his defense look more fearsome, Brett long ago had some fake weapons fabricated. So now half his men were at the barrier aiming empty steel tubing at the hostiles.

He watched as the oncoming force halted some 50 yards away. They'd seen the barrier and his men.

Brett noted a lone woman among the interlopers, though she was unarmed. The woman was white, but the shades of skin for most of the rest varied from dark to darker.

He'd never been one to judge a person by their race, but Brett knew the differences between this predominantly dark-skinned group would create an uneasiness with his own, mostly Caucasian people. Differences aggravated the unknown, and the unknown heightened fear. He had to keep a tight rein on his people if they were going to avoid bloodshed. Something he hoped with all his heart.

The strangers all dismounted and took up positions of their own. Apparently they weren't foolish enough to charge into the field of fire he'd set up.

"Watch the flanks," called out Brett. "They may try and circle around. But no one fires until I give the order. Am I understood?"

Calls of "Yes, sir!" rang up and down the barrier.

"Good. We want to avoid a fight if we can."

One of his daughters chose that moment to come running up to the barrier.

"Savannah, get down! What are you doing here?"

She caught her breath and said, "We can't find Vera. Everyone else is accounted for, but I don't know where she is."

Brett knew his granddaughter liked to explore, and ventured off on her own quite a bit. She could be fine or she could be . . . he didn't want to think about it. He couldn't right now.

"I'm sure she's fine. She's a smart girl. Now you get back with the others and take care of them--and stay down."

She looked like she wanted to object, but realized there was nothing they could do at the moment. She went back.

Brett turned his gaze back on the nomads. One of them--probably their leader--had walked out about ten yards from the rest and just stood there. Brett noted he was unarmed.

"What's he doing?" wondered Jet.

"He wants to parley," replied Brett. "Okay, let's see what he has to say." Brett unbuckled his pistol belt and handed it to Jet.

"It could be a trick," said Jet. "Let me go."

"If it's a trick, our people need you more than a crippled old man," said Brett. "Give my sidearm to a man who can use it."

Brett grabbed his cane and made his way through the barrier. He ambled out, and as soon as the nomad saw him, he drew closer as well. Neither stopped until they were just several feet apart.

The nomad stood in contrast to Brett. His long, thick black hair, held in place by a band of cloth, compared to the short, thinning gray hair of the former naval officer. Though not a boy, he was much younger than Brett, with solid muscles protruding from his sleeveless rawhide vest. He looked much like an Indian from one of the movies of Brett's youth--fierce even without war paint or weapons. Indeed, he looked very much as if his ancestry were Native American.

"I'm Captain Brett Conyers," he stated, deciding it was a good time to use his military rank.

The nomad didn't respond at first, then replied, "I am *Oh'hut Nahgo,* also known as Jim Standing Bear."

"What can I do for you, Jim?"

"Release your prisoner."

That caught Brett by surprise and he was sure his expression showed it.

"We have no prisoners."

"Did you kill him?"

"Kill who? I don't know who you're talking about. We haven't killed anyone. Not since the last time we were attacked by bandits."

"My son is no bandit."

"Your son? Is he missing? Look, those bandits attacked us more than a year ago, and to my knowledge we haven't harmed anyone since. I don't know

127

anything about your son. I've had no reports of anyone being seen by my people."

"Then your people have lied to you. They were seen in the same area where he went missing."

"My people don't lie to me," said Brett stiffly.

"If this is true, let us search your village for my son."

"I can't do that," replied Brett. "Would you let my men into your camp?"

The nomad had no answer for that. He stood silent a moment, then responded resolutely, "I *will* find my son. We will fight if we must."

"That would be foolish of you. I have more men than you, and we're armed with guns. It would be an unnecessary slaughter."

"We won't die as easily as you think."

"Look, Jim. This is crazy. Why don't we work together and search for your son. I was just told my granddaughter is missing as well. I assume you haven't seen her or you would have said something. Let's look for both of them before we start killing each other."

The defiant look on the nomad's face didn't flicker. Brett had no idea what he was thinking--what he might do. A man protecting his family was capable of anything.

Jim Standing Bear opened his mouth to speak, but a nearby sound stopped him. Something was coming through the brush in the East. It sounded like a horse or horses. Brett backed away on his cane, suspicious of treachery. Yet he saw the nomad was surprised as well.

Before either could speak, a single horse trotted into the clearing. On its back was a young man dressed much as the nomad was, though his skin wasn't as dark. Behind him on the horse was Vera.

"Father?" the young man said in surprise.

"Hi, Papa," called out Vera. She smiled and waved. "Look at me, I'm on a horse."

The nomad woman came running out towards the newcomers. "Mother," he said, obviously taken aback again. Brett could tell by the expression on the youngster's face that he figured he was in trouble.

"It appears I was wrong," said the nomad.

"I'm just glad you've found your son," said Brett. "And it looks like I've found my granddaughter as well."

"Yes, I'm sure they have a wonderful story to tell. I can't wait to hear my son's explanation. I hope you will accept my apology."

"I don't know if I can accept an apology from an enemy," responded Brett. He smiled and held out his hand. "But I'd be happy to accept one from a friend."

Jim Standing Bear smiled in return, grasping Brett's offered hand with a grip that could have turned coal to diamond.

Ω

"I had no idea one animal could provide so many uses," said Brett upon hearing a summary of all the things the nomads harvested from the buffalo they hunted. "The glue you make from the hooves could really come in handy."

"I'm certain those who came before us had even more uses we are unaware of," said Standing Bear. "I only know what was passed on to me by my grandfather when he would recount tales of my ancestors."

"Well it's a lot. And trading will benefit both our groups. We get pretty tired of fish."

"As we tire of buffalo meat. Your fish and the vegetables you grow will be a nice change."

"A few horses could come in handy for us as well. I actually worked on my father's horse ranch in Wyoming before I joined the Navy, though I think my riding days are over," he said, brandishing his cane. "We'll likely find many things we can trade as we learn more about each other."

Standing Bear nodded.

After the embarrassment of his aggression, Jim Standing Bear had sent his men back to their camp. Only he, his wife and son had remained, so he could talk peace and trade with Brett. While they spoke, Savannah and Vera took the wife and son on a tour of their village.

"Trading will be good for both of our peoples, but I worry most about bloodlines," said Standing Bear.

Brett caught his meaning right away. "You mean inter-marriage?"

"Yes. It is a concern."

"One I share. Our group may be larger than yours, but it's also older. We have few women of child-bearing age, and too many of our young people are related."

"I suggest then, our people spend time together and . . . ." Standing Bear didn't finish his thought, but Brett did.

"And hopefully nature will take its course and relationships will develop between our young people."

129

"That would be a good thing for both tribes."

"Would you consider a total merging of *tribes*?" asked Brett. "Move your people here and become one tribe?"

"I don't dislike the idea," replied Standing Bear. "But we must follow the herd. It's how we live. If we didn't, you'd still have only fish to eat."

Brett smiled. "I understand. You go where the buffalo go. But you might consider establishing a permanent camp here where your very young, your very old, your sick, could stay while the rest of you follow the herd. They'd be safe here, and we already conduct a school for the children."

Brett saw Standing Bear was considering it.

"I will have to think on it. Maybe, as we learn to trust each other, it could be possible."

"Yes, trust is important," said Brett. "But I believe we've made a good start today."

"We have, Captain Conyers."

"Call me Brett."

"Call me . . . Standing Bear . . . or Jim."

Standing Bear smiled and Brett laughed. "That's good. I think I might have trouble pronouncing your Cheyenne name."

Vilma came up on them while they were shaking hands.

"I'm glad to see you two are getting along," she said. "We missed dinner because of all the excitement earlier, but we have something ready now. Come."

Ω

"El Carrito, help the señora."

John ignored the reference to his childhood nickname, and responded to Father
Diego's request, hurrying to the back of the chapel to help the elderly Señora Martinez to her seat. Father Diego's mind wasn't as sharp as it used to be. Every once in a while his present would slip into the past, or he'd forget things--recent events, work he'd already completed, names of people he'd known for years. John had long ago stopped bothering to correct him on things that weren't important.

He held the señora's arm until she was safely seated, then walked quickly back to his place near Father Diego, who would be delivering the sermon this day.

It was a small chapel, but it was filling up, as it usually did for Sunday services. There were no windows, so the only light came from the open door and the candles scattered around the room. One of his normal duties was to make the candles, out of sheep fat. "Tallow" is what Father Diego called it. Years ago, when Father Diego was teaching him to make the candles, he'd told him God was in everything--even the candles made of sheep fat. "God is everywhere, he'd said. "He's even inside of you, El Carrito."

At the time, John hadn't liked hearing that very much. It was unsettling to think the great and powerful God of Heaven was inside him. It had even made him a little nauseous. Of course he'd come to accept it for its symbolic meaning, though the memory of it still made him chuckle.

When all the seats of the little chapel were full, and many of the men were standing along the back wall, Father Diego directed him to close the door. Any late arrivals would know the chapel was too crowded, but that they could return for the evening service.

Father Diego began his sermon with a story about Jesus. It was a story John had heard and read about many times, but it was one of his favorites. It happened in a place called Bethsaida, where thousands of people came to hear Jesus speak, because, as Father Josiah once said, Jesus told even better stories than Father Diego.

As the story went, night fell and the people became hungry, because few had brought any food. Jesus asked those who had some to share what they'd brought. Five loaves of bread and two fishes were put in a basket and given to Jesus.

John remembered having to ask Father Diego, when he first heard the story, what *fishes* were. He found the idea of an animal living and breathing in water still hard to accept. Their water came from the rain, and from a few deep wells. There were no fishes in the well water.

Of course the five loaves and two fishes weren't nearly enough to feed so many people, so Jesus prayed to God over the food and told his disciples to began handing it out. They kept handing out the food to people, but the basket never emptied, so Jesus was able to feed thousands of people with just those five loaves and two fishes. Father Diego called it a miracle that proved God could do anything.

John had asked Father Diego why *he* couldn't pray to God so the people of the village and the padres of the abbey had plenty of food. He remembered Father Diego laughing at this question, and telling him he was no Jesus.

When he finished his story, Father Diego asked everyone in the chapel to bow their heads, and he began reciting a prayer.

"Oh Lord, we beseech You to forgive mankind for its trespasses, as we forgive those who trespass against us. Deliver us from the evil ways of old. Have mercy on those who have been cleansed by Your heaven-sent fire, and lead us not into temptation, but to better ways and better days. Thy will be done on Earth as it is--"

Before he could finish, a man from the village threw open the chapel door and croaked loudly, "Bandidos!" He tried to say something else, but, instead, fell face first onto the stone floor. From his back protruded an arrow like the kind John had seen used for hunting.

From the open door he heard men shouting and women screaming. Those inside the chapel began crying out, but Father Diego told them very sternly to sit and stay in the chapel. He hurried to the door and walked out to see what was happening. John saw the tense, fearful faces of those in the chapel, then gathered his courage and followed Father Diego outside.

Father Diego was already down the road, trying to direct the villagers he found to get off the road--to go inside. Men on horseback were everywhere-- men with weapons of wood and steel. They were using them against anyone within reach--beating, bashing, cutting--as if the mass violence were a weapon itself. Several of the padres came running out of the abbey, holding garden rakes and staffs. They tried to defend the people, but the bandits were too strong, too many. John saw old Father Josiah knocked to the ground almost immediately, his head a bloody pulp.

Father Diego was struck down by one of the bandits, and John hurried to his side. He grabbed the reins of the invader's horse to try and prevent it from stomping on Father Diego. The animal reared up and the bandit fell. That got the attention of several more attackers. They dismounted and swarmed over John, beating and kicking him. The pain didn't last long. It succumbed to total darkness.

Ω

When John finally woke, his entire body ached and his vision was blurry. He smelled smoke and when he attempted to move, bolts of pain shot through his outstretched arms. As his sight cleared he saw several structures on fire, bodies scattered across the dusty road, and two horse-drawn wagons packed with stolen food and other loot. One wagon he recognized from the village. The other was different, unfamiliar. Behind the second wagon, bound together like a string of goats were many of the village's older children, and even some young women. All around them--all around the wagons--were bandits on horseback. They spoke to each other, calling out directives and commands he only understood bits of. The drivers slapped their reins and the wagons rolled.

He tried to move again, but again the wave of pain stopped him. He looked down. He was naked and held firm against the abbey's wooden door, his feet barely touching the ground. He looked to the side to see how he was bound--why he couldn't move. A red wave of nauseating horror swept through him. His hands had been nailed to the door.

Ω

His father was not happy with him. Since the birth of his daughter, Joe had spent all his time in the village of the river people. That's what his father still called them after all these years. But to Joe, they were his people as much as the nomadic tribe he'd grown up with. But here, by the great river Mississippi, was where his wife was--where his daughter was.

For some time he'd been working with Vera's father and others to improve their community. They'd finished building a windmill that not only pumped water to various spots in the village, but kept the moat around the village filled. The moat was important because it kept out the ants. As a boy he'd seen great columns of the bugs migrating across the prairie, but they'd never crossed paths with his people--never been a problem. However, over the last few years there had been some minor incursions by swarms of the ants either trying to invade the village or just get to the river. So they'd dug a protective trench around the community and connected it so that it was an extension of the river. Not only were they protected, but it allowed the tiny creatures access to water without crossing into the village.

As an extra measure, they'd come across a container of hydramethylnon, an ant poison according to the faded label. So they'd spread that on the ground just inside the protective line of the moat. If neither the moat nor the poison stopped the ants, their next course of action was to light the brush on fire and hope the wind was blowing the right way so it wouldn't spread to their homes.

He enjoyed the work--even digging the trench. He found he had a knack for construction. He felt useful. He was never as good a buffalo hunter as his father and many of the other men. He was more at home with a hammer or shovel in his hands than a bow or a spear, despite having grown up with them and becoming a fair marksman.

Now they were working on a much larger project--a steamboat they'd use to travel up and down the river to explore. The project had stalled though, due to a lack of wood. They were going to have to range further away to find new sources.

Even though his father had established a permanent camp within the village, he thought Joe should be following the herd with the rest of the men and women who'd be gone for days or even weeks at a time. He'd done that for many years, but now he preferred to stay in the village.

He'd helped to build wagons for the hunters to haul their bounty back to the village, but he didn't want to be away from his wife and daughter for as long as the hunts sometimes took. Though he thought of the village as a safe place, and Vera as a strong woman, he was very protective of his family. His mother understood. His father didn't.

He was even more protective after his daughter was born. He doted on her. He thought Saverra must be the most beautiful baby ever--even though he knew every father must think the same.

At first he wasn't sure about her name because it was so different, but he came to like it for the same reason. It combined the names of her mother and grandmother, with the V in the center paying homage to her great grandmother--at least that's what Vera said. It was the way her great grandmother Vilma pronounced it with her accent and the rolling *r* sound that led to them spelling it with the double *r*. *Saverra*--he liked the way it rolled off his tongue.

He liked life in the village, he liked building things, and he liked playing baseball on those rare days when Vera's grandfather would organize a game. There was always much work to do, so a game was a rare treat. He liked the competition, the swatting of the ball, the running of the base paths. He liked it because he was good at it--like he was good at building things. He wasn't nearly as good at reading, but Vera continued to try and teach him. It was often embarrassing, because there were children who read much better than him. At least he was good enough now to read some of the village's books-- even if sometimes he needed help with a word or two or three. He'd even learned about building things by reading the notes some of the seniors had scrawled into the books' margins. He hoped, one day, to build the kind of house he read about in books. A great house for the great big family he planned to have.

#

Water had become the pressing need for the colony--particularly for its verdant ally. The queens knew this, but it was constantly being reinforced through the biological exchange of their pheromonal imperatives. Scouts had been sent out and had discovered a source, but it wasn't enough. The slender stream was traced to an even larger body of water, one that would satisfy their needs. Getting to it only required bridging the narrow waterway between them and their ultimate goal, or they could go around--a minor detour that was insignificant when compared to the incalculable distance they'd already traveled.

It was decided it would be easier to move the colony around the obstacle, but then something happened. Something began interfering with the chemical signals by which the queens communicated. Sonic cues alerted of danger, but they too were erratic. There was something noxious . . . venomous.

Whether this blight was spread by returning scouts or carried on the wind, there was no way to know. Not only were directives lost in a maelstrom of polluted confusion, but hundreds died. There was chaos.

It took time, but once discipline was restored, the directives to the workers had been corrupted--chemical signals altered. Orders were relayed. Workers were massed. Bridges were created. Scouts were deployed. More confusion and death. Hundreds more died clearing pathways for the colony. Soldiers were mustered. The decree was clear. Nothing must stand in the colony's way.

Ω

She'd come a long way since the Sanctuary--both in distance and time. For the most part, she remembered her underground home fondly. All of the mothers and uncles who taught her, were kind to her, cared for her. It had all been a pleasant if artificial existence until . . . until she'd fled the cold mainframe reasoning of Farkas, whose harsh, transistorized silicon and graphene logic circuits required she take part in breeding a new generation.

That, however, had not been her only reason. Her flight had also been motivated by a naive quest to find her birth mother, banished years earlier by Farkas. Her impetuous decision had almost led to her death. Yet here she was, so many years--so many miles later, alive, and not only a mother of seven children, but also a grandmother. She didn't know if the joke was on Farkas, or on her.

She had no complaints. She'd been lucky and she knew it. The life she lived, relative to other survivors on this decimated planet, had been good . . .

135

was good. Being bought by Jim was the best thing that ever happened to her, though even to think of it now sounded funny to her.

"Go say hi to Grandma."

Erica turned to see Brett Conyers release the hand of his great granddaughter and nudge her forward.

Brett was a good man who liked to take Saverra with him when he went fishing at the river. She'd squeal with delight whenever they caught a fish, and liked to tell grandma Erica all about it. Today, Brett had been playing his flute for Saverra. He used to play it all the time to help put her to sleep when she was a baby, and she still clamored for him to play her a tune whenever she could.

"Go on. Grandma Erica's waiting. Papa Brett needs to lie down somewhere and rest his old bones."

The little girl hesitated at first, then rushed into Erica's arms. Erica hugged her tightly. The little girl smelled of sage.

"Oh, Saverra, you're getting more beautiful every day," said Erica.

She didn't believe it was just something any grandmother would say. Little three-year-old Saverra wasn't just cute as most girls her age were, she was strikingly beautiful. The mix of her various bloodlines had hit the right combination thought Erica.

"Play hide-and-seek, Grandma?"

"Of course," replied Erica. "I'll close my eyes and count to ten while you go hide. But don't go too far."

She closed her eyes, heard Saverra scamper off, and began counting to ten very slowly. When she finished counting she opened her eyes and looked around. If she knew her granddaughter, the girl would pay no attention to her admonishment not to go far. So Erica set off away from the village in the direction of the area with the most scrub. Saverra was likely to be crouched in there somewhere.

Erica didn't move as fast as she used to. Life on the plain had taken its toll. Her knees ached and her back was always a bit cranky. But she wasn't going to let her granddaughter down.

"Here I come!" she called out. "I'm going to find you, and then I'm going to tickle you."

She heard a little squeak of pretend dread and followed the sound. After a few steps she saw part of a little leg sticking out of the brush. She snuck up slowly and grabbed the leg. Saverra squealed and Erica grabbed her and started tickling. Each joyful laugh was tonic for Erica's aches and pains. When she finally released her, the little girl ran for the village, expecting Erica to follow. She started to, though at a much slower pace, but then she saw something up the hill. Her eyes weren't as good as they used to be, but it looked like something moving. Her first thought was it was only the wind blowing the weeds. Then she heard someone cry out, "Ants! They've crossed the moat!"

The once bountiful Earth, left barren and dormant by fate's havoc, woke to new princes . . . new messiahs. Wealth, notoriety, beauty, ambition, social connection--all the icons and iconic pursuits of an erstwhile civilization were as irrelevant as yesterday's wind. All that mattered today was the soil's yield. Crops were king. The harvest was god.

SUBSISTENCE

IF KONNER WAS GOING DO IT, he knew he needed to get dusting. He'd been thinking about it for days, and now it was already Holiday Eve. But *flies and fleas*, he didn't know how he was going to keep his promise to Gramps, and still do what was right.

The right thing seemed like the wrong thing, and the other way round. It was way too much for a scrawny sprout of only eleven harvests to figure out, so he put his hand in his pocket and grabbed hold of his lucky goldstone. He hoped it would help him think better.

Gramps had given Konner his goldstone just before he became one with the south field. He said it had come from Faraway. Konner used to love to fold up on the porch and listen to Gramps talk about Faraway, and the things he called cities. Cities, he said, were giant-sized communities with more people than you could count--and Konner could count all the way to a hundred and beyond. Of course Gramps hadn't lived in a city since he was a sprout even younger than Konner. He said once upon a time there were thousands of cities, until the rainfire destroyed them. Konner knew all about the rainfire, the ant swarms, ol' Demon Drought--those things were landstory. They were part of the soil, they were in every seed, every drop of water. But cities? Konner wasn't sure if he believed in them. Someday, though, he wanted to have a looksee for himself. After one or two more harvests, he was going dust a trail to Faraway and see what he could see.

Right now he had a promise to keep.

It was a cool day, but warm enough in the sunshine. The wind was playing with the chaff in the south field, swirling so it looked like a dance. He'd been out there saying *Hey* to Gramps like he did sometimes, even though Gramps couldn't say anything back. That's what reminded him he couldn't put it off any longer.

So he made a trail back to the hub. On the way he saw a bunch of girls carving up their Holiday jack-o'-hearts. His sister, Heather, was there, and so was his mom, who was showing them how it was done right. They were all giggling and smiling and carrying-on strange-like. Heather herself had been acting funny of late. He didn't know if it was 'cause she was older than him or 'cause she was a girl. She sure wasn't the same Heather he used to have mud fights with. All Konner knew was she had her eyes on Billy Wagoner, and that lately she always seemed to smell of honeysuckle.

"Konner!"

His mom waved him over, but he didn't want to get too close to them silly girls, so he shuffled his feet as he walked, and let the dirt run up over his toes. He was going so slow, she came over to get him.

"Konner, where are your brothers?"

"Don't know."

"Well, I want you to make sure they're not getting into any trouble. You know how your brothers are."

"Ah, flies and fleas, Mom. I've got better things to do than looking after those sprouts."

"Go on now," she said. He heard the sternness in her voice. "You find out what kind of mischief they're up to, and put a stop to it."

"Alright."

Her expression softened then, and so did her voice. "Are you excited about Holiday?"

"Yeah," he said, bundling in his real excitement.

"Well, you be sure to have fun now, okay?"

"Sure, Mom."

He noticed she was wearing the walnut shell pendant Dad had given her a long time ago. She was particular about when she wore it. Konner liked how when it caught the sunlight, the tiny piece of crystal inside the shell would sparkle all different colors. He thought it made her feel special.

"It won't be long, Konner, before you're all grown up. So you have fun while you can."

"Don't you and Dad have fun on Holiday?" he asked, not caring to think about the day when he wouldn't have any fun.

"Sure we do. It's just a different kind of fun. Have you thought about your Holiday wish yet?"

"Yes." He'd known for a long time what he was going to wish for.

"Well good. I hope you get your wish. Now you make a trail and find out what Kobey and Kory are up to."

"Okay."

He headed off, meaning to do what she said, but the Trouble Brothers would have to wait. He had something else he had to get done first. Something more important.

Closer to the hub he saw most of the trees and bushes were already wearing their Holiday clothes, though some of the final decorating was still going on. Some women were moving about, here and there, putting on hats and belts and scarves and anything else they could make fit. He knew those clothes would scare Pestilence away for another harvest, but he couldn't figure how. They didn't scare him. Some looked so downright odd, he had to laugh. Maybe that's how they worked. Maybe ol' Pestilence didn't care for laughter.

As he approached the elders' lodge, Henry Olmstead walked out and cornered him.

"Konner Grainwell, what are you up to?"

"Nothing, Mr. Olmstead," he said, hoping he didn't look as nervous he felt.

"Shouldn't you be out practicing your cupid bow?"

"I'm not old enough for the shoot, Mr. Olmstead."

"Rainfire, boy! I wasn't any bigger than you when I took my first shoot. Well, anyway, you go have some fun." He reached into a bowl he was carrying and held out his hand. "Here's a sweetstick for you. Take it now," he urged, "and don't tell Ms. Olmstead I gave you one before the party." He winked and walked off towards the hub where lots of folks were busy getting ready for Holiday.

"Thanks, Mr. Olmstead."

He just waved the back of his hand and kept trailing.

Konner hesitated. He was right there--right outside the elders' lodge. All he had to do was sneak in, grab Gram's marker, and sneak back out. It was all he had to do to keep his promise to Gramps. He put his hand in his pocket and grabbed his goldstone. He told himself it was okay, that nobody would be hurt by it. But he stood there way too long, trying to make himself believe it, and picking at his courage.

"Konner?"

It was Grams with little Hazel in tow.

"Konner, I need you to take Hazel home. She's tired and I still have lots to do."

Flies and fleas! He'd been so close.

It wasn't that he didn't like his little sister. In fact, she was his favorite--not much trouble usually--not like Kobey and Kory. She was only five, and not mooning after boys like Heather. Konner thought Hazel was just the cutest little thing, with her big, wide-open blue eyes and corn silk hair. Right now though, he had something more important to do.

"Do you hear me, Konner?"

"Yes, Grams." He knew there was no way round taking Hazel home. He'd just have to sneak back later.

"That's a good boy, Konner. Your Gramps used to say, 'We can always count on Konner.'"

That made him feel good, and it also reminded him of his promise. It was funny Grams said that, 'cause she didn't know anything about the promise. That was just between Gramps and him.

He liked Grams well enough. She was a nice old lady who spent most of her time smoking weed and talking with the other elders. But whenever he saw her, it made him think of Gramps. Before he became one with the south field, Gramps would spend a lot of time with Konner, telling him stories and singing old songs. Konner missed him, but he wouldn't forget his promise. After Gramps was chosen, he asked Konner to be sure and take care of Grams when he was gone. He made Konner promise when her time came, he'd make sure she was laid with Gramps. Konner promised he would, and he always tried to keep his promises.

Ω

The sun had fallen to that point where the sky took on a more serious attitude--beautiful and grim at the same time. Konner could never figure out how it changed itself. One moment it's this soft, friendly blue, then the next time you looked up it's got these angry streaks of red and orange. He figured it was like a warning. *Here comes the black night--beware!* He didn't waste much time looking at it though, 'cause Holiday Eve was in full bloom.

He heard the music long before he dusted off for the hub. Anyone with any kind of instrument would be playing tonight. When he got there the dancing had already started. He thought dancing was for girls, though he saw some older boys trying to step with the music. Of course he'd seen older boys do crazier things where girls were concerned.

His eyes went right to the tables, where all manner of good stuff was laid out. He saw sweet breads and pies, jams and tater crisps, and enough spiced cider to drown ol' Demon Drought himself. Konner couldn't wait to stuff his belly, but he had to make a careful trail. Those darn jack-o'-hearts were strung up all over the place, candles burning inside them so they were aglow. He saw some girls lingering under their carvings, biding their time, hoping for a kiss. They reminded him of trapdoor spiders, just waiting to pounce.

Konner wasn't planning on kissing anyone, except maybe his mom or little Hazel, so he avoided those orange gourds like they were Pestilence himself. He figured he'd have a little snackdo first, then he'd sneak back to the elders' lodge when it was dark. He'd just grabbed himself a taste of sweet bread, when he spied Kobey and Kory under another table. They had their peashooters and were popping girls in the head when they weren't looking.

It might have been funny if he wasn't sure he'd be the one who'd suffer for their mischief. So he dusted over, grabbed the two of them, and relieved them of their shooters. Both were filthy-looking. Kory stood there scratching his butt as usual. Kobey tried to look defiant.

"You two cause any trouble and you're gonna be at one with your sister, Henna, in the east field." He didn't like to think about his dead baby sister, Henna, who was born still and never had a chance to even see the sun, but he knew it would scare the fertilizer right out of those two sprouts. "Now both of you go wash up, or I'm gonna find Dad and tell him what you've been up to, and that'll be the end of your Holiday."

He let go of them and they dusted off like a couple of field mice. He figured chances were about even they'd actually get clean. He thought he'd better take care of what he had to take care of right then. Afterwards he could--

He was standing there thinking when all of a sudden this girl swoops in like an autumn wind and kisses him. Her lips were pressing against his before he could even see who she was.

Now, the truth is, except for the shock of it all, it wasn't as bad as he thought it would be, though it was the first time any girl not family had kissed him. When she pulled away he saw it was Dandy. He should have known. Even though she had seen one more harvest than him, Dandy had been making eyes in his direction for some time. Now she stood there grinning.

He looked up and there it was. A big ol' jack-o'-hearts, smiling down at him just like Dandy was doing--like he was a rooster, all plucked and stuffed and ready for mealtime. *Darn those sprouts!* Trying to keep them out of trouble had landed him square in Dandy's trap.

Dandy looked like she was about to say something when his mom walked up with Hazel.

"Hello, Dandelion, happy Holiday," said his mom, then looked at him and smiled that smile moms get that make you think they know everything.

"Happy Holiday, Ms. Grainwell," replied Dandy all sweet-like.

"Konner, it's time for the sing and I want you to take Hazel with you."

He took little Hazel's hand, figuring it was a good excuse to get away from Dandy. But she followed them to where the others were getting in line for the sing. Still, he did his best to ignore her.

Konner didn't care much for the sing, but if you weren't joined you were still considered a sprout as far as the sing was concerned. It was the only time he wished he had a wife like his big brother Kyle. Konner didn't mind singing the songs, 'cause they were both scary and fun. He just didn't like having to parade round the hub so all the grownups could *coo* and *ahh* about how cute they all were.

He didn't know who started it, but they trailed off real slow in a line as soon as the first song began. He noticed Dandy was right behind him, but he didn't pay any attention to her. He held onto Hazel as he sang, and watched her trying her best to remember the words.

> *Tell me, tell me landstory.*
> *Back when fire burned the sea,*
> *Rivers wept and mountains roared,*
> *Hot winds sang a frightful chord.*
> *Tell me, tell me landstory,*
> *About when people had to flee,*
> *Swarms came with no warn,*
> *Laying bare where once was corn.*

Ahead of him Heather was walking real close to Billy Wagoner. He figured if Billy wasn't careful, they'd be joined before another harvest. Looking round he saw the Trouble Brothers. They were behaving themselves, acting more serious than usual. But he knew why. The songs still scared them a little.

> *Tell me, tell me, tell me please,*
> *That someday there'll be more trees.*
> *Say ol' Demon Drought is dead,*
> *Then I'll lie down on my bed.*

Round and round they trailed and sang. Konner knew it would have been a real good time to sneak into the elders' lodge, 'cause they were all watching the sing. But he couldn't very well get away with Hazel in tow and everyone watching–especially Mom and Dad. They were holding each other, touching and kissing, and looking so happy when us sprouts trailed by. Dad was usually all leather and salt, except when he was around Mom. It was a sight to see how she could soften him up no matter what his mood.

> *Keep ol' Pestilence away,*
> *He won't eat this Holiday.*
> *Say the poppers will fly right,*
> *And grant the wish I wish tonight.*
> *Tell me, tell me landstory.*
> *How I wonder what I'll be.*

When the sing ended, Konner noticed some of the elders headed back to their lodge. He knew then he'd have to wait until morning to do what he had to do. It was like a weight bearing down on him had been lifted. Since he wasn't worrying about it anymore, he stuffed as much of that good food into him as he could while doing his best to avoid Dandy.

When once he spotted her heading his way, he dusted off in the other direction. Keeping to where it was dark, he made a trail round the hub to the other side. As he did, he spotted two older kids all twisted up together like Gram's special pretzels. He recognized it was Burt Ploughhorse and Lily Landesgard. They were half naked and kissing, and he knew by the way they were moving and the sounds they were making that they were planting seed.

Konner knew what they were doing was for the good of the community, but it still seemed silly to him. He stayed out of sight and made his way back to the party.

It wasn't long after that when Mom and Dad began rounding up everyone for bed. The Trouble Brothers tried to sneak off, but Dad snatched them up by their shirts and lifted them off the ground till they stopped squirming.

"You sprouts need to get to sleep soon, so the Santa will come," said Grams as we trailed off towards our lodge. Kobey and Kory started whispering real excited to each other, and Hazel looked up at Grams, her big blue eyes filled with wonder. Last harvest Konner had snuck out early and saw it was the elders who actually hid the candy. So he figured the Santa must have been at one with the earth for many harvests, and that, so all of us sprouts weren't disappointed, the elders kept doing his good work for him.

When they got to their lodge, everyone else went inside. Konner stayed out so he could look at the moon. It was full and kind of orange. It made him think of Dandy's jack-o'-hearts, and that got him to remembering the kiss. That made him think about the pair he'd seen planting seed. He'd heard talk from the older boys that it was a fun thing. But it sure sounded painful, and he couldn't see the sense in it--except for making babies. Of course he knew the more sprouts, the better for the community. So when a boy and girl got together and started planting seed, the elders always acted all happy.

He put his hand in his pocket, took hold of his goldstone, and stared at the moon. He didn't want to think about girls, he wanted to think about Faraway, and what he might find when he got there. He sure hoped he'd catch a popper and get his Holiday wish. He was worried if he didn't--

"You need to get to sleep, Son," said his dad, stepping outside and looking up at the moon himself.

"Dad . . . ?" he said, then hesitated.

"What is it, Son?"

"How important is a promise?"

His dad looked at him as if he were sizing up a new calf. "A man's only as good as his word, Konner."

He already knew the truth of that. He guessed he just wanted to hear it said.

"Don't forget you got your chores to do tomorrow."

"But, Dad, tomorrow's Holiday," he protested, even though he knew it would do no good. When did he ever *not* have to do chores? Never, that's when.

"It may be Holiday, but the pigs still have to eat, and the tools still have to be cleaned."

"I know, Dad," he said, getting up to go in. But, as he did, he gave one last thought to Faraway. He thought about how when he dusted off to Faraway there wouldn't be any more chores to do. He couldn't wait for that day to come.

Ω

It was Holiday, and just 'cause he didn't believe in the Santa anymore, didn't mean he wasn't going to get up early and find as much candy as he could stuff in his pockets. Mom helped Hazel and the Trouble Brothers were on their own, so he did pretty well. Afterwards he hid it all in his secret place, so Kobey and Kory couldn't get their dirty hands on it.

Then he did all his chores, and by the time he was finished he knew the Holiday shoot had started. So he made a trail to the gully where the older boys, with their cupid bows, were trying their best to hit whichever jack-o'-hearts was carved by the girl they were sweet on. Some weren't even coming close. Others were so bad they were splitting open the wrong pumpkins, much to the frustration of some girls. He saw Heather get all excited when Billie Wagoner shot one right through the heart-shaped mouth she'd carved. That was about all Konner could take.

Most all of the elders, including Grams, had pulled up chairs to smoke their weed and watch the shoot. So he knew it was now or never. He dusted a trail to the elders' lodge, squeezing his goldstone the whole way.

As he neared the lodge, the sky grew dark. The wind passed over him and he shivered. A dusky, mean-looking cloud was blowing in from the East. He could see a big old bull in its shape. He kept watch for a minute, then snuck inside as slow as an earthworm. It didn't seem like anyone was there.

He'd never been in the elders' lodge before, 'cause sprouts weren't allowed. It looked like any other lodge, only bigger. Searching for where they kept the markers he spied a picture hanging on the wall. It scared the fertilizer right out him. Either that or the candy he'd eaten that morning was disagreeing with his insides. It was a creepy-looking thing, painted in more shades of brown and red than he knew existed. It was some kind of monster, all fangs and claws but almost like it wasn't really there--like a monster made of wind. He guessed it must have been somebody's idea of ol' Demon Drought.

Even though it was just a picture, he backed away from it real easy-like. That bumped him right into what he was looking for. All the elders' markers were in this big bowl sitting there on the table. Quick as he could, he found Gram's marker and put it in his pocket. He started to go but got this queer itch to take a last look at ol' Demon Drought. The thing's eyes gave him the shiver-tingles. Konner was sure the ol' demon knew what he was up to. So he dusted it out of there before he gathered any other strange thoughts.

Once outside, he made a trail back to the family lodge, going real slow like everything was okay. But everything wasn't okay--at least not with him. It was more than ol' Demon Drought eyeing him. Konner knew what he'd done wasn't right. It wasn't fair. But he didn't know any other way to keep his promise to Gramps. He just hoped some day he wouldn't feel as bad as he did right then.

Ω

By evening, everyone had gathered at the hub for Last Supper. Konner couldn't help but notice something was in the air—something you could almost feel, like a thick morning dew. Nothing he could see, but he could sense it. It was more in the way folks were talking--or not talking. They were a bit bridled, not as free and easy, as if they were waiting to be set loose. He knew what they were waiting for.

Before anyone could eat, the Harvest Christ had to be chosen. His dad and Mr. Landesgard made a trail to the elders' lodge and brought back the big bowl with all the markers. Konner tried not to show it, but he was feeling real bad about then. He didn't want to be there, but he knew he had to be. Young or old, sick or cripple, everyone took part in the choosing of the Harvest Christ. Konner knew it was a great honor to be chosen, and that only doubled his guilt.

Since the bowl was filled with all the elders' markers, or was supposed to be, none of them could pick. So, after everyone quieted down, Mr. Landesgard reached in, stirred his hand round, and pulled out a marker. Konner's hands were in his pockets--the right one clenched round his goldstone, the left Gram's marker.

"Henry Olmstead," he announced, holding up the marker for all to see.

Everyone started clapping and shouting and Konner looked over to old Mr. Olmstead to see how he was taking it.

He was all smiles, shaking hands with everyone. He looked happy, but . . . there was something about his smile Konner couldn't quite figure. Something different--like he was trying too hard.

Anyway, someone had put the harvest wreath on Mr. Olmstead's head and a big knife in his hand, and everyone was coaxing him to get Last Supper going. He waved the knife above his head and the gesture was greeted with more clapping. Then he brought it down and began carving the Eater Bunny.

Konner was sure it was the biggest rabbit he'd ever seen. Even skinned and barbecued up nice and juicy like, it was as big as a ki-yote. It was such a grand scene, full of laughter and fine-smelling food, it made Konner wonder for a moment whether or not he'd get the honor of carving the Eater Bunny some day. Right then, he didn't feel bad at all. *Flies and fleas*, he even let Dandy sit by him for Last Supper.

Ω

It was long after dark when Konner climbed aboard the wagon with the rest of his family. He was about to burst from all the good stuff he'd eaten, and more than ready to get some sleep. But Holiday wasn't over yet. The whole community was loading up the wagons and making a trail out to the fallow north field where the Holiday fire was already blazing.

As Henry Olmstead's body was being laid aboard one of the wagons, Konner started feeling guilty again. Earlier, when old Mr. Olmstead had drunk from the harvest gourd, Konner had turned away so he wouldn't see. He'd squeezed his goldstone and tried not to think about what was in that drink.

Not that there was anything so terrible to see. He'd watched when Gramps was chosen. It was like he'd gone to sleep. But this time he couldn't help feeling bad about what he'd done, even though he'd kept his word to Gramps. Konner knew the Harvest Christ would be made at one with the north field this Holiday, and Gramps wanted Grams to be with him in the south. That's what Konner had promised. So he couldn't let Grams be chosen--not this Holiday--even if it meant maybe depriving her of the honor. Konner was sure she'd be chosen next year when it was time for the south field again.

When everyone had gathered near the fire, Henry Olmstead was gently carried from the wagon. They took off his clothes and carefully laid him into the place that had been prepared. As they covered him up, Ms. Olmstead stepped forward, looking real proud-like, and delivered the Holiday thanksgiving.

"The earth is the land, and we are the earth. Bless this land and the bounty of its harvest. We who take from the land, now give back to the land. May all of our harvests be so bountiful."

Then everyone joined in for the last part.

"The earth is the land, and we are the earth."

After that, everyone trailed off to stand round the fire. No one said a word, 'cause we weren't supposed to. The littlest sprouts were shushed if they tried to speak, and even the Trouble Brothers knew better than to make any noise.

Konner already knew what his Holiday wish was, so he tossed his popping corn into the fire like everyone else. As he stood there, waiting, hoping to catch one of the poppers so he'd get his wish, he thought about Faraway and Gramps and Grams and old Henry Olmstead. He wondered if they celebrated Holiday in Faraway. He sure hoped so, 'cause he'd miss all the food and the fun. Who knows, he might even miss getting kissed under a jack-o'-hearts.

The poppers had started flying all round him. He waited, ready to grab one if it came his way, 'cause you had to catch them on the fly to really get your wish. He saw Heather catch one and get all excited, then *pop*! One shot off to his right, but he was quick. He caught it, wished his wish again, and tossed it into his mouth.

He was feeling real good when everyone began loading back into the wagons. Just knowing he'd get his Holiday wish made everything he'd worried about seem okay. Maybe he wouldn't get it right away, but some day . . . .

149

In less than a century nature's comeback seemed all but certain. The Earth flourished, its people multiplied, both animal and insect life established firm footholds. Townships grew and some even instituted laws. Societies formed after the fashion of their environments, leaders began to govern, and mankind, its proclivities as robust and irrepressible as ever, turned to the reliable pursuits of profit and pleasure.

RESILIENCE

"WHERE'YAT WIT YOUR MIND? Y'all quit your daydreaming out here, missy, and come see tuh pass duh mop. Dese floors ain't gonna clean dere selves."

Saverra stood and promptly replied, "Yes, Mamam."

"I didn't save your hide so y'all could while way duh day like a lizard sunning hisself on a rock."

"No, Mamam. I'll gets tuh it."

"Mais you'd better."

Mamam went back inside, leaning on her walking stick, and Saverra followed close behind.

She tried to be a good girl and do what she was supposed to, because, by all accounts--meaning what Mamam had told her--Mamam had saved her. Saved her from what, wasn't real clear. Saverra didn't remember much. The passage of years from when she was very young were endless footsteps lit only by a shadowy blur. Only bits and pieces of her history made brief appearances in her awareness--usually at the strangest of times. The rest was a haze of unwanted emotions and dark forgetfulness. But she knew Mamam had come along when things were about as bad as they could be. She'd been hungry, filthy, living in a hole in the ground, hiding out from some very bad people who she was sure were going to eat her. At least that's how she remembered it.

That was many years ago. She'd been with Mamam ever since, and she'd learned she had to work for her keep. She didn't mind working, but sometimes she liked to go off by herself to think--to try and remember the time before she'd run and hid. But the shreds of those memories were few and frightening. She remembered shouts, people screaming, fire, ants--always there were ants in her memory--monstrous blood-colored ants. They swarmed over her recollections like they swarmed over everything in their path.

She had a vague recollection of an old woman--*a grandma?*--gathering her up and running. Where they ran and for how long, she couldn't recall. Neither could she remember what happened afterwards. She knew, that at some point, the woman had died, but when that happened, where and why, she had no memory.

From then on it was always about finding food--eating all manner of strange things--hiding, avoiding packs of dogs, staying far away from the ants, though they still haunted her dreams.

She hadn't seen many ants since she'd come to *Maison Boogalee,* which is what Mamam called her place of business. She hadn't seen much of anything except dirty dishes, dirty bed sheets, dirty floors, dirty walls . . . she figured if it weren't for her and Rosalee, the *Boogalee* would be the dirtiest place in the whole world.

Rosalee was the old woman she helped do the cleaning. She was pretty nice, when she wasn't being bossy. Then she could get real mean. Still, they got along, and she could ask Rosalee just about anything and get an answer she could understand.

What she couldn't understand was why Rosalee told her she shouldn't be in any hurry to grow up. Because Saverra couldn't wait to grow up so she could be like the other women employed by Mamam. They hardly did any work, except at night when the men came. From what she could hear, it sounded like they were having fun . . . at least most of the time.

Rosalee said she hoped when Saverra got older she'd meet a nice man and get married, and that he'd take her away from the *Boogalee.* But Saverra had been there so long already, it was hard to imagine leaving. It was even harder to imagine what kind of life there'd be with a strange man living in a strange place. She guessed it might be okay, as long as it was a place with no ants.

Until then, she didn't mind the men joking at her and asking Mamam how much for her. It made her proud, even though Mamam always shook her head and told those men, "Y'all couyon or pie-eyed. Mamzelle too young, too little, not her, not yet."

The men didn't just come to the *Boogalee* for the company of the women. They came for the food too. Mamam herself worked with the cook to make her gumbo and bouille and ponce--which was pig stomach. Saverra liked it all until she learned the bouille gravy was made from all sorts of animal innards. Once she ate it and got so sick it was like the brown gravy was coming out of her other end. Mamam said she had the fwas. All she knew was she never wanted to have the fwas again, so she never ate any more bouille.

Once Mamam fed some folk who said they could play music. She told them she'd let them "sing for dere suppa." They actually only sang a little, but they had all kinds of music-making tools they used for their songs. Saverra liked the music--liked it more than anything. After Mamam saw her swaying to the music once, she started teaching her to dance. Rosalee helped too, and soon Saverra was dancing for the customers. Sometimes they'd throw silver coins at her or even small pieces of gold. Saverra liked to dance, and liked the attention it got her, even if Mamam kept most all the "tips" as she called them.

The other women at the *Boogalee* started getting jealous of the "Catin"--which is what some of the men started calling Saverra. But Mamam quashed that jealousy with several stern words, telling them they could earn their keep elsewhere if they liked. It was Mamam who actually started calling her Catin. She said it meant "pretty girl" or "baby doll." Saverra didn't like being called a "baby" at all, but she delighted in being told she was "pretty."

Sometimes when she danced, some pie-eyed fellow would try to grab her, and Mamam would smack his hand with her walking stick and call him a "cochon"--which was her word for pig. Saverra liked that Mamam watched out for her, but Rosalee said she was just protecting her investment.

Saverra didn't care why it was Mamam took care of her, she just loved to dance. Not that it got her out of cleaning, but once in a while Mamam might give her a little silver coin to buy something at the market. She said it was her "reward" for putting on a good show.

Once, at the market, she found this necklace she really liked. It was a shiny red rock held by a leather cord. The old woman selling it offered both the necklace and what she called a "reading" for her silver.

"What's a *reading*?"

"A reading is milay--the future. I will read the cards and divine tu fortuna. Tell you what will happen por tus dias siguientes."

Not certain, but intrigued, Saverra nodded.

The old woman removed some cards from the pocket of her dress and began mixing them about. It wasn't easy. The cards were old, torn and creased, their colors faded. But when she was finished, she placed three of them on the ground between her and Saverra. She studied them intently. Each card had a picture. The first was a woman with a basket on her head, birds flying in the distance. The second was a spider on a web of stars. The third a man in a fancy feathered outfit and a horned hat.

"The primero, the first card, is you--the Maiden of Vessels. It is invertido, which means blinded by illusion, seductive but un momentáneo slave to la pasión. Next is the card of Stars which speaks of spiritual balance and enlightenment, but says la pasión can cloud perception. Last is the Shaman card. It is life, even if it may be a harsh or dark life. It speaks of poderio-- power through balance, a healing of the soul."

"What do dey mean?"

The woman closed her eyes and waved her hands over the cards. When she opened them, she said, "You will meet a man--a man who is yohan-- extraño, strange. A strange man with strange ideas. There will be koolo dang- gim--an attraction between you. But another will intervene--dugay namja-- two men." She held up two fingers. "You will have to decide--passion or preservation--illusion or enlightenment."

Saverra shook her head, not understanding.

"When will dis happen? When dese two men coming?"

The old woman shrugged and said, "That is all the cards say." She picked up the trio of cards and put them back with the others. She looked at the young girl, but said nothing else. Saverra took it as a sign the "reading" was over, so she stood and headed back to the *Boogalee*, unsure of what to make of it all.

Ω

One otherwise dull humid evening there was some kind of ruckus outside the *Boogalee*. It got so loud Saverra just had to see what it was. She left her dirty dishes half unwashed and followed a couple of ladies and their customers who'd heard the noise too. Much to her disappointment, it turned out to be nothing much. Just this strange man, dressed in a raggedy assortment of clothes, standing outside next to his mule and talking bad about the *Boogalee* and its business.

" . . . this house profaned by harlotry. Those that glory in such immorality will suffer the everlasting consequences. For neither fornicators, nor idolaters, nor adulterers, nor thieves, nor the covetous, nor drunkards, nor revilers, nor swindlers will inherit the kingdom of God."

Saverra didn't know most of the words he was spouting, and she guessed neither did most of his audience. That didn't stop them from mocking him, and laughing at their own jests. Many of the women from the *Boogalee* were questioning both the nature and size of his manhood. Some even opened their blouses and gave him a free look they'd normally want payment for.

They called him a "preacher man," a "fairy friar," a "rat-faced revivalist" and all kinds of things Saverra had never heard of. The truth was, she didn't think he was "rat-faced." He was a fairly young man with a regular face, accentuated only by thick, dark eyebrows over deep-set eyes. But she didn't understand why he was doing what he was, and what he hoped to accomplish.

Despite the continued insults, the stranger kept talking, kept preaching his words.

"Make not the mistake of your forbearers," he shouted. "God destroyed Sodom and Gomorrah, he destroyed the Earth with a great cleansing fire, and he will destroy you if you do not repent your sins and the sins of your ancestors."

It didn't take long before the man's audience dwindled. Folks tired of hurling insults at him and returned to their own pursuits. Saverra returned to her dishes, but she could still hear him as she went.

"Couyon!" exclaimed Mamam, shutting the door to the *Boogalee*. "Nuff of dat couyon. He bad for business."

Saverra figured Mamam was right. He was a crazy person, no doubt. Still, that night she couldn't get the crazy man out of her mind, so she asked Rosalee about it.

"Who dis God fellow dat man be talking bout?"

Rosalee shook her head. "You don't want no truck with no God," she said. "He's not your business."

"He must be bad if he done caused duh great fire," said Saverra. "Why would he burn duh world?"

"He's bad . . . and he's good," replied Rosalee, unsure of her own words. "Malo y bueno. I mean, he's supposed to be good, but he's got a temper, like Mamam when she furioso."

"Will he really destroy duh *Boogalee*?"

"Por supuesto no, he's not real--not anymore I think. Un cuento sola. He's just a story used to scare little girls. Now go to sleep and don't think about it anymore. It's mala suerte--bad luck."

Saverra didn't want any bad luck, so she stopped thinking about that God person and the stranger.

Ω

The next day she went for long walk outside of town, even though she was supposed to be sweeping out the rooms of the *Boogalee*. She walked along the little river that ran nearby because she liked all the greenery that grew up around it and the tinkling sound it made as it rushed by. She had a hazy memory of living close to water when she was little. She didn't remember much about that place, but she did remember some man taking her fishing. She couldn't recall much about him, except that he was a very old man.

A nice breeze blew along the riverbank--just enough to keep her cool. She didn't think about anything in particular as she walked, she just enjoyed her time alone, away from Mamam's orders to do this and do that. She liked the quiet sometimes, and *Maison Boogalee* was rarely quiet.

She considered picking some of the yellow and orange wildflowers she saw along the river's bank, but decided they'd only be evidence to Mamam that she wasn't where she was supposed to be and doing what she was supposed to do. So she reached down and picked up a stone to toss into the river. Before she could throw it, something stung her hand. She dropped the stone and saw an ant, its pinchers fastened to one of her fingers. Quickly she brushed it off. Even so, a little red spot on her finger began to burn.

It had been one of those large red ants--the same ones that frequented her dreams. She looked to where it might have fallen, afraid it might bite her again, but she couldn't find it. When she looked up she saw something else. Something that sent a wave of unexpected panic through her body. It was a procession of the same ants--hundreds of them. A red column marching perpendicular across her path. Fear froze her. She watched them go by, barely able to breathe. Before she could gather the will to retreat even a little, she saw the carcass of a dead animal being carried along by the ants. What kind of animal she couldn't say, but it was the size of a small dog. It seemed to float weightless atop the regimented column, moving along until it disappeared from her view into a thicket of green bushes.

Saverra stood there, still as the ground beneath her. Trying to decide on a course of action, she heard a strange sound--a whistling. The breeze had intensified and, at first, she thought what she heard was only the wind. But the whistling notes were coming from the bushes where the ants ventured.

The sound that emerged wasn't random. It was a ragged sort of tune. If she listened carefully, she could make out a cohesive melody. She didn't know why, but the song struck a memory. She'd heard it before--somewhere, sometime--but couldn't place it.

That's when she saw him--that crazy preacher fellow. He was on his knees next to those same bright green bushes. His head was bowed and his eyes were closed. She couldn't tell if he was saying something or not. She was about to speak up and warn him about the ants when she saw several more of the bugs near her feet.

An abrupt scream escaped her lips. She turned and ran. Her flight was fueled by abject terror, and with no concern for the terrain. She ran without looking back, ran until her feet tangled in an unseen obstruction and she cascaded to the ground.

Dust covered her damp face and powdered her tongue. She sat up, spit the dirt from her mouth, and wiped her face. Still half-panicked, she searched the ground around her, but saw none of the wretched insects.

"Are you alright, my child?"

Saverra looked up to see the preacher man.

"Are you hurt?"

She shook her head.

"You were running like the devil himself was chasing you," he said, offering her his hand. "Let me help you up."

Saverra hesitated, looked at his hand and saw a dark red scar there. She ignored his offer of help and stood on her own.

"So what form of evil were you running from with such haste?"

"Ants," replied Saverra.

"Ants are not evil," he said. "Ants are but one of God's creatures, put on this Earth for a reason. They are the scavengers of His will. The cleaners of the Earth--the gleaners of the apocalypse.

"All God's creatures have a purpose. Even you."

When she didn't respond, the preacher asked her, "Are you familiar with God, my child?"

Saverra shook her head.

"God is the world. He is the air you breathe, the food you eat, the ground you walk on . . . or, in your case, fall on." The briefest of smiles crossed his face, accentuating the weather-beaten wrinkles around his eyes. "God is almighty, and He is the father. God is great, and He is love."

"Rosalee says dis God fellow is bad . . . and he's good too, and he's gots a temper on him."

The stranger chuckled. "God can indeed be wrathful."

"Is dat why he burned duh world?"

An expression of solemnity passed across the preacher's face, and he held up his hands as if to garner her attention. Saverra couldn't help but notice he had similar nasty scars on both palms. She quickly looked up into his eyes so he wouldn't think she was staring at his ugly wounds.

"God purified the Earth because of mankind's multitude of sins. He purged the malevolence and brought forth a new day--a new world." He lowered his hand and his expression softened. " Yes, God can be wrathful, but He can also be forgiving. He will forgive your sins and wash them away if you let Him."

Remembering what Rosalee said, Saverra responded, "God's not my business."

"God is everyone's business, my child. Would you like to learn more about Him? I can teach you many things."

Saverra considered it--for all of two seconds. But she didn't care for the way the preacher fellow was looking at her.

"What y'all doing out here?" she asked him warily.

He smiled at her suspicion and replied, "I was making an offering, a small gesture to those who set me on my path. And I was communing with God."

"What does dat mean?"

"It means, dear child, I was planting some seeds--some special seeds that remind me where I came from--*who* I came from."

"Seeds tuh grow food?"

"No, seeds for the soul. Sayeth the Lord, whatever one sows he shall reap."

Seeds for duh soul? Saverra figured this fellow must really be couyon like Mamam said.

"I gots tuh go. I gots work tuh do and Mamam is gonna be as angry as God if I don't gets it done in one hurry."

With that, Saverra took off running and didn't look back.

Ω

She was too busy working to think much about her encounter with the preacher, but that evening he was outside the *Boogalee* again, causing another ruckus.

Earlier in the day, Mamam had given her something new--something to use when she danced. She called it a "pandeiro." Rosalee said it looked like a tambourine to her. Mamam shushed Rosalee's sass and showed Saverra how to use it. It wasn't easy. It was going to take lots of time to figure out how to dance and shake or hit that pandeiro at the same time. Mamam told her she'd better practice.

Saverra had just been ready to begin her dance that night, and maybe use her pandeiro just a little, when the commotion began. Everyone ran outside to see. What she witnessed was the stranger being roughed up by a couple of the *Boogalee's* regular customers. They knocked him down and kicked him as other onlookers continued to mock him and laugh.

"Dat's nuff. Y'all don't need hurt dat couyon," called out Mamam. "He's just touched in duh head."

The men didn't want to go against Mamam, so they picked the stranger up off the ground and tied his hands behind him.

When he'd caught his breath, he shouted, "Repent, sinners! God is watching!"

The men lifted the preacher onto his mule, but they put him backwards, facing the tail not the head. They used some more rope and tied him to the animal. All along, he kept talking, kept preaching.

"Let the righteous come forth and be heard. God praise the righteous, for they will be glad when they see sinners punished. They will wade through the blood of the wicked. They will say, 'The righteous are indeed rewarded. There is indeed a God who judges the world.' Repent and be on the right side of the Lord's judgment."

Once he was tied to the mule, the men slapped its rear and sent it running. They kept after it for a spell, chasing it out of town. All the while, Saverra heard the stranger continuing to preach his words--even when she could no longer make them out. She kind of felt sorry for the fellow, though she didn't understand why she felt that way. Maybe, if he was touched in the head like Mamam said, it wasn't really his fault he said such crazy things.

Ω

Whenever Saverra got another piece of silver, she'd visit the old fortune teller woman. But she didn't want her own fortune told again, she wanted to learn how it was done--the magic behind the telling. When she first told this to the woman, the fortune teller cackled with laughter.

"Why do y'all laugh?" asked Saverra.

"Because no one ever wants to know how. They only want to know about themselves. Bien, if you can pay, I'll teach."

158

So Saverra spent much of what little free time she had, and most of her silver, with the old woman whose name she learned was Daemo.

"Each of the talo ka-day--the tarot cards--has its own meaning," she began the first lesson. "Each has its own poderio--its own power.

With each visit, Daemo would explain the meanings of some of the cards, and would test Saverra each time to see if she remembered what she had learned. Fortunately, Saverra had an uncannily robust memory, and rarely forgot anything she was taught. She learned the cards had different meanings, depending upon whether they were right-side up or upside down. There also could be slightly different meanings if they were paired with certain other cards. One time she might turn over three cards, another time four. Sometimes Saverra thought Daemo was making up the meanings as she went along, and often noticed as she watched Daemo tell the fortune of some customer, that she strayed from what she'd taught her. It seemed the meanings could fluctuate with the desires of the person whose future was being told . . . and what Daemo wanted to say.

Saverra spent more and more time with Daemo, even once she learned all about the cards. The old woman wasn't well, and Saverra often helped her with various chores. One uncommonly foggy day, Saverra went to visit Daemo, and found her slumped over her cooking pots. She was no longer breathing.

Saverra was saddened by the loss of the woman she thought of as her friend. She didn't have any other friends--unless you counted Rosalee. But she wasn't so sad she didn't search for Daemo's cache of silver--most of which had come from Saverra. She took the silver, and the tarot cards, and said a quick goodbye to the old fortune teller.

Ω

One particularly hot night, Saverra couldn't get to sleep. The heat was actually only one reason. The sounds coming from the room next to hers was the other. The noise was emanating from Lily's room, where she was obviously entertaining a customer. It was a little louder than usual, so Saverra figured they must have been having lots of fun. Someday soon she hoped to be having that kind of fun, but so far Mamam said "No!"

Mamam told her she was still a mamzelle, a catin. Saverra didn't like being told she was a little girl or a baby doll. After all, she thought, didn't she dance for the men? Didn't she make plenty of silver for Mamam? Maybe she could make even more doing what Lily and the others did. It wasn't like she didn't know exactly what to do. The women of the *Boogalee* had taught her plenty. She'd be ready whenever Mamam would let her.

After a time, Saverra began to hear other noises, and at first she thought it was just more of the women and their customers. Soon though, she realized the shouts and screams she heard were not normal. She figured something unusual must be happening, just about the same time as she smelled the smoke.

Saverra rushed out of her room and opened the door to Lily's room. The customer was on top of her, still going at it despite the screams. Saverra just stared, and before she could say anything, Rosalee ran by yelling, "Fire! Get out, Saverra, get out!"

Lily and her customer heard that, and jumped up from the bed as Saverra ran back into her room and grabbed her fortune cards and pandeiro. She hurried, trying to follow where Rosalee had gone. But the smoke blinded her--got her all turned around. She coughed and fell, tripping over something. When she got back up, she saw the flames on the ceiling above her. She kept moving and kept coughing until she finally found her way outside.

It was quite a sight--the *Boogalee* ablaze, engulfed in scarlet flames that danced to a tune of their own, smoke rising up to disappear into the black night. It grew so hot, Saverra held up her hand to shield her face and moved back with the other survivors. She couldn't tear her eyes away from inferno though. It mesmerized her . . . at least until she heard the sound of weeping.

It was Mamam.

She'd never seen the old woman cry before, but now she was on her knees, sobbing as though the world had come to an end. Saverra figured, in Mamam's eyes, it probably had. The *Boogalee* was everything to her--everything she had. She'd lost everything.

Saverra didn't have that much to lose. What few clothes she had were gone now, but she held her cards and her pandeiro in her hands. Fortunately, she'd buried her little cache of silver just outside of town. She could buy new clothes with that. Maman couldn't buy a new *Boogalee*.

Saverra looked around to see who'd escaped. Rosalee was there. So were Lily, her customer, and most of the ladies of the *Boogalee*. She also saw someone standing near the rim of the intense red glow--a man half in shadow. For a moment she thought she recognized him--thought he looked like the preacher man who'd been laughed out of town weeks ago. But he slipped back into the darkness before she could be sure.

She thought no more of it because so many townspeople were milling about everywhere. Later though, she recalled that even though she didn't get a good look at his face, there was something about the way the fellow had stood there, staring at the fire. It wasn't with the shock or astonishment of the other onlookers, but with expectation.

After the dark swept over the world, little light remained. Few records of mankind's achievements lingered. Those that did were praised and cherished by wise men, while suffering at the hands of simpletons. Interpretation was everything. The past could represent evil, or it could provide a beacon that would guide humanity into the future. The time came when that guiding luminosity began to dim. Pockets of rational thought and insight still existed, but they were few and scattered.

ENLIGHTENMENT

THEY'D BEEN HUNTING HIM SINCE SUNRISE--four vague shapes on horseback--always skirting the horizon, always looming ominously. He didn't know if they were part of the marauding band that had thundered into his community or not. All he knew was running. He'd run when they first attacked--when he saw Will Landesgard cut down with a long metal shaft that shimmered in the moonlight as it struck. He'd run and he'd hid, fear an acrid scent in his nostrils, and then he'd run some more. How long he'd run, he wasn't certain. How long he slept, collapsed with fatigue, hidden in a patch of scrub, he had no idea. *How much time had passed? A day? Two? How many sunrises had there been?*

At one point, Konner thought he'd escaped, but then he'd seen the four riders in the distance--four menacing silhouettes posed against a backdrop of his own panic. So he ran again. When he was too exhausted to run any more, when his legs gave out, his lungs burned, and his feet cried out in pain, he'd found another place to hide. Not that there many places to hide on that hilly plain. He picked the best place he could find and lay flat, unmoving, as still as the Harvest Christ prepared for planting.

When he couldn't hold his eyes open any longer, he found himself awash in a chaotic dream. Everywhere he turned, his people were under attack. He saw his father butchered like a hog, his mother attacked, his little sister Hazel scooped up like a frightened animal, roughly bound and slung over the back of a horse. When she screamed he woke with a start.

Try as he might to sort through the horrific images, Konner couldn't remember. *Had it actually happened like that? Was it only a dream, his imagination, or had he seen it all with his own eyes?*

He sat up and looked around. There they were--the four horsemen--still a ways behind him, mounted on a hill as if surveying the terrain, no doubt searching for him. Konner thought he saw one of them point in his direction. One of the horses reared up and they all started down the hill toward him.

He surged to his feet and ran.

He ran as fast as he could, slowing only once to glance backwards. He no longer saw his pursuers, only an uneven terrain studded with high brush and endless cacti. He turned his eyes ahead just in time to feel the loss of contact. He'd taken to the air, and for a brief second Konner thought he was flying. He wasn't flying. He was falling--falling off the edge of an eroded bank. He flailed at the air in vain and landed hard, his left knee crashing against a rocky outcropping. The pain was unlike anything he'd experienced. He curled fetal-like, grabbed hold of the knee, and tried to muffle his cries of agony.

He lay there for a long while, unwilling to test his injury--afraid to move. He kept expecting the riders to come upon him and put an end to the pain. He was resigned to it--almost welcomed it. After a time, when no one came, he imagined they must have ridden by him. He decided to test his leg. It didn't take long to discover he could put no weight on it at all. The knee had already begun to swell.

He needed something to lean on. He tried hopping, but instead fell back into the dust and whimpered in pain. He knew he was going nowhere, so he rolled onto his back and lay there, staring at the sky. He reached into his pocket and felt his lucky goldstone. It was still there--for all the good it had done him. He began wondering if it was lucky at all. He wondered about a lot of things that were . . . and things that were no longer.

When a sudden wind kicked up with intense fury, he turned his head and shielded his eyes. After it passed, he opened them and stared straight ahead. Not more than six paces from him lay an ancient-looking corpse, as desiccated as the sand that blanketed it. Part skeleton, part dusty leather, he wasn't sure if it had been a man or a woman. The initial shock of seeing it there, so close to him, gave him the shiver-tingles and made him want to get up and run. He tried, but could only shriek in pain. So he just lay there staring at it, wondering who it might have been, and what kind of life he or she might have lived.

It wasn't long before he heard the clomping of horses. Desperately he tried to crawl into the shade of a scrawny bush where he thought he might hide. He held his breath.

"What have we here, Banshee?"

The voice was so near, Konner knew he'd been discovered. He scrambled to sit up.

He saw no horses and only one man. An old man--at least as old as his gramps had been before he got put in the south field. He even had white hair and a scraggly white beard like Gramps. Konner had to blink twice to be sure it *wasn't* Gramps. Of course it couldn't be.

This old fellow wore a hat with a wide brim and a dimpled crown. It was dusty brown in color--or covered with desert dust--he wasn't sure which. He didn't look like one of those raiders but Konner couldn't be sure. Not that there was much he could do about it. He couldn't run any more.

"I heard you cry out, boy," said the old fellow. "What's wrong with you?" Konner stayed silent.

The stranger stepped closer and looked down at him with penetrating silver-gray eyes. "You think he doesn't speak English, Banshee?"

Konner wondered why the fellow spoke as if he were talking to someone else, and then saw the little animal sitting off to his right, a few feet away. It was akin to a skinny rabbit, but with shorter legs and ears, and a longer tail. Its thick fur was a patchwork of gray and orange. It just sat there staring at him. He half-expected the strange creature to answer the old fellow.

"Habla Español? Neoneun hangug malhani? I see lights on, Banshee, but it doesn't appear anybody's home." He bent down and took a closer look at Konner's leg. "That knee doesn't look so good. How'd you manage that?"

Konner looked back to the old man and blurted out, "They were chasing me. Four of them, on horses. They--a bunch of them--attacked our home, killed my . . . ."

The old man looked at him with an expression melding both concern and skepticism. He turned and with surprising vigor, clambered up the nearest hill. Konner saw him turn and look in every direction.

When he came down, he said to Konner, "I don't see any riders. Whatever happened, you're safe now." He turned to the animal. "Well, Banshee, I guess we can't just leave him here."

The little furry beast rose from its haunches and whipped its tail about in response.

"What's your name, boy?"

Konner hesitated, but when he couldn't think of a reason not to respond, he said, "Konner . . . Konner Grainwell."

"Alright, Konner Grainwell, let's get you up and over to my wagon."

Ω

The stranger's wagon was larger than any Konner's folk had used for harvesting, and it was enclosed like a little square house. The house part was painted with peculiar swirls and symbols, and blotches of various bright colors. Inside it was packed with things he could only guess at. Pulling the wagon were two horses the likes of which astounded Konner. They were rust-colored, tall and brawny--much bigger and more muscular than any horse he'd seen. When he wanted them to get going, the old man called the horses by their names--Dodge and Durango.

Those weren't the only animals the fellow had with names. There was that funny long-tailed rabbit he called Banshee, and three more of the little critters waiting for him at the wagon. Konner wondered about them, but didn't say anything until he'd managed, with the old guy's help, to get up on the wagon's seat. His knee still hurt real bad. It hurt like the time he stepped barefoot in some cook-fire coals.

Up on the seat, the Banshee creature sat between them, while two of the other little beasts stayed back in the wagon. The third one, doing what seemed impossible, scampered right up the side of the wagon in a flash of leaps, all the way to the top when the old man called out, "Frodo, up high!"

"He's the best damn lookout there is," he said when he saw Konner's astonishment.

"What kind of funny rabbits are those?"

"They're not rabbits, they're cats," he replied. "Haven't you ever seen a cat?"

Konner shook his head.

"Well, I guess maybe you wouldn't have. There aren't many still around, though I once met a fellow who had dozens of them, and names for each one."

"Do yours have names?"

"Sure--of course. You already met Banshee here. The chubby black and white one is Bilbo. The gold one up top is Frodo, and that scrawny all black one is Gollum."

Konner thought the names were strange, but he didn't say so. He did wonder about them though. Horses were work animals, but cats?

"What do they do, these cats?" he asked. "Do you eat them?"

"Eat them?" The stranger's response exploded from his lips, then he burst out laughing. "Of course I don't eat them," he said, still chuckling. "They're my friends--my traveling companions. Oh, now and again they'll catch a rodent or a lizard and bring it to me. If it's big enough I might even cook it. But their only job is to keep me company."

Konner never heard of anyone keeping company with any kind of animal. That's what people were for. Of course, the old guy *was* all alone--maybe even touched in the head a bit.

"So where are you from, Konner Grainwell?"

Konner looked around at the landscape, at the overhead sun, and realized he was no longer certain which way was home.

"I . . . I don't know. I'm . . . not sure."

"How long since you left there?"

"Uh, two days . . . I think."

"You think? It must have been a rough time if you're not sure. You said some men attacked your village--men on horseback. How many men?"

Konner shrugged.

"What *do* you remember?"

Konner didn't respond right away, but when he did, anger swelled into his voice.

"Fire . . . blood. They were killing folks, burning things. It was . . . ." He turned and looked away from the old man.

The stranger didn't ask any more questions--didn't say anything else until they stopped for the night in a small grove of palm trees. Until then, they rode in silence, though Konner's thoughts were anything but tranquil. They were populated with flashes of carnage, a cacophony of screams, and shadows he didn't want to discern. Instead he tried, without much success, *not* to remember.

Ω

They never came upon any horsemen, any people from his community, or the community itself. Konner guessed they were traveling in the wrong direction, though which way was the right direction he couldn't tell. He knew the sun rose in the East, set in the West, and thereby knew which ways were north and south, but that didn't help him. He'd been so panicked when he'd run, he'd never bothered to keep track. He ran much of the first night, and likely hadn't gone in a straight line.

As the first twilight in the company of the old man approached, they stopped and the stranger spent some time unhitching his horses before helping Konner down. Konner's knee still hurt when he put any weight on it, so his new companion fashioned him a crutch from an old tree limb. Soon they were sitting near a fire the old fellow had built. He ate what he was given--something that tasted like part bread, part weed. It was peculiar but filling, and his stomach had been empty for some time.

He watched the stranger, his odd little animals sitting next to and all around him, wondering where the fellow had come from--how he'd ended up out here all alone.

"Have you ever been to Faraway?" Konner asked, breaking the silence.

The old guy looked at him. "Where?"

"Faraway. My gramps used to tell me stories about Faraway. I wondered if you came from there, or ever went there."

"I don't know of any place with such a name, though I've journeyed far and wide, wandered off the beaten track, taken the road less traveled, and rambled through no man's land." He smiled as though he'd said something funny, then paused for a few seconds to think. "No, can't say that I've been there, though I've certainly roved here, there, and just about everywhere."

"You mean you're not really going anywhere--any certain place?"

"Ah, not all those who wander are lost," he replied with a smug look. "All journeys have destinations, even if the traveler isn't aware of them."

Konner wasn't sure the man's words made any sense. *How could you not expect to end up where you go?* He decided that's what he needed to do right then, was to go relieve himself. He stood with some difficulty and a fair amount of pain, got his crutch under him, and turned to walk away from the fire. As he did, the crutch knocked against something laying nearby on the ground.

"Careful there!" exclaimed the old fellow, jumping up and hurrying over to the fire. He plucked something from the flames and quickly doused the embers on it that had begun to smoke. "You almost burned this, boy. We've lost too many to fire already."

Konner understood the old guy was upset, though he wasn't certain why. He didn't even know what the thing was, though this fellow acted as if it were something precious.

"I'm . . . sorry."

"It's okay," he said calmly. "No harm done. But a book will burn pretty quick when it gets going. Then all those words will be gone forever."

"Book?"

"Yeah, *this* book. I was going to read some later." The stranger looked at him, realization dawning. "You don't know what a book is--do you?"

Konner shook his head.

"Hell's bells, boy, you've got a lot to learn."

"What is a *book*?"

"A book is . . . well a book is the purest essence of a human soul--the soul who wrote it. Books are the quietest and most constant of friends--the most accessible and wisest of counselors--the most patient of teachers."

"How does it do all that?"

"How? Well . . . ." He stopped, not sure how to respond, scratched at his beard, then gathered himself. "You don't know how to read, do you?" Konner shook his head. "Well, books are for reading. Sometimes for storytelling. They can be entertaining--full of wonderment and adventure--or they can be about truth--about what happened, how and why. Books are full of words--you know what words are."

Konner nodded.

"A book is a bunch of words written in the proper order to describe something, teach something, or just tell a tale. Here, look at this book you almost kicked in the fire. What's the color you see here on its cover?"

Konner could see, even by the firelight, it looked like a bunch of trees and was mostly one color. "Green," he said.

"Okay, you know the word green. Well, there are a group of letters--symbols--which make up the word *green*. You see this at the top of the book. These are all letters. They make up words. The name of this book is actually like two words put together." He covered half the letters with his hand. "You see this word? This is how you write *green* using these symbols. If you wanted to describe the color of this book as green, you'd write it like this." He moved his hand to cover the portion that read "green."

"Now this part of the word says *Ever*. You know, like if you say, 'The horizon seems to go on forever and ever.' Or if you ask, 'Is that pig ever going to stop eating?' You know what a pig is, right?" Konner nodded. "Now, if you put the two words together," he said, taking his hand off the book and running a finger under the letters, "it says 'Evergreen'. That's the name of this book--*Evergreen*. The word means something that is always green, like a tree or a bush that's green year-round. Get it?"

Konner's expression mirrored his bafflement.

"I know, it's not easy to understand at first. But words can be powerful things when linked together in the right sequence. Don't worry, I'll teach you to read."

"Why?"

"*Why?*" he echoed with a hint of consternation. "Because reading is knowledge, and knowledge is power. That's why."

"Okay," replied Konner, and limped off to relieve his now powerfully bulging bladder.

Ω

They were everywhere he turned--wherever he dared look. Terrifying men on horseback, black wraiths with red eyes trampling newly-planted fields, brandishing weapons and torches, maiming, killing, burning. He saw the bodies of his father, his mother--even the Trouble Brothers lay bleeding in a ditch, their eyes unmoving but still mocking him. He tried to run, but each way he turned they were there--grinning, grimacing, howling, each face looking every bit like the picture he'd once seen of ol' Demon Drought. No matter how fast he ran, there was no escaping them. He fell, a horse reared over him, a blade glinting in the moonlight rushed down at him . . . .

"Wake up. Wake up, Konner Grainwell. You're safe."

Konner opened his eyes, jerking awake. The old man was leaning over him.

"That must have been quite a nightmare," he said. "But that's all it was."

Konner sat up and looked around. It was sometime after dawn. He saw the wagon, the two unhitched horses grazing, and one of the cat animals, Gollum, looking at him. He realized it had just been another dream--another horrible dream.

Gollum stopped staring and sauntered under the wagon. Konner watched him go, saw him leap up and disappear. Curious where he could have possibly gone, Konner scooted to where he could see better. There was an opening under the wagon's structure with some kind of door. Fully open, Konner thought he could fit through it. Little Gollum had jumped right through and disappeared inside the wagon.

"That's my cat door . . . and my escape hatch," said the old man. "You should always have a good escape plan." He winked. "Come on, let's get you something to eat. A little food will fill your belly and put your mind in a good place."

Konner ate what was brought him without paying much attention to what it was. The truth is, he was trying not to think at all. Then he blurted out, "I don't know your name. What do I call you?"

"My name?" The stranger seemed momentarily puzzled by the question. He was quiet for a few seconds as if trying to think of an answer--to recall his own name. "You can just call me Teacher, since it looks like you've got a lot to learn."

One thing Konner learned pretty quickly was that Teacher was brimful of words he didn't understand. Even if he knew all the words separately, sometimes the way the old guy put them together made no sense. Like when he got his first lesson in reading, and Teacher said, "A journey of a thousand miles must begin with a single step." Yet they weren't going anywhere. They were just sitting there next to the wagon. When Konner hesitated to try and read his first word because it seemed all those words were going to be too much for him, Teacher said, "The secret to getting ahead is getting started." Konner didn't know what *head* he was talking about, or why he'd want a head. Was he talking about Konner's head?

Ω

The howling of the sandstorm had been so furious, it made Konner think of the coriolis storms he read about in the book *Dune*. Even though it had been hard to read, it was his favorite . . . so far, and Paul Muad'Dib was his favorite character, because, he too, had been thrown into a world he knew nothing of. That's what Konner felt like every time he picked up a new book. All the pages, all the words were a new world he'd never visited.

The sandstorm passed before midday, and before long the sky settled on its habitual blue, dotted with a motley patchwork of clouds. A short time later, Konner noticed there was no wind at all, and the horizon in all directions was as silent and serene as a pool of shallow water. It was as though the fleeting storm had pacified the harshness of the landscape. Nature's wrath and nature's calm divided by a handful of heartbeats.

Konner didn't know exactly how long he'd been with Teacher--how many Holidays he'd missed--but it had been long enough he'd grown some. He realized one day he no longer had the planting, the caring, and the harvesting to mark time. He was also aware he no longer wondered about his family or his previous home. They were a distant, though still painful, memory. A place he'd left behind, untold miles back. Home was now wherever Durango and Dodge took them. Home was just over the next rise. Home was in the pages of the next book.

Teacher had dozens of books, and on a rare occasion they found new ones. Konner had only read about half of them, and only fully understood half of those. But he could read them all now--only once in a while having to ask Teacher what a certain word meant.

Once the storm passed, and they exited the shelter of the wagon, Konner propped himself up against its shady side. Gollum and Banshee curled up next to him as he read *The Complete Poems, Lyrics, and Musings of James Douglas Morrison*. It wasn't easy. He found poetry, often times, was the hardest thing to understand--even if it had the fewest words. Teacher said a poem was usually less about information, and more about the images it formed in your mind or the emotions it forged in your gut. Konner found this Morrison fellow to have some strange images, and some even stranger ideas--at least what he could understand of them.

So much of what he read was set in a strange, outlandish world--a dead world he'd never known. It was hard for him to picture highways packed with mechanical automobiles or cities with millions of people. Some of things he read about--the devices, the cultures--were difficult for him to even imagine. Yet teacher told him these things were real, and not just flights of fancy.

Konner looked up from his reading when Dodge suddenly whinnied and stomped his right front hoof a couple of times. It looked as if the horse was counting. It was unusual enough that Konner put his book down and stood to have a look around. Teacher had gone off with Durango to look for water. The horse had a good nose for it, and had saved them from dying of thirst more than once. Frodo and Bilbo had tagged along, though they had no particular skill at finding anything other than the occasional lizard.

Konner didn't see anything on the horizon, though he did wonder about Teacher. He'd been gone quite a while. He was about to sit back down with his book when Frodo scampered into their camp. He was breathing hard, He'd run quite a distance. Gollum and Banshee raised up to peek at him through sleepy cat eyes as well. Konner looked in the direction the cat had come from, but he didn't see anything unusual.

He didn't think much of it--the cats were always running about wherever they wanted. He propped himself against the wagon wheel again and was about to pick up his book when Frodo walked over and cried out in way Konner had never heard. It was definitely strange--strange enough Konner took hold of the cat and looked him over to see if he was injured.

He seemed alright, but when Konner put him back down, he cried again, and ran off in the direction he'd come from. He was acting peculiar enough that Konner decided to follow him.

His knee had healed long ago, but on occasion it still bothered him. Some days it was fine and he could run like the wind, and other days, especially when it was damp and cloudy, it nagged him with its aching. Today, with storm clouds on the horizon, he felt a twinge as he walked across the uneven ground of the sandy mesa.

It wasn't too long before he saw Durango in the distance, but no sign of Teacher. He also saw, off in another direction, the signs of an ant migration. There were thousands of them traveling together in a massive column--a dark red river of ants. He got the shiver-tingles just seeing them.

Konner had learned such a river brought only death with it. Teacher made certain they traveled far out of their way to avoid such a migration, and whenever he came across a singular ant--a scout he called it--he'd be sure and kill it. He didn't want the scout leading the rest back to wherever he and Konner were at.

Konner was worried. The ants were too close. They needed to pack up and move on. He had to find Teacher right away.

As Konner got closer to the horse he finally spotted Teacher, lying on the ground. "Flies and fleas!" he exclaimed, breaking into a run despite the pain in his knee. He quickly knelt next to Teacher, who seemed asleep but began convulsing, his body as wildly agitated as an animal in the throes of death. In fact, Konner thought Teacher must be dying to act so. He didn't know what else to do, so he tried to restrain Teacher's movements. Shortly, the convulsions stopped and Teacher opened his eyes.

"What . . . ?" he asked, dazed and disoriented.

"Are you alright?" asked Konner. "You were shaking something awful."

"Yes, I'll be okay in a minute. Just let me gather myself."

"What is it? What's wrong?"

"Don't worry. It's something I've lived with for a long time. It's a disease that only flares up on occasion."

Konner looked more worried than ever. "A disease?"

"Don't worry, I'll be fine. And you can't catch it. It's something I was born with--called epilepsy."

"Are you sure you're okay?"

"I will be. Hand me my hat and help me up now. We still have to find some water."

"I don't think we have time. The ants are on the march."

Ω

It wasn't what Konner expected. Of course he didn't know what to expect. When they approached the large settlement, Konner had been anxious to see other people. It had been a while since they'd seen anyone else, and they'd never come across a place as populated as this one.

He was surprised by the wary, suspicious eyes with which the townspeople regarded them. An old man and a boy shouldn't have looked dangerous, but you wouldn't have known it by the inhospitable stares aimed their way. Many of the residents didn't even come outside. They peered from openings in their gaunt domiciles to get a safe look at the strangers. Their reactions spoke volumes about their previous encounters with outsiders.

Konner discerned by the well-kept fields surrounding the hamlet that it was a farming community much like the one he grew up in, though his recollection of his old home was as hazy as the distant horizon. Of course this one was larger, and in his mind, the first real town he'd ever seen. They'd come upon small encampments and what he thought of as little villages many times. But he thought of this new place as a town--maybe because of the all books he'd been reading and the line of gutted, decrepit old buildings that formed its center. It *looked* like what he pictured a town should look like.

Teacher said these places were the seeds of a new civilization, but Konner wasn't so sure. There didn't seem very much new about them. Like this one, they were often constructed upon the relics of the world that once existed, but now few could remember. Ancient brick walls were conjoined with those constructed of newer adobe, and roofs were patched with a variety of scraps, material from both now and then.

Teacher had long ago told him about how the old world ended--about what he and his people used to call the "rainfire." It was indeed a rain of fire that had scorched the entire world . . . at least as far as Teacher knew, and he'd been there to live through it. He said he once figured out how many days it had been since the end of everything, and reckoned there were about 20,000 of them. Konner had never heard of such a number, but he knew it was a lot more than he could count.

Here and there in the town, Konner saw the cross signs. It wasn't the first time he'd seen such, but he'd never seen so many. Teacher had told him all about the story of God and Jesus, and he knew that so many crosses meant

173

these were a god-fearing people. From what he knew, he still wasn't sure why people feared this God person. Teacher said it was a complicated subject he'd learn more about as he read more. He did know there was something in this religion thing similar to the Harvest Christ his own people had celebrated. Teacher told him the Jesus character was also known as the Christ. How it all worked, Konner wasn't sure yet.

Once they got over their suspicions, the people started coming over and talking with Teacher. They paid special attention to Dodge and Durango, and Konner noted he hadn't seen any other horses in the town. A handful of children came out to stare at the giant beasts, but were soon distracted by the cats resting aboard the wagon. When Bilbo began sniffing at Banshee's hindquarters, she took exception and smacked him with her paw. That prompted several laughs, and the children giggled amongst themselves.

Teacher learned the last time a pack of bandits had come through, they'd taken all the town's horses . . . among other things. So he worked out a trade, whereas they got some food in exchange for letting the townspeople borrow the horses, under his supervision, for some hauling work. And, as he often did, Teacher offered them other things he'd found in his travels to make more trades. He called them *doodads* and *gewgaws.*

When they finally settled down for the night at one end of the town, Konner built a fire to cook the meat they'd gotten in trade. Teacher didn't tell him what kind of meat it was, and he didn't ask. They hadn't had much lately so he wasn't going to *look a gift horse in the mouth*--an expression Teacher liked to use. Konner wasn't sure why anyone would want to look in a horse's mouth. He'd done it once, and what he saw wasn't pretty.

"That was good," said Teacher, when he finished his meal. "Not as good as chocolate, but close."

"What's chocolate?"

"Just something I was thinking about from long ago. You've never tasted chocolate, have you? Of course not. You're too young. I remember when there was nothing better than chocolate. The last time I ate a chocolate bar I was still driving around in my Dodge Durango. Must have been close to fifty years back. Found it in a vending machine. If I close my eyes I think I can still taste it."

Teacher closed his eyes.

"You were driving Dodge and Durango even back then?"

"Not the horses," said Teacher, opening his eyes. "That was when I still had an automobile that ran. It was a Dodge Durango. You've read about automobiles--cars--right?"

Konner nodded.

"I was just a little older than you back then. I met this girl and she . . . well, that's a story for another time."

Teacher picked up his book, a signal he was done talking, and rested against the wagon. Frodo, Bilbo, Banshee, and Gollum had especially appreciated the meat scraps they'd gotten for dinner, and were still busily licking their coats clean when Konner and Teacher settled back to read by the firelight. But it was tough to concentrate because they kept hearing this crying noise. Konner had heard such crying before, many times when he was young. He was sure it was a baby in distress.

Finally, exasperated, Teacher closed his book and got up. He set off into the town without a word. Konner decided to follow him. The crying got louder and louder, and finally they found the source of it. It was indeed an infant, and after speaking with the child's mother and father, Teacher marched back to the wagon, mixed together one of his concoctions, cooked it up into soup, and then took it back to the family.

Konner overheard Teacher tell the parents that his "tea" was made of sacred herbs blessed by God himself. He told them how much and how often to give it to the baby. They thanked him and by the time he and Konner had got back to their campsite, the crying had stopped.

It all left Konner confused. It wasn't unusual that Teacher provided someone with some kind of healing ointment or potion. He'd done that before--usually in trade. But he knew Teacher took no stock in God talk or religion, and wondered how he'd gotten herbs that were blessed. When he asked Teacher about it, the old man just sat and picked up his book.

Without looking at Konner he said, "The baby had colic--a common enough ailment. I made a tea out of chamomile and ginger. It should soothe the child's stomach."

"But why did you tell them you used sacred herbs blessed by God? Where would you get such herbs?"

Teacher looked at Konner with mild disappointment. "I've taught you better than to believe in such, boy. You know there's no such things as *sacred* herbs. There's probably not even a god. And if there is, he's got better things to do than spend time blessing dried weeds."

"Then why'd you say it?"

175

"You never contradict someone's superstitions. Sometimes it's better to use those beliefs to help the person . . . or yourself. A little hocus pocus never hurt. Don't forget that."

When the baby's parents brought a chicken for Teacher the next day, thanking him for curing their sick child, Konner figured Teacher was right. It was a lesson he promised himself to remember.

Ω

Konner had seen many pregnant animals before--mostly livestock--but he thought Banshee looked especially funny. It was as if the cat had swallowed something large and round, making her legs look even skinnier than usual. He wove a basket out of yucca leaves for Banshee to birth her babies in, but every time he put her in it, she wouldn't stay.

"Why doesn't she like the basket?"

"I don't know," said Teacher, "but never try to out-stubborn a cat. Women and cats will do as they please. Men and dogs should relax and get used to it. She'll have her kittens wherever she wants. I'm just glad she's pregnant. I doubt there are many cats left in the world. It wouldn't hurt to have some more."

"Who do you think the father is?"

"Could be anyone of those rascals," said Teacher. "I think they all had a go at her when she was in heat."

Konner remembered the noisy nights when Banshee's suitors came a'calling. He thought they were fighting until Teacher explained what was really going on. It was quite a ruckus, but it broke up the boredom Konner often felt during their endless travels. The desolate, monotonous prairie took its toll on him sometimes. They'd often go weeks without seeing anyone or anything, before coming upon some new settlement. Cats weren't the only thing there weren't many of. People were a rare sight too.

Those folks they *did* find were usually friendly, if a little suspicious at first. It helped he and Teacher were obviously not much of a threat. They'd trade some of the knickknacks and gewgaws Teacher had found on their journeys, or offer a potion or salve or some kind of healing herb to someone who was ill. He knew how to set a broken bone or stitch a wound closed. There were always sick folks, suffering from one malady or another. Usually Teacher could help them with something, even if it was just "giving them a positive attitude" as he liked to say.

It had been weeks since they'd last seen anyone else, and Konner was resting in the shade with his latest book, one he'd recently found in some old ruins. He was fascinated with what he thought of as "the tricks" he read about in *Mindfulness and Hypnosis: The Power of Suggestion to Transform Experience*. Some of them reminded him of how Teacher talked to strangers when he was selling something. But these tricks went beyond that. It seemed, if you knew how, you could get people to do what you wanted them too . . . even if they weren't inclined to at first.

It took him some time to appreciate it, but Konner now fervently believed what Teacher had told him long ago, that books were the "wisest of counselors." He relished most of them, and always looked forward to immersing himself in another. To find a new book, as he had this one, was a joyous occasion.

It wasn't just books and the pleasure of reading Teacher had introduced him to. He'd taught Konner how to live off the land. How to find water, which plants were edible, which ones could cure, and which ones could kill. Konner had learned how to deal with strangers--when to be bold and when to blend in. He was no longer the terrified lost boy he'd been when Teacher first found him. His horizons had been expanded in all the ways that seemed important. He was confident in his knowledge, though his confidence was always tempered by something Teacher once told him. "You're only ignorant of what you don't know."

As he was reading, he heard Teacher climb to the top of the wagon where Frodo and the other cats often lazed in the sun on a cool day. He didn't know why Teacher was up there, and was too taken by his book to find out. But it wasn't long before Teacher called him.

"Konner. Come up here."

Reluctantly, Konner put down his book and made his way onto the wagon's roof.

"What is it?" he asked. But, as he spoke, he saw Teacher gesturing toward the western horizon.

Konner shielded his eyes from the sun and looked in the direction Teacher was pointing. What he saw was a massive ant migration. Even though they were far off, he knew it was ants because of its size and the way it flowed gently across the plain. But there was nothing gentle about a horde of ants. Ants were part of the landstory he'd been taught as a sprout. But this was the largest migration he'd ever seen. He couldn't begin to guess how many millions of ants were on the march. It was an imposing sight.

"Seems like they're always moving. Where do you think they're going?" asked Konner.

"Wherever they want," replied Teacher, still staring into the distance. He watched them for a moment longer. "You know they're much bigger than they used to be."

"Bigger?"

Teacher nodded and said, "When I was boy, ants were tiny little insects. The biggest ones I ever saw would fit on my fingertip. Now they're the size of crickets, and smarter than they ever were.

"Smarter?"

"That's right. I've watched them over the years, and I'm sure of it. They've changed more than just their size. It has something to do with the bobbin plants."

"That's the bush with the purple berries you use for medicine?"

He nodded. "After the comet hit, the bobbins seemed to flourish, and they definitely attracted the ants. I used to think it was something sweet they must like, but the more I watched, the more the ants changed. I've come to believe it's something else--that somehow the bobbins have had a mutating effect on the ants. What's stranger, is that they protect those plants as if they were protecting their own queen. I once saw a man cut off a bobbin branch loaded with berries instead of just picking some. He was swarmed by ants and dead before he could take a half dozen steps."

"Why did it only happen after the comet?" asked Konner. "You think the comet changed the bobbin plants somehow?"

"Maybe," said Teacher, still staring at the distant migration. "Or maybe it brought the bobbins with it."

Ω

Teacher had been ill for many weeks, but in the last few days it had gotten worse. He was having frequent pains in his chest and trouble breathing. When it got so bad he couldn't move around much, Konner made a place for him to lie inside the wagon and asked what he could get him. Teacher said there was nothing that would help. He said he'd tried everything he could think of, but none of his herbs or potions had worked.

"What about some bobbin berries?" asked Konner. "You said they're good for lots of things"

"I don't have any more, and I doubt they'd cure what ails me. This is . . . something else."

"But there's a chance--right?" asked Konner. "They *could* cure you. I could go find some more."

"No, no, it's too dangerous. I'm just old, my boy. There's no cure for old age."

Konner had been traveling with Teacher for many years, but he had no idea of his mentor's exact age. He knew he was very old--certainly older than his gramps was when he was planted in the south field. Konner had accepted the death of his gramps as the natural way of things--the way of Holiday and the Harvest Christ--but now he was fearful Teacher might die. Maybe because he'd gotten used to the old fellow--or maybe because of what he learned from Teacher's books. Or maybe because he didn't want to be alone in the world.

"Konner." Teacher called to him from inside the wagon.

Konner hurried to him. Teacher had propped himself up inside the wagon, and was stroking Gollum, who lay on his lap. The cat was very old as well, and not moving around as well as it used to.

"Do you need something?"

"It's hard for me to hold a book up for very long. Would you to read to me?"

"What would you like me to read?"

"Anything. Whatever you've been reading."

So Konner retrieved his current book, *The Wit and Wisdom of Mark Twain*, and sat on one of the storage boxes in the back of the wagon. It wasn't a story book like most of the ones he read. It was filled with short little bits of philosophy and humorous anecdotes. Some of them made sense to Konner, but others belonged to a time and a place he had no reference to.

He began reading out loud, and occasionally Teacher would chuckle. Sometimes he would cough and Konner would get him a drink of water. But Teacher kept telling him to "Go on. Read some more."

Konner didn't stop reading until it appeared Teacher had fallen asleep. He moved to leave the old man in peace, but Teacher opened his eyes.

"Did you finish?" he asked.

"No, but I thought maybe you needed to rest."

Teacher nodded. "Help me lie back down."

Konner helped him lie flat, and even with all the squirming around, Gollum didn't move.

"Alright, get some sleep. I'll be here when you wake up."

Teacher didn't respond. He fell asleep almost immediately.

Ω

As Teacher grew more ill, Konner became more determined to find some bobbin berries for him. Even if it was dangerous, Konner felt he had to take the chance. He couldn't just stand by and let teacher die. He wasn't certain he could even find any, but he'd convinced himself he had to try.

One day, after teacher fell asleep and all the cats were napping, Konner set out with a canteen full of water and no idea which direction might be best. He snuck away as quietly as he could so none of the cats would try to follow him, choosing the direction they were least likely to see him when he left.

He walked a long time, seeing neither bobbin bush nor ant nor much of any living thing other than sage and mesquite. Several hills dotted the horizon, so he turned toward them, hoping maybe to find a hidden water source. During their travels, they'd observed large stands of bobbin hedges close to ponds and streams. It made sense to him that's where they were more likely to grow.

He felt more assured with a destination in mind, as opposed to wandering aimlessly. He'd search the hills, spend as much time as he could, but promised himself he'd return before nightfall. He didn't want to leave Teacher alone for too long.

Nearing the base of the first rocky knoll, he searched the slopes for the bright green bobbins. He wasn't really watching where he was walking and almost stepped right into a column of ants. He'd come close, but apparently not close enough to distract them from whatever task they were about. They paid no attention to him.

The procession traversed in two directions. One was almost straight back the way he'd come. The other led deeper into the hills. He followed the latter, paralleling its path and never getting too close. He knew how dangerous swarms of the ants could be. If they changed direction, came after him, he'd have to run, hoping he wasn't running into more of them.

Watching carefully where he stepped, almost holding his breath as he walked, it wasn't long before Konner let escape a sigh of relief. The ants had led him to a thicket of bobbins. They were the largest ones he'd ever seen, higher than his head and grown so close together they were like a wall. He guessed there must be water nearby, but he didn't care about that now. He just had to get close enough to pick some of the berries and get them back to Teacher.

There was a single large ant mound on one side of the hedge--that's where the column was headed, and where hundreds of other ants were coming and going. So Konner circled around the opposite side, still watching where he stepped. He knew, despite the bustling activity around the mound, there could be ants anywhere nearby.

Approaching the edge of the bobbin growth, he heard a strange sound. He thought it was only the wind until he got closer and saw a collection of hollowed-out stems atop the hedge of bobbins. There was no question in his mind the whistling tune was coming from those stems, but the fact that what he heard was an uneven but recognizable melody astonished him. Not that he knew the specific tune as anything he'd heard before, but it definitely sounded like something of human origin. Because the sounds and their volume rose and fell with the wind, he was certain it was the gusts that powered the song. But he couldn't figure out how the variation of notes could possibly be created in such a harmonious pattern.

Then he saw something else--something that sent the shiver-tingles racing right through him. The extremities of various animals were half buried right up next to the stalks of the bushes. The tops of two rabbit ears poked out of the ground, along with what looked to be a woodchuck's tail and possibly the hind legs of a dog or a ki-yote. No ants swarmed on them as you might expect. Instead, they were just rotting, right up next to the bobbins, almost as if they were an offering.

The wind died down and the music it fed grew silent. Cautiously, Konner continued closer, found some berries, and began plucking them and placing them in a small pouch he'd brought. He didn't think he needed many, but wanted to be sure he had enough to cure whatever it was that had made Teacher ill.

When he was satisfied he had plenty, he turned carefully to leave. Before he took a single step, he froze in place. Fear swept through his rigid form like a chill in the air. He was surrounded by a red swarm--more ants than he'd ever seen in one place. They'd fanned out across the ground in front of him, blanketing the area. There was nowhere for him to run. The bobbin thicket on one side, the ants spread across the other.

Konner held his breath. He didn't dare move. Even though it was apparent they were there to fence him in, he hoped against reason that if he didn't move, they might go away. They didn't. He wondered briefly if the music had summoned them, but he didn't know if ants could even hear.

For what seemed like forever, they didn't move at all. He kept expecting them to rush him, swarm all over him. He stood there, sweating, trying not to imagine what such a horrific death would be like. He fought against the terror, against a surging panic shouting inside his brain, *Run!*

One grouping of ants abruptly moved away from the others. A score of the scarlet creatures, each almost the size of his little finger, marched toward him. But they stopped a few feet away. Konner was still afraid to move. He watched as the menacing bugs formed a line, following one after the other. The line began to curve and when they halted their march, they'd formed a circle--a perfect circle of ants.

Konner was dumbfounded. He looked down at the red ring, not sure of his own senses. His first thought was it couldn't be real. He was seeing something that wasn't really there. The circle dissipated and the ants reformed. He watched in amazement as the same group formed a square, five ants to a side.

Konner had no idea what they were doing. He only knew such behavior in any creature was amazing beyond words. He wondered if they trying to communicate. If so, what were they saying? How was he supposed to respond?

Konner took a chance. He bent down as slowly as he could. The ants didn't move.

Using his finger, he drew a square in the dirt, doing his best to approximate the size and perfection of the shape the ants had formed. When he finished, he stood back up. As he did, the squadron of ants reformed on the lines he'd dug into the ground.

For a minute that seemed to last for hours, the ants remained in the shape of his square. He had no idea what was next, so he waited. When minutes passed, he decided to try something else. He bent down again, and this time he drew a triangle into the soil. When he straightened up, the ants moved to his triangle and copied it exactly.

Because of its size, two of the ants were not needed to complete the three-sided shape. Instead, after seeming to inspect the border of the triangle, the two ants scurried off through the bobbins towards the mound on the other side of the thicket.

Konner waited. None of the ants in the triangle moved. Neither did the thousands spread out before him. They were waiting also. Waiting for what, Konner had no idea. But he also had no choice but to stand there. He was afraid the slightest move might be interpreted as a provocation.

While he never saw the two ants return, a sudden activity stirred the bugs. The ants forming the triangle moved off to join the giant swarm. Then, with no forewarning or signal he could recognize, the sea of ants before him parted. The wave of red moved several feet on each side, creating a pathway through them. Konner stood there, amazed once more, but he didn't stand for long. While he struggled to comprehend what was happening--how it was happening--he was certain this path was meant for him. Slowly he moved onto it, warily watching the ants on either side as he went. He didn't run, he walked as calmly as he could, until he no longer saw any ants behind him. Then he ran.

Ω

That night, after he'd had a chance to calm down, Konner thought about the ants. But the truth was, he didn't know what to think. To accept the little bugs were somehow intelligent defied everything he knew. But he didn't know how else could they have done what they did. And then to show him . . . what? *Mercy?* They'd let him go when they easily could have killed him and buried him next to the bobbins like the other animals. *Why?* All because he drew a couple of shapes into the ground? Maybe it wasn't just the ants, thought Konner. Maybe Teacher had been right when he suggested the bobbin plants had changed them. Had they somehow modified the insects' brains? Had they made the ants more intelligent? Intelligent enough to understand geometric shapes? Or was it the bobbins themselves that were intelligent, and the ants were only following orders?

Konner found any of the possibilities difficult to believe. In all the things he'd read, only in fiction did anything come close to what he'd witnessed. But it wasn't fiction. He'd seen it with his own eyes. It had been real.

When Konner gave Teacher the bobbin berries, Teacher didn't say a word. He just stared at Konner for a moment with his rheumy gray eyes, then shook his head with a hint of disappointment. He swallowed the handful of purple berries with an expression that read, *They won't help, but since you went to the trouble.*

Konner wanted to tell him about his strange encounter with the ants, but he thought that might make Teacher even angrier with him. Only silence separated them for a long minute, then Teacher put his hand on Konner's arm.

"You know I'm dying, don't you, Konner?"

"But the berries might--"

"The berries won't help," he said harshly before Konner could finish. Then, more gently, he added, "There is no miracle cure, my boy. I'm beyond even the powers of the bobbin bush. I told you that, but you . . . you were determined to help me, and I appreciate that. Even so, you need to be ready--to be smarter. You're going to be on your own soon. I don't know how long I have now. Not that any of us ever do. We're mortals all."

A tear ran down Konner's face. Teacher reached out and caught it with a fingertip.

"Don't cry, Konner. Crying does no good. What's important is remembering." He leaned back and looked straight up at nothing. "I remember when my father was dying, he made me promise not to let the words die with him--all the words in mankind's books. I kept my promise and now I've passed the words on to you. You're my legacy."

Another set of tears formed in Konner's eyes, but he quickly wiped them away.

"Are you . . . are you afraid?"

Teacher chuckled. "You know what Mark Twain once said about that? He said, 'The fear of death follows from the fear of life. A man who lives fully is prepared to die at any time.' I've lived a strange life, Konner. Not the life my father or mother would have imagined for me, but I've lived it as fully as I could. As another writer once said, 'In the end we'll all become stories.' I've been part of many stories, so I can't complain. I'm part of your story, and you're part of mine. Some day you'll have dozens of your own stories."

Konner nodded and said, "I'm glad you were part of mine. There's so much I wouldn't have learned without you."

"And I was glad to be your teacher."

Konner thought about how the old fellow had been more than just his teacher. He'd been like a father--the father Konner had once had but lost.

"There's one thing I've always wanted to ask you."

"Well there's no time like the present."

"What's your name--your real name?"

"My name?" Teacher paused for a few seconds. Whether he was remembering or just trying to form the sounds in his mouth, Konner wasn't sure. "In another life, my name was Adam."

Ω

Adam, whom Konner knew for so long as "Teacher," died that night. When Konner found him in the morning, Gollum was lying lifeless by his master's side. Konner didn't know which of them had gone first, but he hoped they'd gone together.

He spent half a day digging a hole. After he managed to get Teacher in it, he placed Gollum on top of him. The other cats had taken turns smelling the bodies, but didn't react otherwise. Konner figured they accepted the loss of their friends as a natural part of life. Konner himself was not so accepting. He looked down at the corpses, hesitant to cover them. He put his hands in his pockets and felt his goldstone, the little rock he'd kept all these years. He no longer believed in luck, or in any "superstitious nonsense" as Teacher used call it. In a sudden fit of anger he pulled out the stone and made to throw it as far away as he could. But something stopped him. Instead of throwing it, he dropped it into the hole with Teacher and Gollum.

He knew he'd have to cover them up soon, but he felt like he should say something first. He had no idea of what he should say, until he remembered something from his past.

"The earth is the land, and we are the earth."

The sciences were forgotten arts. Literacy was rarer than gold, but valued less. No real education existed beyond what was needed by the next generation to scrape a meager subsistence from the earth. Into this void of knowledge marched religion and superstition. The twin yearnings of hope and faith found man's hardships fertile ground in which to plant its spiritual figments and nurture its dogma. Gods new and old flourished, and those men and women blessed with an eloquent tongue, a way with words that could dazzle and delude others, rose to prominence and power. It didn't matter what they were selling, as long as someone was buying. Oracles, hucksters, soothsayers, spiritualists, diviners, flimflammers, self-proclaimed messiahs, all thrived.
Life was hard, for most it was short, and these prophets all promised something better . . . whether it was in this life or the next.

DISSEMBLANCE

SHE'D HEARD OF THIS PREACHER--this Elcaro--even before she'd come to this place. She'd heard the name in mumbled curses and whispered prayers. Word of his followers, his promise of salvation, had spread across the territory, though the utterances were such they left her uncertain whether or not he was even a real person . . . or just a name from the before times that people bandied about. Yet it had no relation to why she was here--she hadn't even known this was where a church was being built in his name until she arrived.

There was no real reason why she'd journeyed here. She certainly hadn't come because of any spiritual beliefs. This was simply another town--another stop for someone who had no place of her own.

Often she felt separate from the rest of the world, with nothing to hold onto, nothing to connect with. She'd lost her family when she was very young--so young she no longer remembered them. She'd lost Daemo--the old woman who was her only real friend. And she'd lost Mamam and her home at *Maison Boogalee*--the only home she remembered.

Once she'd considered maybe it was *her* that was lost. She never admitted to herself outright, but she was always looking for a place to belong to, an attachment stronger than just survival. So she kept on the move. Always looking but never finding. By nothing more than chance she came to this ramshackle town with no name. It had simply become known as the place where the preacher had put down roots, and to where his believers and other pilgrims trekked.

Saverra wasn't a believer. She didn't believe in much of anything. Though she'd been there many days, she'd never bothered to seek out this preacher. She'd seen what he was building only from a distance. It wasn't much. Three half-built walls rising up from the red brick bones of some more ancient structure. It was a hodgepodge of sandstone and adobe built around a skeleton of tall, rusted stanchions. She didn't figure there was much inside those ragged walls, but curiosity and boredom eventually seduced her. When she saw the flocks of believers streaming towards the supposed holy place one day, she decided to follow.

The sun was bright and the cloudless sky foretold of the day's heat to come. Though it was late morning, warm gusts of wind already swept through the town sporadically, rearranging the dust and playfully twirling her skirt. When the wind picked up, the woman walking in front of her had to shield the baby at her breast. Saverra glanced at the infant with more than casual interest. She'd long ago suppressed the yearning for motherhood, but there were times when she couldn't seem to help herself.

She'd been with men before--sometimes because she wanted to, sometimes not. But she'd never caught--never had a baby of her own. She had no idea why it was, but she was certain it was something that would never be.

She followed the woman and others to the open end of the would-be church and saw rows of crude wooden benches inside for the believers to sit on. There must have been more than a hundred folk already gathered. Not quite half the town, but more people than she'd ever seen in one place before. The seats were almost all taken, so Saverra stood in the back with others that were milling around, waiting for the preacher.

They didn't have to wait long. He appeared suddenly on the upraised dais at the other end of the church. From where he came, she wasn't sure.

Hushed silence spread through the throng like fire across tinder. There was nothing particularly daunting about his appearance, and Saverra wondered what it was that gave him such command over the crowd.

He wore a plain brown cassock tied at the waist. It was threadbare but clean, its hood thrown back. He had thick, dark eyebrows and short black hair, cut as if someone had placed a bowl over his head. His eyes were dark as well, and even from a distance Saverra could see *that* was where his power emanated from. His gaze was piercing, commanding. He looked somewhat familiar to her, but why, she had no idea.

He walked out and stood in front of a table covered with fine white linen. On the table was a small statue of a woman holding a child, mottled brass candlesticks, and a standing cross, at least two feet high, that looked to be made of gold. Upon seeing the cross, Saverra couldn't imagine how many fortunes she'd have to tell, or how many dances she'd have to dance, to earn that much gold.

"Sin!" abruptly cried out the preacher, his voice seeming to echo through the throng.

He searched his audience, his eyes staring, accusing. He let them stew under his gaze for a long moment before he continued.

"Sin is the reason," he said more serenely. "Sin is what brought us here." He gestured to the world in general. "Is it right that we bear the burden of our fathers' sins? Of our fathers' fathers' sins? Is it fair?" The preacher pointed skyward and the volume of his sermon rose. "Only *He* can decide what is fair. Only *He* decides what is right.

"This world was built upon the decaying pillars of avarice, pride, lust . . . ciphers and sums, science and tech knowledge. When they crumbled we were left to climb from the spiritually desolate pit that was the old world. Have no doubt the Lord, in His righteous wrath, destroyed that old world--cleansing it with the flames of perdition. It was a world not worthy of Him, so He chose to start anew. We, my friends, my brethren, *are* the new."

He walked to one side of his stage and looked down at those gathered there.

"Although He is slow to anger, He is great in power. His fury is the whirlwind and the storm, and the clouds are the dust of his feet. He rebukes the sea and makes the rivers run dry."

As he spoke, he paced back and forth across the limits of his stage as would a caged animal. His hands gesticulated like dancer's, and his expressions ran the gamut of soft smiles to angry glares.

"But why does He do this?

"He does it because He is waiting. He waits for you . . . and you . . . and you . . . and you . . ." he said, pointing at random faces in the crowd, " . . . and you." He pointed directly at Saverra--or at least it seemed like it to her. "He waits for a beacon in the wasteland. He waits to see a bright light of faith emerge from the darkness. He waits for the roots of devotion to spring forth from the barren earth, sprout leaves like angel's wings, and blossom beneath the fullness of His divine wisdom."

The wind chose that moment to howl like a beast in pain over the heads of the gathering. As the preacher spoke, it gradually increased in both strength and endurance. The table cloth whipped about, but no one noticed. They were entranced--more so by his voice than his words.

"He does this because He loves you. God so loved the world that He gave His one and only Daughter, that whosoever believeth in Him should not perish, but have eternal life. For He did not send Her into the desert, naked and alone, to condemn the world, but to save it, sacrificing Her to wash away the sins of mankind."

The preacher paused and looked into the distance for a moment. Saverra thought he seemed to be staring off as if remembering something.

"Eternal life in paradise--that is what the Lord offers those who believe. Life everlasting in the land of milk and honey.

"Therefore, do not be anxious, asking 'What shall we eat? What will we drink? When will it rain? How will we live?'

"Your Heavenly Father knows your needs. Patience is the virtue He looks for--patience and faith and obedience.

"Consider the buffalo. They neither sow nor reap. They have neither storehouse nor barn. Yet God feeds them. Are you not more worthy than buffalo?"

Several murmurs of assent rose from the crowd, some calling out "Yes!"

"He will provide for you as He provided the fishes and loaves in the time of the Christ. You only must have faith and sow righteousness wherever you go. Have faith and you will reap the fruit of His unfailing love.

"What must you do?" He cupped one ear with a hand as if trying to hear them. His believers responded on cue.

"Have faith!"

"What does God say?"

"Have faith!"

"What is the answer to all your woes?"

"Have faith!"

The preacher smiled at his audience, even as some began shielding themselves from the wind and blowing dust. Loose bits of construction blew about or swayed in place. The white linen flew up, uncovering part of the old table.

"Let us pray," he said, bowing his head and closing his eyes.

Likewise, his followers bowed their heads and closed their eyes. Saverra mimicked them, but furtively watched those around her.

"Heavenly Father, we who are building this tabernacle in the wilderness do so for You. We, the faithful, ask for nothing in return but Your love and forgiveness."

The wind slowly but steadily churned into a frenzy. Dust blew among the believers, who bowed or fell to their knees more for protection than abeyance. The preacher raised his voice to compete with the bluster.

"Yet we pray in Your name for the water of life that has been denied us. Give us rain for our crops. Wash away the iniquity of the past. Let our souls be cleansed and our spirits shine bright enough to be seen in heaven."

The howling wind and buffeting dust became too much for the congregation. Most were already retreating, seeking shelter before the preacher could finish. He tried to continue, but had to hold up his arm up to shield his own face. The golden cross Saverra had admired blew over with a *thud.*

Protecting herself as she moved, Saverra glanced at the preacher and saw his expression as he watched his flock disperse. Whether his displeasure was for the people or for his god, she didn't know. It was only for a moment that he stood there, then he too sought refuge from the encroaching sandstorm that engulfed them all.

Ω

The windstorm's intensity lasted long enough to scatter the town's residents, who sought what shelter they could. Saverra didn't make it back to her tent, but found safe haven along with several others in one of the marketplace shops. When it was apparent the tempest had subsided, blowing off to the East, she ventured outside. It was still breezy, but the sand had settled, and people were already shaking the dust from their clothes and their wares.

Emerging from cover she saw a large wagon approaching the town from the West, riding in on the sandstorm's tail. A single figure sat aboard, holding the reins to a pair of horses--one gray, one russet. They were strong-looking

190

beasts, but they moved ploddingly, as though their burden were a heavy one.

The wagon rolled leisurely up the coarse dirt road, collecting intrigued stares from the people it passed. Its sides were colorfully decorated, though the colors had long faded. Its driver wore a wide-brimmed, dust-colored hat over long black locks that fell to his shoulders. Draped over him was an ebony blanket with a hole cut in it to fit his head through. A pale yellow design zigzagged across the front of the ragged cloak. Several days growth of beard gave his face a ragged look, but the mustache that flared across his upper lip and dropped to frame his mouth had a more commanding presence.

On the seat next to the stranger was a small furry animal like a squirrel, but with longer arms, a skinny tail, and bright blue eyes. It was tan in color except for the tips of its feet and tail which were black like the mask around its face. How the stranger had trained the creature to sit there calmly like it was enjoying the ride, she had no idea.

The bolder children issued forth from their shelters to watch the wagon's passing. Some followed it. As it wheeled past Saverra, the driver glanced in her direction and touched the tip of his hat in a gesture that was clearly meant for her. But he drove on without another look, not stopping until he'd nearly reached the other end of the settlement.

Saverra overheard an old man close by say to his friend, "Healer."

"How you know?" asked the friend.

"I seen that wagon before--elsewhere. He's a healer alright."

The two men headed off in the direction of the wagon, following others who were curious about the stranger.

Saverra had heard of healers, but had never seen one. Half the stories she'd heard said they were traveling magicians who could perform miracles. The other half said they were tricksters, cheats. She didn't know the truth of it, but decided to follow the men down the road to see for herself. She stayed back from those clustering closely around the wagon, watching from what she felt was a safe distance . . . just in case some hoodoo was being thrown around.

The stranger, however, was nowhere to be seen. The little animal had jumped to the top of the wagon and sauntered back to the rear, its long tail held high. That drew most of the people to the back of the wagon, watching the unusual creature. But it didn't do anything. It just sat on its hind legs, swishing its tail occasionally.

The curiosity had almost worn off when everyone but the cat was startled as two doors at the rear of the wagon flew open and the stranger burst out onto a step just below the doors.

"Ladies, gentlemen, friends, fellow beings, good tidings to you all. I come to you today bearing vast wonders and helpful hints. I have with me the greatest collection of potions, salves, pills, detoxins, concoctions, and cure-alls you will ever see in this world or any other." The stranger spoke in a rapid-fire burst that left no space for interruptions. In each hand he held a tiny glass bottle--one amber, one clear as crystal--and waved them about as he spoke. "I have medicine for the mange, an antidote for the plague, and a healing agent guaranteed to combat infections of all kinds.

"For those of you with extraordinary and exotic maladies, I have incantations and spells, rituals of sun and rain to call forth the elements, and lyrics to cleanse your souls."

"You a healer?" called out the old man Saverra had heard before.

"I've been called that, friend, along with many other things." The stranger grinned as he said it, but his expression quickly reverted as he searched the crowd and pointed to one person after another. "Now, who has an ailment that needs treating? Does your back ache? Does your skin itch? Do your gums bleed? You there, how's *your* life? What about your wife? I have potions of passion and elixirs for sleep, arcane herbs to smoke or eat. Pay me in silver, gold, or coin of the realm. I accept fruits, eggs, baked goods, and tasty treats of all kinds. A traveling man always has an empty belly."

Some of those watching wandered away, but others approached the healer, asking for this cure or that. Saverra was intrigued, but since she didn't need any healing, she turned away to head back for her tent and see if it had withstood the storm. It was sheltered between a couple of buildings, so she had hope her few possessions hadn't been scattered to the wastelands.

Ω

In a natural clearing, framed by a semi-circle of mammoth boulders, a crackling bonfire carved a niche out of the damp, black night. Around the edges of the clearing sat a score of townsfolk--mostly men. One of them sat cross-legged, holding a crudely-fashioned string instrument from which he forged rich, melodic sounds. But the music his gittern made was not the focus of attention. All eyes were on Saverra.

She spun and twirled and danced barefoot around the fire like a woman possessed. Her skirt flapped and fluttered with each movement, delighting the onlookers with a glimpse of her bare dancer's legs. In her right hand she held an oval sphere, shaking it until it jingled, slapping it against her thigh, and pounding it with her other hand in rhythm with the string melody and her sensuous gyrations. A couple of spectators began clapping their hands to the beat, and soon everyone joined in.

Around and around the fire she whirled, seemingly as unrestrained and spontaneous as the flames themselves. But it wasn't as impromptu as it looked. Saverra had danced this dance, with slight variations, a thousand times. She knew it as well as she knew how to walk or eat. Yet familiarity didn't diminish her zeal for the performance. For it was only when dancing she felt truly alive--with no worries, no troubles, no tomorrows to bind her.

Faster and faster she spun and leapt around the fire until in a climax of music and motion, she swirled in place, rapping the pandeiro high over her head, her dress of faded sunset colors flailing out in an ever-widening disk until she collapsed like a broken doll. She lay still as death, legs split, head bent to one knee, arms thrown out wide.

The audience clapped and howled their approval. The show over, they stood and most walked past a basket lying on the ground next to the musician, dropping coins, food, and other offerings into it. When they were gone, the musician went straight to the basket. Saverra hurried over. They argued briefly before dividing their take.

He took his gittern and left. Saverra looked over her share. It wasn't much, but she'd eat the next day.

She sat next to the slowly dying fire, pulling her legs underneath her, and for some reason she thought of Mamam--the woman who'd taught her to dance. She hadn't thought of Mamam in a long time, but tonight she remembered her as a benefactor, despite the harsh ways she'd been treated at times. She wondered what had happened to the old woman after the *Maison Boogalee* burned to the ground. She remembered how the old woman's spirit had been broken, and how, shortly after the fire, she'd vanished. Where she'd gone, no one knew.

Sitting there, lost in thought, Saverra saw someone standing in the shadow of a massive boulder. At first she believed it was a trick of the light, the flare of a dying ember. But then . . . .

"I see y'all there. Don't be trying tuh hide now. Y'all not so sneaky."

The shadowy figure stepped forward just enough that Saverra realized it was the healer. He was no longer wearing his hat, and he'd shaved off everything but his mustache, so she could see the rawhide tan of his face more clearly now. It was hard to tell his age. He looked younger than herself, but there was something about him, something other than his facial features that suggested he was very old.

"I'm not hiding," he said, "I'm just watching you."

Saverra jumped up, putting one hand on her hip and pointing at him with the other.

"Y'all watch my dance, but don't pay for it?"

"And you dance beautifully. You dance like the fire itself dances."

She spurned the feeling his words pleased her, aborted a smile and summoned a frown.

"Don't try and color your words tuh me"

"But words have only the color your ears give them."

She thought about the meaning of that for a second before challenging him again. "Y'all watch duh dance, like duh dance, must pay for duh dance."

"What's your name?" The voice came from behind her. Saverra turned and looked. No one was there.

When she turned back, the healer had moved closer. She saw him more clearly now in the rim of the firelight.

"How y'all do dat? Y'all stand dere, but your voice come from over dere."

"It's a simple trick." He warmed his hands over the fire. "I believe you were going to tell me your name."

She wasn't, but she did.

"Saverra."

"A beautiful name for a beautiful dancer. Do you live in this place, Saverra? Do you have a family?"

"No family. I live here now. Sometimes I live other places."

"Ah, a fellow traveler--a dancing gypsy."

"Gypsy?" She'd never heard the word, but liked the sound of it. "Y'all be a healer?"

"That's what some call me."

"Why y'all do dat? Why y'all travel round and heal people?"

"Why does the sun rise in the East only to disappear in the West? Why does the wind caress the mountain tops? Why does a moth fly into the flame? It's what I know. It's what I can do."

"Don't y'all gots a family somewheres?"

He turned his head and called out, "Nomad!"

She was about to ask what a "nomad" was when the strange little animal that had been sitting next to him on the wagon strolled in from the shadows, its tail held high. It sat on its haunches next him, its blue eyes staring straight at her through the black mask of its face.

"Nomad is my only family," he said, seeing the quizzical look on her face. "He's a cat."

"I know it's a cat," said Saverra indignantly. She'd heard the word, but never actually seen one before. "I heard dey's bad luck."

"Only the black ones." He laughed. "His full name is Nomad Muad'Dib. Nomad, meet Saverra."

She half expected the beast to say something, but it just sat there.

"Mais, y'all still need tuh pay for my dance."

"What would you like in payment? I can give you pills to make you dream impossible dreams, a potion to heal your body or put your mind to rest, a poem to soothe your soul, an incantation to--"

"A poem," she blurted out, interrupting his list of choices. "Pay me wit poem."

Saverra had no idea what a "poem" was, but that's why she chose it. This healer had many words she didn't understand, and she didn't like not knowing what he was talking about. It unsettled her.

"Sit," he said loudly, more command than suggestion. Then softer, "Sit, and I'll give you a poem. A special poem for a dancing gypsy."

Saverra sat, but she watched the healer carefully as he moved closer to the fire. She didn't entirely trust the man, but she didn't really trust anyone. She didn't know what this "poem" thing was, but she was ready to protect herself from it should need be.

With a sudden flourish of both arms, he began.

"Wild child, full of grace, savoir of the human race, your cool face.

"Natural child, terrible child, not your mother's or your father's child.

"You're our child, screaming wild."

He paused, turned to the side, and looked out across the gloom-shrouded horizon.

"An ancient lunatic reigns in the trees of the night," he said softly, as though talking to himself.

Saverra stared at him, then started to say something when she thought he wouldn't go on. But he whirled back around and stared straight into her eyes. The projection of his voice and the intensity of his gaze pieced her inner armor and slashed her psyche.

"With hunger at her heels and freedom in her eyes, she danced on her knees, pirate prince at her side, staring into the hollow idol's eyes."

Again he paused, then continued in a gentler tone of voice.

"Wild child, full of grace, savoir of the human race, your cool face, your cool face."

He bowed his head briefly, signifying an end, and walked around the fire to where Saverra sat mesmerized. His approach splintered her reverie and she smiled.

"Dat good," she said. "I like dis poem. Y'all know lots of words. Some I don't, but dey still be pretty. Dey flow like water," she said, waving her hand like it was the flow of a river. "Almost   . . . " She thought for a moment. " . . . almost as if'n dese words done belonged tuh music."

"Maybe they did . . . once upon a time."

He bent down to sit crosslegged near her and winced in pain, grabbing his left knee.

"Your leg be hurt?"

"It's an old injury. It bothers me on occasion."

Saverra wondered how that could be. "If'n your leg hurts," she asked with a tone of suspicion, "why don't y'all heal it? You're a healer."

"Some things are better left as they are," he replied. "Even a cracked barrel has its uses. The pain in my knee talks to me on occasion . . . and I listen."

She looked at him, puzzled, not really understanding how his knee could talk to him, or for that matter, what good a cracked barrel was. Then she flashed a smile, trying to add a touch of allure to it.

"Y'all give me more poem now?"

"But I've paid you for your dance. You must have something else to trade if you want another poem."

She frowned and jerked her head around in a mock tantrum. She stared into the darkness, purposely ignoring the healer's presence. She waited for him to speak, but when only silence greeted her, she turned back around. Her expression quickly morphed from irritation to astonishment. The stranger was no longer there.

Saverra jumped up and looked all around. The healer was gone. Only his cat still sat on the other side of the fire, watching her.

"Nomad!" called a voice from the darkness.

The funny little animal stood, stretched for a moment, and then bounded off into the night.

Saverra grabbed a handful of dirt and with a frustrated whine flung it into the direction the animal had disappeared.

Ω

He sat with the grieving parents for a time, but there wasn't much solace he could give them. Still, he tried his best. He reached out and gently placed his fingertips on the dead infant's forehead.

"I understand, little one, why you may not have wanted to stay in this world, even if you were so wanted, so loved by your mother and father. God understands too. It's a hard world--harder even for one so small. We don't blame you for not wanting to stay when it's so much easier for you to rise into the Kingdom of Heaven."

Elcaro took his hand from the baby and grasped hold of one hand each from the mother and father.

"I cannot tell you not to weep, not to mourn. But your innocent child is indeed in a better place now--a place at God's side. In time, I hope you will rejoice for her. Have faith that the Lord's choice was for the best. Let us bow our heads in prayer."

After a brief minute of silent prayer, he stood and told the grieving parents, "I will leave you with your child now, so you may say your final goodbyes. If your faith falters, or you have any need, seek me out. I will be there for you. *God* will be there for you."

The preacher pulled aside the hovel's flap and walked out into the sunshine. He wandered aimlessly for a while, dealing with an anguish as real as that of the child's own parents. Yet he knew there were others who needed him. The day before it was a dying old woman. Today it was a child who'd ascended much too soon. Tomorrow it would be someone else--something else. He was shepherd to an entire flock, and he could not wallow in grief forever. He had to be strong. He had to have faith God's judgment could not be questioned.

Even so, there was so much misery, so much blight upon the land, upon the people. There were times when even he could not bear it. There were times when even he grew angry and filled with doubt. He was angry now, though he kept the rage bound tight against his soul. However, it slipped free and taunted him when he spied the harlot speaking with a trio of his believers. What ungodliness she was up to, he didn't want to guess. Elcaro strode stiffly, purposely, towards her. He was the Lord's soldier--ever pressing onward.

The men she was talking with saw him coming and quickly walked away. He flashed them an accusing stare as they retreated, then turned his attention to the woman.

"You profane yourself in the eyes of God, my child. What would your mother say if she saw the way you live?"

Saverra didn't flinch. She responded with equal rectitude.

"I never knew my mother, or my father. Dey were gone when I was still little. What would your mother say, if'n she knew what y'all do?"

Her mention of his mother only fanned the flames of his ire.

"My mother was a saint--Saint Janelle--the Lord's child. She set me on the path I still follow." His voice calmed and he added, "But, like you, I never knew my mother. She died giving me life."

"Mais, aren't we just a couple of sad cases," replied Saverra with more than a hint of sarcasm. "I didn't have a mother tuh teach me, but I had Mamam. She taught me how tuh live. How tuh make the most of what I had. How tuh survive."

She turned to go, but Elcaro grabbed her arm and held tight.

"Let me show you another way to live, child. Let me show you God's way."

Saverra tore her arm free of his grip. He held up his hands to show he meant no harm. That's when she saw the marks--the deep red scars on his palms.

He was used to people's reaction when they saw this, but this woman's response was different. Her look was one of frightful recognition. He dropped his hands.

"I know you," she said. "I've seen you before."

Where she'd come across him during his travels, Elcaro had no idea. But he didn't understand the fear in her eyes.

"There's nothing to be afraid of, my child." Out of habit he reached out to place his hand on her shoulder to comfort her.

"Don't touch me, y'all couyon. Stay away from me," she said, fleeing in a near panic.

Elcaro watched her go, not understanding her reaction, but saying a prayer for her all the same. He reminded himself, *We're all God's children*.

Ω

" . . . Dorothy was so mad, she grabbed a bucket of water and threw it on the wicked witch. To her surprise, steam bellowed from the witch, and the old woman began shrinking right into the ground. 'I'm melting!' she cried."

Hearing something out of the ordinary, Saverra had followed the sound and come upon the healer, surrounded by a group of children, and even some adults. Their faces revealed how fascinated they were--their attention locked on every word. He was telling them a story, occasionally punctuated by their *oohs* and *ahhs*.

"Sure enough," continued the healer, "the wicked witch was melting like a candle under a flame." He waved his hands in the air, and suddenly there was a flash of light like a sheet of fire that was there, then it wasn't. It was magic in Saverra's eyes, and his audience was so startled they might have run off if it hadn't happened so quickly. He continued with his tale before they could even question the flash. "In the blink of an eye, the wicked witch was no more than a puddle of goo surrounding the ruby slippers."

He paused as if the story might be over.

"Then what happened?" bravely asked a little girl who was listening.

The stranger looked straight at the girl with his dark eyes and replied, "Dorothy grabbed those ruby slippers and put them on."

"Did she fly home after she put them on?" asked another girl.

"No, she had to go see the Wizard of Oz first. So she and Toto and the Scarecrow and the Tin Woodsman and the Cowardly Lion all got back on the yellow brick road and headed for the land of Oz."

"Then what happened?" asked the first girl.

"Then it was time for everyone to go to bed," said the healer and laughed. "You'll have to wait for the rest of the story tomorrow."

Groans of disappointment sounded in response. The healer responded to them, saying, "I want you to imagine what happens next. You can imagine can't you? What do you think happens to Dorothy and her friends?"

There were more moans of exasperation, but the healer waved them off, smiling, saying "Tomorrow, tomorrow," as he walked away.

Saverra joined him and he greeted her with a smile.

"Well, if it's not my dancing gypsy," he said, spotting her standing there. "Good evening to you."

Saverra smiled at the word "gypsy" and nodded.

He started to say something else, but then spotted a woman carrying something. He approached her and asked, "What have you there, my good woman? Are those books in your arms?"

"Yes," she replied tentatively, unsure why he would care. "I'm taking them to the preacher," she added defensively. " They're old evil--he says so. He's gonna burn them."

The healer's smile contorted into a mask of anger, but Saverra recognized restraint in his voice.

"I'll buy them from you right now. Here." He pulled a few silver coins from his pocket and offered them to her.

She hesitated, looked around to see if anyone was watching, then quickly took the coins, handed him the books, and hurried away.

The healer called after her. "Spread the word. I'll buy any books anyone has."

She didn't acknowledge the healer's words as she retreated, and he didn't bother to repeat them.

"What are dese books?" she asked abruptly. "What y'all gonna tuh do wit dem?"

"Right now I'm going to put them where they can't be burnt," he replied derisively. "Eventually I'm going to read them."

"Read dem? Is dat some kind of hoodoo magic?"

"It's not magic at all. I could teach you to read if you wanted."

Saverra looked aghast that she would want anything to do with such inexplicable mysticism.

"Books tell of all the wonders there used to be." The healer gestured as he described those wonders. "Once upon a time there were buildings built high enough to touch the clouds, and people traveled through the air in great flying machines. So many people--more than raindrops in a storm--and more books than you could read in a lifetime," he said wistfully. "It was a different world--a better world."

Saverra didn't know if it was a better world, but it was certainly a stranger one.

Ω

Elcaro was not deaf to the rumblings of the town's farmers. Their dissatisfaction loomed higher and heavier with each passing day. They were desperate for rain.

Despite all his prayers, God hadn't seen fit to bless them. He wondered if the people of this place weren't righteous enough. He wondered if *he* wasn't.

Even his sparse Mescalito patch was wilting, despite the water he regularly anointed it with. He'd only shared the secrets of its bounty--its spiritually curative powers--with his closest followers. They were the small cadre of true believers who'd followed him to this place. But even they didn't know everything--even they didn't commune with Mescalito as he did. No one but he and God knew everything.

When he overheard a group of farmers talking, he grew angry. They were discussing the stranger who'd come to town, and how he was curing folks with his medicines and potions. Someone said the stranger had mentioned calling forth rain. Elcaro knew this was a preposterous notion, but before he could confront farmers and dissuade them, they were off, headed to find the outsider.

He considered going after them, trying to stop them, but what would he say? God had not been forthcoming. How could he convince them not to? Better to let the stranger fail, then he would be run out of town.

So Elcaro followed the farmers from a distance. He stood near a street vendor, pretending to examine the vendor's wares, but near enough to the stranger's wagon so he could hear the farmers make their desperate plea. The wagon, the horses, struck a familiar chord within him. The sight of them reminded him, ever so faintly, of a vision he'd experience long ago during his romería. The memory was not a strong one, and he dismissed it at once.

"You want me to make it rain?" The tone of the stranger's voice showed the request had caught him off guard. He turned slightly and his hand reached down to his left knee.

"Our crops are dying," said one of the farmers. "We need rain. We need it soon."

"What makes you think I can make it rain?"

"I heard you," said another farmer. "The day you first came. You said you had 'rituals of sun and rain.' I remember."

"So I did," admitted the healer somewhat reluctantly. "So I did. You have an excellent memory, sir."

"Well, can you do it?"

"I have, on occasion, aided the natural processes. But tampering with such powerful forces is dangerous. It's not a matter I conduct lightly or effortlessly."

"We'll pay you."

The healer once again squeezed his knee. "I will have to think on it," he said. "The conditions must be just right before I could even attempt such a thing. I make no guarantees. Mother Nature is more potent than any incantation I carry."

When the farmers continued their plea, the healer held up his hand to quiet them. "I said I will think on it," he declared with a touch of command in his tone. "If I can, I will. Go now. Leave me to confer with the forces of nature."

The farmers wandered off, but Elcaro stayed where he was, watching the healer, assured now the man *was* a charlatan, a heretic. He saw it on his face. He had no powers. He knew he couldn't make it rain. When he didn't deliver, the people would turn once more to Elcaro for salvation. They would turn back to God when this devil failed.

Ω

Saverra remembered seeing it down in the lower parts of the cave she'd discovered some time ago. If he liked such things so much, she figured she'd go get it for him. So she lit a torch from a nearby cook fire and hiked the short way to the cave. It was partially concealed by a large stand of cacti and scrub brush, but she found it right away. All sorts of unusual things were scattered throughout the outer cavern, but she was only interested in one. She went all the way back to where she'd seen it before. The rear of the cave slanted downward, and looked as if it fed into a tunnel that plunged even deeper. But a pile of rocks and other debris had blocked it off.

She found what she was looking for and examined it closely. She opened it and turned it this way and that, as if some new angle might unlock its mysteries for her. But it was still a garble of strange marks and symbols no matter how she looked at it.

As she was studying it, something else caught her eye. A column of large red ants were streaming out from the obstructed tunnel. The sight of them so close to her sparked old fears. She panicked, threw the torch at the ants and ran out into the light.

Once she'd composed herself, and was certain the ants hadn't followed her, she went in search of the healer. He wasn't at his wagon, and someone said they'd seen him walking out towards the wasteland. Why he'd be out there, she didn't know. There was a lot about this stranger she didn't understand. Yet something deep inside her trusted him, despite his peculiarities. Something inside her was drawn to him.

It didn't take long before she spotted him. He hadn't gone far. But what Saverra saw shocked her momentarily. There was an expansive pool of water where there should have been none--a small lake sitting on what had been desert land. Yet that wasn't what shocked her. It was the healer. He was walking across the top of the water, without sinking, without a splash.

Saverra stood there, her mouth open with astonishment. The healer saw her and changed direction. As he got closer, he was no longer on the pool of water. He was walking on sand, and she was no longer certain she saw any water.

"What is it?" he asked. "You look like you've seen a ghost."

She pointed to where she seen the water. It was now only desert. "Y'all were walking on water!"

The healer laughed. "There's no water out there--just dry sand. You must have seen a heat mirage. It's a trick of the light, a reflection of the sky that fools the eye."

Saverra shook her head, not comprehending.

"What have you got there?" he said, pointing at what was in her hand.

"It's a *book*." The world was strange on her tongue, but she was certain she'd said it right.

"Where did you get it?"

"I'd seen it before. Y'all said it was a good sometin."

"It certainly is. May I see it?"

"It's for y'all."

"It is? Thank you, Saverra. A better gift you couldn't give me."

"It's no gift," she said because she had no reason to give him such. "I just don't gots any use for it."

"Let's see what it's all about."

He opened the book and looked through some of the pages as they walked back to town.

"Can y'all read it?" Read was another strange word to her, but she remembered it.

"Certainly. It's not a long book. It's actually a diary."

"A die or e?"

"A *diary*," he said carefully. "It's a book someone wrote in every day to explain what happened to them each day--what they were doing or thinking about."

"What does it say?"

"Well, it's from long ago--from just after the cataclysm."

"Cat-what?" Saverra wondered if it had anything to do with the cat, Nomad.

"The cataclysm is another word for the end of the world that used to be. This was written just after the comet Smith-Kim collided with the Earth. The woman who wrote it lived underground with some other people--a group of scientists who were prepared for what happened. They were planning on doing what they could to rejuvenate the planet--bring back some of its plants and animals."

Saverra only understood about half of what he was saying, but she was intrigued.

"What happened tuh dis woman?"

"I'm not sure. It says they started taking orders from a computer--a machine--and then things went bad. People died. It ends there. There's nothing after that."

Saverra thought she knew what a machine was, but she didn't know how could it give orders. *Why would people do what a machine said?* She was more certain than ever the world from before must have been a bizarre place indeed.

Ω

The healer was standing near his wagon in the mid-day sun, peddling his cures to a couple of locals, when Elcaro found him. One of the townspeople mumbled "Preacher" when he saw Elcaro approach. The prospective customers all grew silent and moved away.

"Your scowl is bad for business, my friend," said the healer. "What is it that I can do for you? Mayhap I have a potion that can turn that frown upside down."

The healer's jovial quip slowed Elcaro, but didn't diminish his glare.

"You're the preacher, aren't you?" the healer asked, though it was apparent he already knew the answer. "How do I address you? Reverend? Father? Your Holiness?"

"My name is Elcaro."

"Elcaro? Yes, I've heard of you. You get around almost as much as I do."

"This is my home now. These are my people. Make no mistake, stranger, I *will* protect my people from your fraudulence."

"On what do you base such an allegation?"

"You've told the people you can make it rain. That's a lie--as bold a lie as I've ever heard. No man can make it rain. Only God can do that."

"You've misquoted me, Padre. I never said I could make it rain--not exactly."

"You're playing with words. You're a charlatan, a trickster, a swindler. You sell people false hope."

"You may call me a prevaricator of sorts. I prefer to think of myself as a raconteur, a teller of tales, and yes, a word man. Let's face it, priest, we're both peddlers. Only I sell knowledge, science, poetry. I trade in hope. But you, you barter in fear and superstition."

"You dare call praise of God's word *superstition*?"

"I do. I'd also ask, what makes *you* the voice of your god? How is it you speak for him . . . or her?"

The question disconcerted him for a moment--but only a moment.

"I have studied the word of God," responded Elcaro. "I've been immersed in faith since the moment of my birth. My pilgrimage on his behalf has taken me across this desolate world and back again. I've seen what his fury has wrought. I know the sins of mankind."

"Sin lies only in hurting others unnecessarily. All other *sins* are invented nonsense."

"You speak the blasphemy of a barbarian."

"I'm a barbarian because I don't bow down to your religious precepts? Yours is not the only theological doctrine riding roughshod over this planet. Do you know what the newest religion is? I came across a group of folks who worship a certain kind of plant. A vegetable god, as it were."

Elcaro held his immediate reaction in check. He knew of this sect. He'd been a part of it himself for a brief time. His days with them had proved illuminating, if only to convince him they knew nothing of God's true plan. They were ignorant of scripture, of the meaning of faith. God wasn't just in the Mescalito, He was in everything. The Mescalito bush was simply an embodiment of His holy being--a conduit for His wisdom.

"Do you know how religion began?" The healer continued. "It started when men first began to till the soil. They became dependent upon the weather for their crops to grow. The spirits of the sun, the rain, the earth, had to be appeased and pacified. Then some smart cookie decided he could control the actions and beliefs of others by saying he had a direct relationship with the gods. That's what you have with your followers--right? Control."

"You think I wanted this?" declared Elcaro with more than a hint of anger. "You think I asked for this?" He held up his hands so the healer could see the scars in his palms. "You think your elixirs can heal this?"

The healer stared at the marks, his expression revealing he was caught by surprise.

"It's a hard world, Padre. We've all got scars. Some are just more visible than others." The healer offered a half-hearted grin. "They build character, don't you think?"

"What do you know about building character? Developing morals? I'm the shepherd of my flock. I guide them through deserts of unrighteousness onto a path that will lead them to Heaven and the ultimate reward on the day the Savior returns."

"No eternal reward will forgive us now for wasting the dawn," said the healer. "Besides, how do you know *I'm* not your savior? After all, the Lord works in mysterious ways--right?"

It was Elcaro's turn to be unsettled, but he didn't let it show.

"More blasphemy. Your feeble words mean nothing to me. They're as empty as--"

"Your promises of salvation?"

Elcaro took a breath and let himself be restored with calm. With a measured tone, he responded, "God is not mocked, for whatever one sows, that will he also reap. The resurrection *will* come. When it does, your soul, healer, will be damned to Hell for eternity."

"Fortunately, my soul is not governed by you or your mythology. Or, as one ancient philosopher once said, 'Go to Heaven for the climate, to Hell for the company.'"

Elcaro had had enough of this heathen, this unbeliever.

"I see it plainly now. You're lost, healer--cursed by God. I couldn't save you if I tried. You could wander the wastelands for a hundred years and still not find your way. I pity you."

"Reverend, we're all wandering in the wasteland of life. The only curse is that I have no cure for the sanctimonious."

Elcaro wasn't even listening to the man now. He ignored him and said, "Your tongue plots destruction as sharp as a knife's edge, as treacherous as a worker of deceit. For you, there will be no salvation. When you turn your back on God, He turns His back on you."

"Then I guess you'd better cancel my subscription to the resurrection."

Elcaro turned slowly and walked away. As he did, he silently prayed to God for forgiveness--forgiveness for his ire, his raging indignation. The stranger had provoked him in a way he was unused to, but that was no excuse. He must do penance for his lack of control.

Ω

She found she enjoyed listening to the healer talk. Even when she didn't understand everything he was saying. There was something soothing about his voice, something reassuring in his lilting laugh and the cheerful spark in his eyes when they met hers.

He'd been talking about the place he was born, about his family, when he spied a man, a woman, and a little boy waiting at his wagon. Nomad was there, sitting on top again, watching them. The man sneezed and wiped at his dripping nose. His voice was cloudy as he explained his illness to the healer, who asked a few questions, opened his wagon, and came out with a small glass bottle. Saverra wondered what kind of magic was in it.

"A common enough ailment you have my friend. But you're in luck. I have the cure. All you need do is drink this, don't walk about under the cold glare of the stars, drink buckets of water, and rest as much as you can."

"This and water?" asked the fellow in amazement.

"Yes, *lots* of water. In a couple days, you'll be as loud and proud as a bear."

"A bear?"

"A ancient creature as big as a horse and twice as mean."

As the man's wife paid the healer with ears of corn from a basket, Saverra watched the boy staring up at the healer's cat.

"Wha . . . wha . . . what is tha . . . that?"

The boy had something wrong with his tongue. Saverra wondered if he'd been injured.

The healer turned his attention to the boy. "That, my boy, is a cat. His name is Nomad. Would you like to touch him?"

The boy nodded.

The healer reached up and called, "Nomad." The cat leapt into his arms.

"Let me introduce you," said the healer. "What's your name?"

"Sa . . . Sa . . . Sam."

"Nomad, this is Sam. Sam, this is Nomad. Just reach out and pet his head like this." The healer demonstrated and the boy mimicked him. "He likes to be scratched between the ears too."

"What do you think about Nomad, Sam?"

"I . . . I li . . . li . . . like him."

The healer turned to the boy's parents. "Has Sam always had this problem speaking?"

"No," responded the mother. "Only about two harvests."

The healer knelt down, put Nomad on the ground, and let the boy pet the cat some more.

"Sam, do the other children make fun--laugh at the way you talk?"

The boy nodded.

"Would you like to change the way you talk?"

He nodded again.

"Alright. I'm going to sing a song, and I want you to listen carefully, so you can sing it with me when I'm done."

Another nod.

"Twinkle, twinkle, little star," began the healer, singing softly, "how I wonder what you are. Up above the world so high, like a diamond in the sky. Twinkle, twinkle, little star, how I wonder what you are.

"Alright now, Sam. I want you to sing it with me. Okay?"

The boy looked unsure, glanced at his parents, then nodded. They both began singing, with the healer helping him with the words. After a few tries the boy was singing without any stutter, just as smoothly as the healer himself. His parents looked astounded.

"Good job, Sam. That was excellent. Now whenever you talk . . ." The healer began singing his words instead of just saying them. ". . . I want you to sing the words like I'm doing now. It doesn't matter what the song is, just sing them. Now you try. Tell me the names of your mother and father. Sing them to me, Sam."

It took a couple of words for him to get the hang of it, but soon the words were flowing from his mouth.

"My . . . my . . . my mother's name is Rachel, and my father's name is Bill." He was so happy with what he'd said, the boy repeated himself.

"That's how you do it, Sam. Whenever you have trouble speaking, just think of it as a song, and sing the words."

Sam's mother took hold of the healer's hands and said, "Thank you, thank you, Healer. Here, let me give you more corn."

"No, no. It was my pleasure to help Sam. If he keeps practicing, maybe someday he won't have to sing at all." The healer smiled. "Unless he wants to."

Both parents and Sam, thanked him again before leaving.

"How y'all do dat? Was it magic?" asked Saverra.

"Did it look like magic?"

She shrugged.

"It was science not magic. By thinking about singing, Sam used a different part of his brain to speak. It was something I read about once. I really wasn't sure if it would work. But it might help him to speak normally if he keeps at it."

She shook her head. "If'n it's not magic, den how y'all cure folks?"

The healer sighed. "Sometimes my herbal remedies work their own kind of natural magic, but sometimes it's just the power of belief that cures people. If I'm convincing enough, if I sell the cure with enough flash, enough showmanship, people will believe enough that they cure themselves. It's mind over matter--the placebo effect--the power of suggestion."

He looked at Saverra. "You have no idea what I'm talking about, do you?"

She shook her head slowly.

He shrugged. "One man's science is another's magic."

Ω

Saverra woke late the next morning and stayed in her tent a while. She'd hurt her leg dancing the night before and was trying to massage it. It wasn't until she heard a bit of a commotion that she peeked out. Various town folk were gathering in small groups and then heading off in the same direction.

Her curiosity got her out of the tent. She stretched her sore leg and rubbed it some more. As she did, the bright sunshine overhead vanished. She looked up. A bank of dark clouds had blown in, covering the sun's glare. The wind propelling the clouds had a bit of a chill to it, and Saverra realized she hadn't seen such ominous clouds in some time. She didn't think too much about it. She was more interested in where everyone was going, so she followed them. When she was close enough, she asked one of the women what was happening.

"It's the healer. He's making rain."

A sense of urgency pushed her. The stranger hadn't told her he was going to make rain. She hurried, following the people to an open field outside of town. All the farmers, as well as many others, were gathered there, a safe distance from the healer, who stood alone, his arms limp at his side, eyes closed, chest bare, his long black hair whipping about in the wind. His whole posture was slightly unnatural--like a scarecrow in a trance. Seeing him there, posed like that, sent a shiver through Saverra's body that was more than just a reaction to the cool breeze.

"He's been standing there a long time now," said one of the farmers. "I don't think he can do it."

"Look at those clouds," said another. "Where do you think they came from? He can do it alright. Just wait."

Saverra didn't know what to believe. The stranger had denied using magic, but how else, she thought, could he make it rain? He spoke of the power of belief, of something he called "showmanship," but neither, she reckoned, would cause water to fall from the sky. Would he use that other kind of magic he called science? She couldn't deny the sky had taken on the aspect of a storm. If he really made it rain, it must be some kind of hoodoo.

A powerful gust blew across the field, sending many scurrying after their hats. Others pulled their coats tighter around them as the horizon darkened even more. Saverra heard several people murmuring fearfully.

"Look at him--he's sweating!"

Indeed, despite the cold wind, Saverra could see glistening rivulets of sweat running down the healer's lean ribcage.

The wind suddenly howled like a forlorn beast, and, without warning, the healer flung his arms wide, opened his eyes and looked up at the sky. The crowd fell into silence. Some backed a few steps away.

"We're getting tired of hanging around!" bellowed the healer. His voice seemed to come from every direction at once. "Waiting around with our heads to the ground!" He dropped one hand and cupped his ear. Softer he said, "I hear a very gentle sound. Very near, yet very far. Very soft, yet very clear. Come today, come today."

For what seemed like longer than it could have been, no sound could be heard but for the growing intensity of the wind. The heavens had grown black and menacing. The people stared at the healer--waiting.

"What have they done to the earth?" Shouted the healer as if an accusation. He raised both hands into the air again. "What have they done to our fair sister? Ravaged and plundered and ripped her and bit her. Stuck her with knives in the side of the dawn, and tied her with fences and dragged her down."

Saverra stared in awe. Rain or no rain, the man was mesmerizing. She couldn't look away. Then the first bit of moisture streaked across her face. She held out her hands to be sure it was rain.

He lowered his arms, bent down to one knee, and placed the flat of his palm on the ground next to it. Though he tried to hide it, Saverra saw him flinch in pain as he went down.

"I hear a very gentle sound," said the healer speaking in a hushed tone. "With my ear down, to the ground."

The sky opened up at that moment--not a drizzle, but a deluge--almost as if enraged by this mortal who dared to disturb it. The rain fell so quickly, so powerfully, the astonished exclamations and gasps of the crowd were drowned out and washed away as everyone ran for cover. A bolt of lightning flashed overhead and a thunderous crack split the sky. Saverra ducked out of reflex and shielded her eyes. The intensity of the downpour almost surpassed the fantastic notion of it. Awe and disbelief warred within her. But she couldn't reject the proof of what she saw--what she felt--an unrelenting onslaught pelting her arms, her face, saturating her incredulity.

When she stood and turned around, the healer was only steps away from her. The solemn, almost contorted expression he'd worn minutes ago was gone. He smiled and said, "Have you no sense, gypsy woman? There's a storm about."

Without giving her a chance to reply, he took her arm and led her across the muddy field to the shelter of his wagon, limping the entire way.

Ω

He stood still as stone, his clenched knuckles rigid and white. His robe drenched, hanging on his wiry frame like a suit of sagging armor. He couldn't believe what he'd just seen, despite the onslaught that battered him. His fists were clenched, his teeth locked. His only thought was, *it isn't possible.*

It didn't matter if he'd witnessed it, along with dozens of others. It didn't matter if his clothes were already soaked and he could hardly see through the blowing wind and rain. It couldn't be. It was an illusion of some kind--the blackest of magic.

Despite his disbelief, Elcaro held up an arm to shield himself from the elemental assault, and hurried away to find shelter. As he ran, lightning continued to crackle and thunder assailed his ears. Though it was further away, he ran for his tabernacle, ignoring several dwellings he passed. He must speak with God. He must understand what had happened and why.

Before he could reach the entrance, a bolt of lightning struck directly in front of him, blinding him momentarily. He opened his eyes when he heard a loud *crack*, and saw a portion of his church collapsing from the force of the electrical strike.

He ran inside. Disillusionment fought with disbelief. He saw the destruction of what had taken so long to build. He fled the tabernacle, sprinted through the wind and rain, dashed across rivulets of silt and muck until he came to his Mescalito patch. He fell to his knees in a puddle of mud before the impassive shrub.

"Why?" he demanded. "Why?" he pleaded, ignoring the rain assaulting his face. "Haven't I done all You wanted? Haven't I done more?" He held up his hands, bearing his scars to the heavens, and shouted over the storm. "Where have I failed You? Tell me, Lord. Tell me what You want of me. Tell me what to do."

He dropped his hands to the mud, bowed his head, and didn't move until the rain had stopped.

Ω

By the light of a single candle, Saverra removed her wet clothing and wrapped herself in a blanket given her by the healer. Though he was outside checking on his horses, his cat was inside, watching her every move. The flickering candlelight forged a flash of perception onto the otherwise cryptic look of its black-masked face. The way it stared at her was both unnerving and captivating. She made herself look away.

Instead, she stared at all the brightly colored bottles, ornaments, and charms stored randomly about the inside of the wagon. There were sealed gourds, a pipe carved from a tree root, clear containers full of various powders, an assortment of things she couldn't comprehend, that left her wondering.

Outside the rain still pounded and the wind still shrieked. She heard a noise from the front of the wagon as a gust of wind nearly blew out the candle. The healer was returning, closing the door panels behind him.

Water ran from his hair and bare chest. He smiled at her and grabbed a length of cloth with which to dry himself. He took off his wet pants, leaving him covered in only a kind of loincloth.

"We shouldn't be washed away, at least for a while," he said, still smiling. "But I'd better close Nomad's escape hatch."

She'd noticed the square hole in the wagon's floor, though it had been partially covered by a colorful rug. The healer reached down into the hole and pulled up a door which he fastened closed. The final gust of wind through the opening made her shiver and he noticed. He found a bottle amongst his various treasures and poured them both a drink.

"Here, drink this," he said, handing it to her. "It'll keep the cold from you."

She drank as he did, and felt the warmth spread through her. She'd tasted the like before. Mamam called it moonshine.

"How y'all do dat?" Saverra asked as the healer settled across from her and scratched the cat between his ears. "How y'all done make it rain? What kind of magic is dat?"

"You think *I* made it rain?"

"I saw it. Everybody saw it. Y'all speak strange words and duh rain come."

He laughed, but cut it short when he saw the irate look on her face.

"Sorry, but sometimes laughter is the best medicine, and this rain has really put the ache into my knee."

"Is it talking tuh y'all?"

He smiled again. "You remembered what I told you about the pain talking to me."

"I remember," she replied indignantly. "I'm no couyon."

"Yes, it's talking pretty loud right now," he said, stretching his left leg and rubbing his knee.

They both took another drink and Saverra noticed how the healer was looking at her. She recognized the look and pulled the blanket tighter around her.

"What's your name?" she asked suddenly. "Y'all never done told me your name."

The healer shrugged. "What's in a name? That which we call a rose, by any other word would smell as sweet."

"What's a rose?"

"A flower that didn't survive the holocaust," said the healer. "At least I've never seen one myself."

"Den how y'all know it smells sweet?"

"I read about it in my books."

"In one of dose?" Saverra pointed at a row of books lining a shelf of the inner wagon.

"It might have been in one of those," he replied, a sad expression taking root around his eyes. "I can't keep every book I've ever read. There have been too many. My horses can only pull so much weight. I've had to leave some behind . . . in as safe places as I could find."

"Y'all find poems in dese books?"

He nodded as if he were still somewhere else--somewhere he'd left his books.

"Y'all give me another poem?" she asked meekly. "A special one for me?"

He smiled and replied, "But what will you give me in return? You can't dance in the rain. If I give you another poem, I must get something in return."

Saverra's hopeful expression twisted into a sulk. Then something occurred to her. She tucked her blanket tightly around her and rummaged through her wet dress.

"I'll tell your fortune," she said enthusiastically. "Tell y'all what's tuh happen for your tomorrows."

She pulled a small wooden case from her dress, and from that she removed her worn, heavily creased cards.

"Oh, then you have magic too," the healer said with a twinkle in his eye.

"It's not me," she said earnestly. "Duh magic is in duh cards--not me."

"Alright, but I think we're going to need some more light."

He filled a metal cup from the spigot of a small barrel and, to Saverra's amazement, seemed to light the oily substance with a wave of his hand. The liquid in the cup burned even brighter than the candle.

Saverra began mixing the cards in her hands, while the healer tried to copy the seriousness of her countenance. Even the cat wandered over to get a closer look at what she was doing. Each shuffle, each movement, was ritual. She knew the telling of someone's fortune involved certain tricks at times. She'd learned that from Daemo. Despite all the ruses and wiles Daemo had taught her, Saverra still believed there was magic in those cards. She was certain of it.

When she finished with the deck, she handed them to the healer.

"Hold in your hand," she said. "Duh cards must touch y'all--feel your soul."

He held them a moment, then she retrieved them. She started to place them on the rug before her, then quickly kissed the top of the deck.

"For luck," she said shyly, without looking up at him.

For a long few seconds, she concentrated her focus on the deck of cards, then turned over the top three cards. On the first card was the faded picture of a young man inspecting a pentacle hovering over his hands.

"Duh primero, duh first card, be y'all--duh Page of Pentacles. It means messenger, a bringer of truth, of news--both good and bad. It be a card of much dinking, of loyalty and freedom.

"Duh next card be what stands in your way--your obstacle."

The second card featured a king, sitting in a pose of judgment, holding an unsheathed sword. Behind him was a banner of authority.

"Duh King of Swords be duh card of command--someone strong wit power.

"Duh next card be what surrounds you--where y'all are--duh people, duh place, what y'all gots tuh use tuh overcome your obstacle."

The third card was torn slightly, but pictured a naked man and woman. The woman stood next to a fruit tree and a serpent, while the man was by a tree of fire. Above them hovered an angel.

"Dis duh card of beauty, passion, of obstacles overcome," she said, averting her gaze from him. "Dis be card of joining, but not a joining blessed by all."

Saverra dealt out three more cards, face down.

"Y'all must pick duh last card--duh card which rules all others. It foretells what's tuh come--duh future. Choose one and turn over."

The healer quickly selected the middle card and flipped it over. Saverra gasped loud enough to startle the cat, who'd been nodding off to sleep.

The final card featured a skeleton in black armor astride a white horse and holding a black standard. The horse was stepping over a body on the ground while a priest prayed nearby.

The healer smiled and said, "That doesn't look too good."

Saverra couldn't hide the panic on her face. She reached for the card, but the healer stopped her.

"What is it?" he asked. "Tell me what the last card means."

Saverra shook her head and twisted away from him. The blanket wrapped around her opened, but she gave no thought to her exposure. The healer gently turned her back so she faced him.

"It's okay. Tell me."

"It be duh card of death."

"It's alright, Saverra," he said, locking eyes with her. "Death measures us all--eventually."

She didn't understand his words or the assuredness on his face as he stared into her eyes.

"And I know, it will be, an easy ride," he began. "The mask that you wore, my fingers would explore. Costume of control, excitement soon unfolds. And I know, it will be, an easy ride. Joy fought vaguely with your pride--with your pride."

She didn't realize it at first, but the rhythm in his speech revealed he was giving her another poem.

"Like polished stone, I see your eyes. Like burning glass, I hear you smile."

His hands slid down her bare back, pushing away the blanket and pulling her slightly closer.

"Coda queen, now be my bride. Rage in darkness by my side. Seize the summer in your pride. Take the winter in your stride--let's ride."

He pulled her even closer and kissed her lightly. She hesitated, entranced but wary. Then her arms found their way around the healer and they kissed again with more fervor, brushing against the deck of cards and scattering them across the wagon's wooden planks.

Ω

She woke to find herself alone--alone except for Nomad, who was curled up next to her. She could see it was day by the light seeping through the cracks in the wagon's doors, and thought of looking for the healer. Instead she just lay there, stroking the cat creature, remembering the night.

They'd shared pleasure, but there was also pain. She recalled that during the night, the healer had turned and twisted and called out in terror during his sleep. She'd dealt with her own nightmares, so she knew what he was going through. She thought of waking him, but he quieted down before she had a chance.

Prior to falling asleep, the healer had told her it was time for him to leave this place. He said the wind was calling him, telling him to move on. He said it was never safe for him to stay in one place for very long, though his explanation about why this was, wasn't clear to her. Most of all, she remembered him asking her if she'd like to go with him.

It had caught her by surprise. She'd never been asked such before, and never expected it. She was so taken aback by the question, she hadn't answered right away. So he'd spoken up and said he understood it was a big decision, and that she should think about it. He said he wouldn't leave right away, promising to stay until she decided.

Lying there, in the calm of the morning, Saverra wondered why she'd hesitated--why she hadn't agreed immediately. Nothing held her here. This place was like so many others where she'd lived, and the idea of traveling to new places--learning new things this healer could teach her--was intriguing. There was no denying she was fascinated by him, even when half the time she couldn't grasp what he was saying. Yet, that was part of what appealed to her--called to her inner longing.

The truth was, she couldn't think of any reason *not* to go with him. Except . . . except to go with him was to chance losing him. She'd been by herself for so long--independent for so long. To go with him was a risk. To let herself care about anyone was a risk. Was she willing to take such a risk for this healer-- this man whose name she still didn't know?

In a rash moment of resolution, she decided. She would leave with him. Go wherever he went, as long as he wanted her. But first she'd make him wait at least a day--see if he was still willing, if he still wanted her. Then, before she would leave, she'd make him tell her his name.

Ω

All day he'd been hearing the whispers, the scattered conversations, the hushed talk of the healer and how he'd brought the rain. It was one thing if the non-believers chattered, but even some of his closest followers were talking, though they would fall silent if he was near--unwilling to speak such heresy in his presence. But it was there, simmering amongst the faithful. He knew he couldn't let such doubt fester--such doubt in *him*. He mustn't lose them. He must do whatever God needed to wrestle free their souls from malicious uncertainty.

Yet there was hope. There was a way. He'd heard both awe and apprehension in their voices. Their belief in the stranger's supposed powers amazed them, but also frightened them. It was that fear Elcaro knew he could use.

He'd been preparing for his sunset service all day, while loyal workers cleared the debris of the calamitous lightning strike from his tabernacle's interior. The downpour had stopped shortly before sunrise, but the hours of rain had given him plenty of time to think--to remember. The tumultuous storm had played havoc with his recollections. At one point a clap of thunder cast him back to the day his fellow padres were slaughtered by marauding strangers. It was a day that left more than his hands disfigured. It had also blackened his soul. He had no memory of exactly how long he'd wandered after being freed from the nightmare to which he'd been nailed. He only knew he'd been lost--roving, raving, drifting . . . until he found God again. *No*--until God found him.

The morning after the storm had spread itself bright and clear, as clear as he hoped to leave the minds of his followers. They'd been duped, no doubt. What the farmers had paid the stranger, he didn't know. All he knew was that no man could make it rain. Only God had that power. The people had been swindled, and it was his obligation, his burden, to protect them, even if he must stray from scripture to do it.

Evening fell with the same blaze of fire he felt in his heart. The glorious sunset was a tableau of majestic fury, full of reds and golds and oranges--a magnificent message from God. The Lord had set the scene, now it was up to him to sculpt the moment.

He stepped out onto his stage and those gathered grew quiet. The crowd was not as large as some he'd preached to, but still larger than what it had been when he'd first arrived in this place. It didn't matter. There were enough believers here for his purpose. His loyal cadre stood ready around the congregation, staves in hand, just as he had directed.

He didn't speak right away. Instead he stood there, staring fiercely into the faces of his audience, and he hoped, into their hearts, their souls.

"It is written in the great book that false prophets will rise among the people, spouting lies and spreading destructive heresies. These deceivers will speak with the silvered tongue of a serpent and promise miracles which only the true God can perform. They do this because they are in league with Satan, and Satan, above all, is a trickster who often disguises himself as an angel of light."

Elcaro paused, stepped toward his followers, and shouted, "Believe not in the blasphemy of such demons! For, in their greed, with malignant intent, they will exploit you with false words and empty promises!

"Remember, when the sins of the people grew too great, God sent His holy flames upon the world to destroy the ungodly."

Elcaro turned and walked away from his audience, looking up at the heavens, where the last vestiges of the now ominously intense sunset still lingered. In the shapes and forms there in the sky, he saw his mother--the mother he'd never known--St. Janelle. He was certain he saw her. Certain her presence was a sign he was on the right path.

In an expansive theatrical motion, he threw up his arms and pressed his palms together in an aspect of prayer. He held the pose for several beats before he turned back around, lowering his arms.

"You all know of the demon of whom I speak. You've all seen or heard the stranger who rode into town on the devil's own tail."

Elcaro saw many of his flock nodding in agreement, poking their neighbors in an *I told you so* fashion.

"This vile interloper claims to heal suffering. Has your suffering been healed?"

Many in the crowd shook their heads.

"He claims to control the elements, to be able to call forth heaven's rains. Do you really believe this sinful charlatan, this depraved shaman made it rain?"

More head-shaking and voices crying "No!"

"Of course he didn't make it rain. God made it rain. God answered our prayers." He pointed at his audience with both hands. "God answered *your* prayers. You had more to do with the rain than this venomous stranger who slithered out of the desert.

"What must we do then?" he asked the congregation, provoking numerous responses. "How shall we protect ourselves, our souls, from this serpent of Satan?"

More angry shouts played like music to his ears. The faithful were with him now. Elcaro saw the assent in their faces, in their voices--without even hearing their words. They were ready. They understood the danger. Their fear had been fanned into the flames of action.

"Be strong in the Lord and in the strength of His might. Put on the armor of God that you may stand against the schemes of the devil. Fasten the belt of truth around you and wear the breastplate of righteousness proudly. For this stranger is not of God. He is not a healer, he is a disease, a blight upon our land that we must cleanse with fire--the way God cleansed the world."

At that word, his disciples lit their staves, igniting a conflagration of torches all around the congregation. One of the flaming rods was handed to Elcaro. More torches were lit and passed among the faithful.

"Follow me now," called out Elcaro. "Follow me and we shall show this demon God's light and drive him from our land."

Elcaro marched down the stairs of his stage and the sea of outraged faces parted before him. He had no need to look around to know they followed him on the virtuous path he'd set before them.

Ω

Saverra decided she'd made him wait long enough. Part of her felt like an impatient child, but she knew what she wanted. She had a few misgivings about leaving with this stranger, but they were quelled by the idea of such an adventure--the expectation of discovering new places and learning new things. And, she admitted to herself, she was intrigued by this man, this healer. There was something about him--something more than all the fancy words he used that she didn't understand. She sensed a kindness about him that she'd never known.

She collected what meager possessions she deemed worthy and wrapped them in a bundle. She tossed the bundle over her shoulder and headed for his wagon. Night had fallen, and with it the busy sounds of its inhabitants. But before she'd gone far, she heard a ruckus. It was a dissonance of rage, a convergence of many angry voices. The sound, and what she guessed it meant, terrified her. She ran. She ran until she saw the flames. The sight slowed her. She saw the mob of people surrounding the healer's wagon. Two men had unhitched the horses and were leading them away. The rest of the people were throwing stones at the wagon.

"He's inside," someone yelled. "I saw him go in!"

Another group of people were standing apart, just watching the mad throng. Among these Saverra recognized the little boy, Sam, and his parents. They were holding tightly onto him. Saverra didn't know if they were afraid he'd run to danger, or if they thought the rabble might grab him.

Saverra also saw Elcaro. He stood just back of the unruly crowd, torch in hand, the firelight accentuating his heavy brow, a grim look of satisfaction on his face. It took only a confused moment for Saverra to realize what, *who*, was behind the attack on the healer.

They began throwing their torches against the wagon. *Fire! Flames!* Her mind raced with memories . . . with nightmares. Always there was fire-- dangerous, hurtful, blazing fire. Separating her from her family--destroying the place she lived.

Saverra pushed her way through the mob, screaming, "Stop dis! Stop it!" She slapped and shoved and kicked whoever was in her way. All eyes were on her as she fought her way between the rowdy attackers and the wagon. She held up her arms. "Stop!"

They didn't stop. The stones kept flying, pelting her one after another. She tried fending them off with her outstretched hands, but one hefty rock struck her in the head. She fell in a crumpled heap. She didn't lose consciousness, but her vision blurred and she couldn't get up. She couldn't even feel the blood running through her hair and down the side of her face.

When her eyes briefly cleared, she saw the wagon had caught fire. Before it could really begin to burn, a succession of rapid blinding flashes burst forth all around and above the wagon. A voice that seemed to echo everywhere called out "Stop!"

The crowd backed away, crying out in strangled exclamations as if they'd witnessed a feat of dark magic. They ceased hurling stones and torches, but it was too late. From where she lay, Saverra watched the fire climbing the wagon wheels, devouring the wooden frame. She also saw the hinged door hanging open beneath the wagon.

As the apprehensive crowd retreated, Elcaro made his way to the forefront, raising his hands, trying to calm them.

"God will protect you. Stand your ground. There's nothing to fear. The demon has no more power. God has seen--"

The ground shook, the sky blazed, and flaming debris flew in every direction. Saverra closed her eyes but could do nothing else. She barely felt the shrapnel raining down upon her. When she opened her eyes, she saw Elcaro, trying to rise from the ground, a jagged shard of wood piercing his torso. He stood, looking down at it in disbelief, then looked skyward before he fell back to earth.

Ω

She couldn't see much anymore. Scattered fires still burned, but the light was dimming. There was little left of the healer's wagon. She could hear the crackling of the flames, but nothing else. The people had all run off, leaving the preacher where he'd fallen. There was just enough light for her to see the twisted grimace of death on his face--just enough light to give her satisfaction.

She felt no pain--she felt nothing. Her arms, her legs--nothing would move no matter how hard she tried. Only her ears and eyes still functioned, but even their sensory powers were beginning to wane.

When she saw a figure approaching her out of the dark, she was certain it was a trick of the flickering firelight. Then she thought it was her imagination, only to revise that when she realized it must be Death coming for her. But it wasn't death at all. It was the healer.

He bent down next to her, pulled her hair gently aside, and examined her wound. He closed his eyes ever so briefly. When he opened them he looked down at her, smiling as best he could. The cat creature, Nomad, sauntered up to her, stared with its sapphire eyes, then moved off, out of the range of her vision. She felt a surge of happiness that both the man and his animal companion had survived.

She tried to return his smile, but wasn't certain if she succeeded.

"Your name," she managed to whisper. "Tell me your name."

He had to clear his throat before he could speak. "My name is Konner."

"Konner," she repeated, closing her eyes. She liked the sound of it on her lips.

Saverra opened her eyes and looked back up at him. He was still working hard to hold his smile, but there were tears in his eyes. "Poem," she barely managed to mutter. Then again. "Poem."

He nodded, clearing his throat again.

"Before you slip into unconsciousness, I'd like to have another kiss, another flashing chance at bliss. Another kiss--another kiss.

"The days are bright and filled with pain, enclose me in your gentle rain. The time you ran was too insane. We'll meet again--we'll meet again."

She couldn't hold her eyes open any longer, but she could still hear. The last thing she heard was . . . .

"Oh tell me where your freedom lies. The streets are fields that never die. Deliver me from reasons why you'd rather cry--I'd rather fly."

The last thing she felt were his lips kissing hers.

Homo sapiens had endured and dominated the planet for thousands of years before Smith-Kim. For those who survived the apocalyptic cataclysm and the ensuing hardships, there was never any question humankind would continue its preeminent place in the world.
So thought the dinosaurs.

TRANSIENCE

HE HAD NO DESTINATION--no particular motivation or objective. He'd started walking days ago and, except for sleep and occasional rest, he hadn't stopped. Where he would end up wasn't foremost in his thoughts. He only knew he wanted to go, to get away, to be alone.

Of course he wasn't completely alone. Nomad Muad'Dib still walked at his side--when he wasn't scampering off to chase a butterfly or capture a lizard. Konner appreciated the sporadic company of the feline. It was only humanity he wished to separate himself from. In doing so, he tried not to think too much--tried to keep certain memories buried. At times, though, he found it impossible.

For every recollection that disturbed him, he'd try and recall something pleasant. He pushed darkness and death aside to remember the sweetsticks and poppers of his youth, the satisfying discovery of a new book given him by Teacher, the silky skin of a certain dancing gypsy. It was a game he played with himself. But it was a game with pitfalls. The memory of sweetsticks only reminded him of how hungry he was. Recalling the days of reading with Teacher left him thinking of the destruction of his favorite books. And reliving the feel of Saverra lying next to him was too recent, too raw to contemplate for long. The game always ended with him trying to turn the page to one that was blank. All he could do was put one foot in front of the other and keep marching on. At least there'd been no sign of rain, and his knee no longer hurt.

For the last couple of days he'd been making a trail in the direction of a humble cluster of mountains. They stood there, stolidly on the horizon, where they'd likely rested for centuries. He could have altered his course, gone around, but he saw no reason to. One path was as good as another.

After a time he entered a gorge at the foot of the first few hills, and a short hike through the narrow canyon gave way to a lush valley. The verdant foliage was a pleasant change from the dry scrub and cacti that had stoically ignored his passing over the last several days. The abundant vegetation also meant a likely source of water with which to replenish his nearly dry canteen.

Nomad preceded him and quickly disappeared into the undergrowth, no doubt looking for something to satisfy his hunger. Konner didn't worry about him. He always found his way back. As for his own gnawing hunger, Konner tried to wall if off, ignore it the way he ignored so much of what ate away at him.

The thriving valley he'd come to was much larger than he would have guessed. His first impression was that of a small oasis, only flourishing because the runoff of rain from the mountains had collected in a reservoir of some kind. But the vale stretched off to the East as far as he could see.

Something else he saw surprised him even more. The landscape was dominated by hardy groves of bobbin bushes. The solid green hedges were so substantial in most places they were like impenetrable fortifications. His first thought, upon seeing the bobbins, was of ants. In his experience, the two were never far apart. He scanned the area. He didn't see any, but that didn't quell his fear.

"Nomad!" His first thought was that his companion might be in danger. "Nomad!"

The cat scurried out of the brush with a tiny field mouse locked in his jaws.

Konner exhaled in relief, chastising himself for his panic.

"I see you found lunch."

The cat had no reply. He was already busy making the most of his meal, so Konner waited until Nomad had consumed all he wanted. While he waited, he listened carefully. Though it had been many years, he remembered the eerie melody of the bobbins. So he listened, but heard nothing--no hint of music. He surmised that might only be because no wind was blowing through the hills.

When Nomad had finished with his repast, they continued their sojourn carefully, Konner watching everywhere for the red menace he was sure must be nearby. He never saw a single ant, and that only made him more wary.

He soon came across a stream, filled his canteen, and ate from a patch of wild strawberries he found. He watched and laughed as Nomad tried to lap up a drink without getting his paws wet, and ended up leg-deep in water.

"You needed a bath anyway," he told the unhappy-looking animal.

After Nomad spent several minutes furiously licking his fur into some semblance of order, Konner called to him and they started their climb of the first little hill leading up into the heights.

The ascent wasn't easy. It grew harder with every step, with every loose patch of earth that gave way and every rocky outcropping that caused a detour. There were a few times when, with a mumbled curse, he questioned why he'd chosen to go up instead of around. But, because he had no answer to such questions, he kept climbing. It was exhausting, yet invigorating. The energy and attention required left scant time for idle thoughts or misgivings. It was him, with all his physical inadequacies and inexperience, against the mountain. He slipped more than once, sliding back the way he'd come. At times, out of frustration, it was all he could do not to pick up a rock and throw it at Nomad, who bounded easily ahead of him, and kept stopping to look back as if saying, *Come on, slowpoke.*

After more than hour, he realized he was further than halfway to the top of this particular peak. He needed rest, so he stopped, turned, and looked down the way he'd come. It was a magnificent view, even from this abbreviated altitude. He saw the teeming valley did indeed stretch for miles along the base of the mountain range. Beyond that he saw desert browns and umbers, but the distance was too great to be certain what was really there. Then he discerned something else. Something so strange, so inconceivable, it took him several seconds to accept and comprehend.

From this height, the bright chartreuse of the bobbin bushes stood out against the rest of the landscape. To his astonishment, Konner observed what would have been impossible to distinguish from ground level. The hedges had grown into the shapes of perfect equilateral triangles. Even more astounding, the vertices at the base of each triangle intersected with those of the triangles on either side. Five triangles went round, connecting in a chain, forming an open pentagon in the center and a star-like shape overall.

As far as the open acreage would permit, the apex of each triangle intersected with the apex of another, so that what he saw were scores of green stars, all connected, all spanning the valley, growing ever towards the horizon.

Konner fell to his knees, his exhausted legs suddenly too weak to hold him. Nomad came to his side and rubbed against him as if aware something were amiss.

It took more than a moment, but as soon as Konner accepted the sight his eyes beheld, he recalled his encounter with the ants at the bobbin bush so very long ago. That geometrical communication had been through the ants, but he remembered Teacher had always suspected the bobbin plants were the true intelligence. What kind of intelligence, he had no idea. Teacher thought they might be an alien lifeform--something that hitched a ride on the Smith-Kim comet. What he witnessed now could only support Teacher's theory.

He pondered what these linked triangles meant. Was it a message of some kind? A warning? If so, who was it meant for? Mankind? Was it meant for the simple farmers he was raised by? The savage marauders who slaughtered those farmers? The superstitious mob that destroyed everything he cherished? If the bobbins were trying to communicate, would anyone listen? Would anyone understand? Would anyone care?

Konner figured if the bobbins *were* from another world, then their arrival had coincided with the annihilation of any chance they had for thoughtful discourse. He didn't know if humans had that capacity any more--at least not enough of them--not most of the ones he'd known.

Maybe this geometric progression had nothing to do with humanity. Perhaps man's days were numbered. Maybe ants and bobbins were the new princes of the Earth. It could be they regarded people with indifference--with no more consideration than mankind gave to the life of an amoeba or a virus. But if so, he wondered, why had they let him escape on that day so long ago? Why had they, seemingly, tried to communicate with him?

Konner didn't have the answers to any of the questions he was asking. He doubted anyone did. Maybe someday he'd devote himself to finding them. But right now there was only one thing to do.

He stood, turned around, and began climbing once more.

ACKNOWLEDGEMENTS

I couldn't have created the foundation for this apocalyptic world without the scientific knowledge and advice of several actual scientists. So I'm very appreciative of the time taken to school me by Dr. Donald Yeomans and Dr. David Morrison of NASA; Dr. Clark Chapman and Dr. Dan Durda of the Southwest Research Institute's Department of Space Studies; Dr. Ken Johnson and Dr. Michael Dowler, San Diego State University Emeritus Professors of Biology; Dr. Brian Toon, Professor of Atmospheric and Oceanic Sciences at the University of Colorado Boulder; Dr. Jay Melosh of the Earth Atmospheric and Planetary Science Department of Purdue University; Dr. Roman Schmitt, Oregon State University Department of Chemistry; Ryuzo Yanagimachi of the University of Hawaii; Dr. Loren Riesenberg, Deparment of Botany at the University of British Columbia; and submariner Gregory K. Maxey, Commander USN (Retired). If there are any technical inaccuracies in this book, the fault, dear readers, lies not with these stars, but in myself.

In addition, I want to thank Carolyn Crow for her feedback and editing skills, and a big muchas gracias to Señor Steve Vaughan for his Español expertise. Kudos also go out to Jonny Linder for his great artwork on the book's cover.

Finally, I want to acknowledge the words and wisdom of Samuel Langhorne Clemens, Robert Anson Heinlein, William Shakespeare, Margaret Eleanor Atwood, James Douglas Morrison, Carlos Castaneda, John Ronald Reuel Tolkien, Thomas Carlyle, Lyman Frank Baum, Charles William Eliot, Mordechai "Martin" Buber, and Lao Tze, which are scattered throughout this work of speculative fiction.

ABOUT THE AUTHOR

Bruce Golden's career as a professional writer spans more than four decades and includes nearly 400 published magazine articles, short stories, poems, and books . . . as well as thousands of news and feature stories written for broadcast. Born, raised, and still living in San Diego, Bruce has worked for magazines and small newspapers as an editor, art director, columnist, and freelance writer; in radio as a news editor/writer, sports anchor, film reviewer, feature reporter, and the creator of *Radio Free Comedy*; in TV as a writer/producer; as a communications director for a youth non-profit; and as a writer/producer of educational documentaries on public health for the state of California.

You can find out more about Bruce's other books by searching Amazon.com or going to: **http://goldentales.tripod.com/**

Books by Bruce Golden

Mortals All
Better Than Chocolate
Evergreen
Dancing With The Velvet Lizard
Red Sky, Blue Moon
Tales Of My Ancestors
Monster Town

Made in the USA
Monee, IL
11 April 2020

Made in the USA
Monee, IL
11 April 2020